ANGELS IN DISGUISE

ANGELS IN DISGUISE

#8 of the 'HAWKMAN SERIES'

Betty Sullivan La Pierre

Published by SynergEbooks

Published by SynergEbooks
http://writeronlinebooks.com/genres/ebooks-mystery1.htm
Published in the United States of America

ISBN : 1-4196-3317-1

To order additional copies, please contact us.
BookSurge, LLC
www.booksurge.com
1-866-308-6235
orders@booksurge.com

ANGELS IN DISGUISE

Others in 'The Hawkman Series by
BETTY SULLIVAN LA PIERRE
http://www.geocities.com/e_pub_2000

THE ENEMY STALKS
DOUBLE TROUBLE
THE SILENT SCREAM
DIRTY DIAMONDS
BLACKOUT
DIAMONDS aren't FOREVER
CAUSE FOR MURDER

Also by Betty Sullivan La Pierre

MURDER.COM
THE DEADLY THORN

www.geocities.com/e_pub_2000

Acknowledgment:

I want to thank, Dr. Jeffrey D. Urman, Dr. Robert H. Feiner, Dr. Mehdi Kamarei, and nurses in the Infusion Center of the Kaiser Permanente Medical Group for their help in writing this book.

ANGELS IN DISGUISE
Cover Art by author, Paul Musgrove

TO THE MEMORY OF PATTI GRAY.
AND TO HER FAITHFUL FRIEND
JEAN FORD
WHO NEVER LET HER DOWN.

CHAPTER ONE

After testifying on a client's behalf, Hawkman left the courthouse around noon and decided to stop by Togo's. He ordered a large pastrami and soda to go. Carrying his food in a sack, he jumped into his 4X4 and drove toward the office. The tantalizing aroma swirled around his nose, causing his foot to push heavily against the accelerator. His stomach growled as he parked in the alley behind his office. He jumped out of the SUV and headed up the stairs, but hesitated for a moment and admired the new shingle attached at the top of the stairwell: Tom Casey, Private Investigator. Smiling to himself, he hurried up the steps to his small cubicle above the doughnut shop. His mouth watering, he settled at the desk, pulled the waxed paper away from the delicacy, and directed it toward his mouth. But before he could take a bite, someone knocked at the door.

"Come in," he called, and rolled the sandwich back into the wrapping.

A man, appearing to be in his mid-thirties, dressed in a dark gray business suit, stepped into the office. He had a clean shaven face, square jaw, deep blue eyes, and dark brown hair tinged with gray at the temples. When he approached the desk, his gaze drifted to the food Hawkman had pushed aside.

"Looks like I've caught you in the middle of lunch."

"No problem, it can wait. Have a seat," Hawkman said, gesturing toward the chair in front of the desk. "How can I help you?"

He held out his hand. "My name's Paul Ryan, Mr. Casey. You were referred to me by a friend at the office. I need someone to help me find my wife."

After they shook, Paul sat down and let out an audible sigh.

"You sound a bit frustrated. How long has she been missing?"

"Going on four days. We're separated right now, and my mother called to tell me Carlotta hadn't picked up our daughter and she'd been at her home since Friday. She tried to call my wife numerous times, but didn't get an answer."

"Did you check the house?"

"Yes. The newspapers were scattered all over the yard. And inside, the mail had piled high under the door slot. It looked like nothing had been touched. I felt disgusted at her irresponsibility for leaving our child with my mother for so long without notifying either of us."

"What about your wife's parents?"

"Killed in a car accident years ago."

"Sisters or brothers?"

"None. She was an only child."

"Have you filed a missing person's report?"

Paul shook his head. "No, I didn't want to feel like a fool if she showed up after a swinging time with some boyfriend she'd picked up."

"Have you checked the hospitals or called the police to make sure she wasn't involved in an accident?"

"Yes. She hasn't been admitted for emergency care and the officer I talked with said they had no record of her being in any accidents."

Hawkman raised a hand. "Before we go on, if you want me to take this case, I require a down payment. Then I'll give you a weekly accounting of my expenses."

Paul nodded and removed his checkbook from the breast pocket of his suit. "Will a thousand dollars get you started?"

"That will be ample."

He peeled off the check and handed it to Hawkman. "I appreciate you taking this on."

Hawkman took a large yellow tablet from the drawer. "Okay, first of all, let's go through some routine questions. Then

I'll need more personal information about your wife. To begin, give me both your full names."

"Paul Lee Ryan and Carlotta Ann Ryan."

After asking several questions, Hawkman flipped over the sheet, then glanced at Paul. "Okay, before we go into more particulars on your wife, I want you to file a missing person's report on her as soon as you leave here. She's been gone long enough; the police won't question the time."

"Okay, I'll do that first thing. Is there anything else I need to do as far as police paperwork is concerned?"

"Not at the moment. I'll let you know as time goes by. What's your daughter's name and how old is she?"

"Tiffany Lynn and she's ten."

"Do you have any pictures?"

Paul dug out his billfold and handed him a photo of Carlotta and Tiffany. "This is a recent snapshot of them together."

"Mind if I make a copy?"

"Not at all."

Hawkman studied the images as he strolled over to the copy machine. "Nice looking girls you have there."

"Thanks. I wish I could classify us as a family, but I'm afraid things just aren't working out."

He gave the original back to Paul and placed the copy on his desk. "Okay, let's dig into your life a little deeper. How long have you been married? And when did the problems begin?"

"We've been married almost eleven years and I thought things were going real well until two years ago when Carlotta told me she was sick of our humdrum life. She said we had no excitement left and things were boring as hell. I told her to get more involved with Tiffany at school. She'd roll her eyes and tell me I could drop that suggestion into the garbage can."

"When did you separate and where is she living?"

"She threw me out about a year ago, and I moved into a two bedroom apartment. Carlotta still lives at our original house with our daughter."

"Give me the address." Hawkman jotted it down, then

glanced at Paul. "Do you think she had a lover on the side around then?"

"I'm not sure, but more than likely she's got guys coming and going now. That's why I didn't want to report her missing just yet." He grimaced. "But I will."

Hawkman leaned back in his chair. "Do you suspect she could've met with foul play?"

Paul shook his head. "I haven't the vaguest idea."

"Tell me a little about your mother. Does she take care of your daughter often?"

"Yes, and even when it's my turn to have Tiffany and I get called into work, Mom will come over to my place to watch her. In fact, I didn't even know she had Tiffany this past weekend until she called."

"What does your dad think about this arrangement?"

"Mom's been widowed for years."

"Sorry. Does she like Carlotta?"

"Unfortunately, no. But she adores Tiffany."

Hawkman raised a brow. "Why doesn't she care for your wife?"

Paul sighed. "From the first day we were married, Mother showed her disapproval in several different ways."

"Enlighten me."

"She picks on Carlotta constantly about how she dresses, and handles herself in front of Tiffany. My wife wears sexy clothes which Mother disapproves of vehemently." He chuckled. "Mom preaches to her that married woman don't go flaunting their boobs and legs in public places."

Hawkman glanced at the picture on the desk. "Carlotta appears to be quite a beautiful woman. And it looks like Tiffany is following in her footsteps. However, your daughter looks quite a bit older than ten years."

Paul nodded. "Yes, I know, and Carlotta doesn't put any restrictions on how she dresses, and allows her to wear make-up. This angers my Mom to no end."

"Tell me again about this last weekend when your mother was watching your daughter."

"Carlotta dropped Tiffany off at Mom's on Friday afternoon after school, and said she'd pick her up Sunday evening. Here it is Tuesday and there's been no word from her. Mother tried contacting Carlotta several times, as I said, and even drove by the house, but never caught her home."

"Does your wife have a car? And if so, what kind?"

"Yes, a Camry and it's in the garage. That's the first thing I checked. It gave me a strange feeling in the pit of my stomach to think she's out with some guy living it up."

"Well, you can't be sure, so don't jump to any conclusions yet. She could have gone out of town with girlfriends. Tell me a little more about your mother and where she lives."

Paul gave him her address. "She's a great grandma and has always been very attentive to Tiffany. The child adores her and the feeling is mutual."

"Did Tiffany say anything about her mother's where-abouts?"

"No. She just said Carlotta told her she'd be staying with her grandma for a few days."

"Would you mind if I questioned your daughter?"

"No, not at all."

"I'd also like to make a visit to your wife's house. You obviously have a key. How about taking me over there this evening after you get off work."

"Sure, I'll drop by Mom's and pick up Tiffany as I'm sure she'll want to get some extra clothes or more of her personal stuff. I'll meet you there, say around six o'clock."

"Okay, that sounds good. Tell your mother not to be alarmed if a guy with a cowboy hat and an eye-patch comes snooping around asking questions."

Paul scooted back the chair and and arose. "I'll do that."

Hawkman stood. "I may need more information as the investigation proceeds. But right now, I think I have enough to tackle the case."

"Thanks for taking it on. I'm sure you'll do whatever's necessary to find out what's happened to Carlotta."

After Mr. Ryan left, Hawkman wrapped his sandwich in a

napkin and put it into the small microwave Jennifer had insisted he get for the office. Times like this he blessed her many times for this convenience. He sat down with the warmed food and glanced through his notes as he munched. Very peculiar case. Looked like a communication channel never developed between Paul and his wife. He hoped Carlotta would turn up alive and well. It bothered him to think she might have met with foul play. He'd talk to the neighbors, then search through her phone and credit card bills. Maybe he could pick those up when he met Paul at the house this evening. He needed to get a feel as to what type of woman Carlotta Ryan might be.

CHAPTER TWO

Hawkman left the office at five thirty, figuring that would give him plenty of time to locate Carlotta's address, and survey the neighborhood before Paul arrived.

He pulled into a cul-de-sac and spotted the house. It appeared this fairly new group of tract residences approached the medium price range, and probably attracted young families purchasing their first homes.

After parking at the curb, he noticed a couple of newspapers on the yard, and a flyer hung from the front door. He sat there a few minutes checking out the dwellings on each side. One had a Caravan parked out front, the other a big SUV. Obviously occupied by families with children as bicycles of all sizes cluttered the inside of the open garages.

Soon, Paul Ryan pulled into the driveway in a Lexus. A lovely young girl hopped out of the passenger side and pranced up to the front door without so much as acknowledging Hawkman's presence as he climbed out of his 4X4.

"Hello, Mr. Casey. Hope you haven't been waiting long," Paul said, getting out of the car.

"No, not at all, in fact, I've only been here a few minutes."

They made their way to the porch, where the child tapped her foot in impatience as Paul fumbled for the key.

"Dad, hurry up. I need to get my stuff."

He grinned as he inserted the key, then glanced at Hawkman. "I think we've already hit the teenage years."

The minute he unlocked the door, she shoved it open and stormed into the house, leaving the two men standing outside. Hawkman couldn't help but notice the hip-hugger jeans, the bellybutton ring and the cropped top on this ten year old girl. It made him wonder what role the father played. Or the grandmother, who supposedly disapproved of these styles. Did they not enforce their authority and refuse to let the girl wear them or were they unable to control her? Nowadays it seemed children ruled and not the adults.

They stepped into a well furnished living room with an entertainment center, including everything from a DVD player to a wide screened television. Since Paul furnished the house, obviously money was no object. The recent day's mail lay scattered in front of the door slot, which Paul immediately gathered and stacked on a counter with the rest he'd picked up previously. He glanced around, then raked a hand over his hair.

"It doesn't look like Carlotta's been here since I came by the other day."

"Is there an answering machine on your phone?" Hawkman asked.

"Yes."

"Have you checked it for messages that might give you a clue as to where she might be?"

"No, I hadn't thought about that."

"When you listen, don't erase anything. Might be something on there that will give us a hint."

Hawkman waited in the living room as Paul disappeared down the hallway and turned into a room which he assumed was either a study or bedroom.

Soon Paul returned, shaking his head. "There were eight messages, but most were from my Mother trying to contact Carlotta. A couple of hang-ups and one from Tiffany's friend. Nothing indicating where Carlotta might have gone. Of course, she could have erased those messages before she left."

"True. Mind if I sort through the mail? I'd like to check phone and credit card bills. If they're not here, could you furnish me with the latest ones?"

"Sure."

Hawkman lucked out and found both bills in the stack. "I'd

like to make some copies of these and I'll get them back to you in plenty of time for payment."

"No problem."

"Let's take a look at your wife's car."

The men walked through the kitchen and into the garage. Hawkman slipped on a pair of gloves and carefully searched the interior of the Camry, then reached down on the driver's side and opened the trunk hood. After searching through it, he turned to Paul. "Nothing suspicious here," he said, closing the lid. He took off the gloves and returned them to his pocket. "So far, there's no clue where your wife has gone. Maybe I could talk to Tiffany now."

The two men went back inside to the living room, and Paul called his daughter. "Hey, sweetheart, could you come here for a few minutes."

She slowly wandered in and studied Hawkman.

"This is Mr. Casey. He's a private investigator I've hired to help us find your mother. He'd like to ask you some questions, so please answer truthfully."

She glanced up into Hawkman's face with big brown moist eyes. "I really miss my Mom."

"I'm sure you do, honey. Why don't we sit on the couch." Once seated, Hawkman pulled out a small paper pad and pin from his pocket, then leaned back. "Did your mom tell you why you'd be spending a few days with your grandmother?"

"No."

"She gave you no hint where she might be going?"

Tiffany shook her long pony tail. "No."

"I know this might be painful. But did your mother have any men visit her while your dad wasn't here?"

She shot a look of fear at her father.

"Go ahead and answer, Tiffany. We have to know."

Ducking her head, she mumbled. "Yes. Two of them I didn't like and told her so."

"Why not?" Hawkman asked.

She clutched her hands in front of her. "Because they were mean."

"What did they do?"

Glancing at her dad again, she bit her lower lip and tears welled in her eyes. "One of them pulled my pony tail and told me I was a spoiled brat. When mom told him not to touch me, he just laughed."

"Do you remember his name?"

"Derrick something or other. He had a funny last name."

"Was he just a friend?"

"I'd never seen him before. He came by to fix the toilet when it overflowed."

"Oh, so your mom called a plumber?"

Tiffany nodded.

"Did he pull your hair on his first visit or did he come by other times?"

"The first time he came over, he just took care of the problem and left, but then he came back two or three more times. The last time he came is when he grabbed my hair and yanked it really hard. I think Mom told him to get lost, because he never showed up again as far as I know."

Hawkman jotted down the name on his pad. "So you don't remember his last name or even how it sounded?"

She shook her head. "No."

"Did you see his truck the first time he came by? And by any chance if it had a company name on the side?"

She shook her head again.

"Okay, you said there was another man you didn't like. What was his name?"

"Mom called him Jack Smith. I'm not sure it was his real name because he always snickered when she said it."

"Did he come to fix something around the house?"

"I don't think so, unless he came while I was at school. He walked in with her one day after she'd been shopping. I'm not sure where he came from."

"You said he was also mean. What did he do?"

"He'd tell me to get lost when he came over. Then once he tried to kiss my Mom in front of me. She pushed him away and told him to stop. He twisted her arm until she squealed, then he kissed her anyway."

"I see. Did he come back several times, too?"

"Yes. But I'd run to my bedroom, because I didn't like him at all. One day, he opened my door and peeked in. I told him to get out."

"What'd he say?"

He put a hand on his hip and wiggled his butt, and said. "You're a mighty sassy little girl. Maybe I ought to take some of that cockiness out of you." But about that time, Mom grabbed his arm and pulled him away telling him to leave me alone."

"Were there others?"

"Just Mr. Withers from the meat market."

Hawkman patted her on the shoulder. "Thank you, Tiffany, you've been very helpful."

"Do you think my Mom is with one of those horrible men?"

"I have no idea. But maybe we can find out."

Picking up her duffle bag from the floor, she rested it on her lap, and fidgeted with the strap. "Dad, when are we leaving?"

"As soon as Mr. Casey's done."

Hawkman stood. "I'd like to look through your wife's bedroom."

Paul led him to the end of the hallway, and let out a sigh as he opened the door.

"I'd like you to come in with me and tell me if anything looks amiss."

"Sure," Paul said. "Of course, I haven't lived here in some time, so I'm not sure I'd recognize anything out of sorts."

"Does Carlotta work?

"No."

"So you pay the household bills?"

"Oh yeah. I pay her a healthy monthly allotment to keep things going. And to make sure Tiffany has everything she needs."

"Is she a good money manager or does she keep wanting you to up the wage?"

"Only once or twice has she asked me for more and it was for Tiffany's school stuff."

Hawkman nodded as he slid open the closet door. "There's a large suitcase in here. Do you know if this belonged to a set?"

Paul poked his head around the edge. "Yeah. It has three pieces. That one, a medium size and then one smaller. I don't see the middle one."

"Check the bathroom and see if her make-up is still there."

He went into the small room, opened the medicine cabinet, then checked the drawers and cabinets underneath the sink. "Nope, it's not here."

"Do you think you'd notice if any of her clothes were missing?"

"I doubt it. She likes to shop and had a continuous new wardrobe."

"Do you think Tiffany might know?"

"Possibly." He poked his head out the door. "Tiffany, come in here for a minute."

She moseyed into the room, and flopped down on the unmade bed, her ams folded. "What do you want?"

"Would you look and see if any of your mother's clothes are missing?"

"Hmm, I'll try." She slid off the mattress and went to the closet. Putting a finger to her lips, she flipped through the hung dresses and shuffled through the shelves. "I don't see her real fancy blue dress or her black Gucci handbag. Her jeans are gone along with two or three of her tops." She glanced down at the floor. "Her silver high heels are missing, and her tennies. She quickly glanced under the bed. And I don't see her pair of black floppies she wears a lot around the house That's all I can tell right now. She's always buying clothes, so I'm not sure if she had anything new."

Hawkman raised a brow. "Are you sure it was a real Gucci purse?"

Tiffany grimaced and glanced at Paul. "Dad, don't get mad,

but I was with Mom when she bought it and it cost a bunch. It has the silver logo right on the front."

Hawkman smiled as he flipped his notepad shut and put it into his pocket. "You've been a lot of help, Tiffany. Thank you." He turned to Paul, "The information I've acquired so far will get me going. If I need to come back, I'll give you a call."

Paul grabbed a sack from the kitchen pantry and put the mail inside. "Guess I better pay some of these bills."

As they stepped outside, Tiffany ran toward their car and jumped into the passenger side. Paul locked up the house and picked up the stray newspapers. "Guess I better cancel the Daily News, too."

The two men stood in front of the house for a moment. "I'd like to talk to your mother soon," Hawkman said. "But first I'll go through what I have and see if any interesting clues show up." He patted his pocket. "I'll get these bills back to you tomorrow."

"Have any idea as to what might have happened?" Paul asked.

"Right now it looks like she took a long holiday without telling anyone. I'll speak with some of the neighbors. Who knows one of them may have dropped her at the airport. I'll do a quick study of those bills, and perhaps find she bought a ticket on her credit card or made some informative calls. They might reveal something."

Tiffany tooted the horn. "Hurry up, Dad...it's hot in here."

CHAPTER THREE

Hawkman went back to his office, copied the bills and made notes of more questions. He wanted Paul to check his bank statement, especially if his and Carlotta's names were on the same account. It was possible he'd taken her off because of the monthly payments. Hawkman needed to make sure no money had been withdrawn without Paul's knowledge and if so, when.

Next, he hastily checked through the credit card bill and saw no sign of a plane ticket purchase. There were lots of clothing shops and restaurant charges, but nothing out of the ordinary that caught his attention. The phone bill proved a little more interesting. Several long-distance calls were made to the same number and many to one local residence. The digits looked familiar, so he flipped through the sheets of notes he'd taken during the interview with Paul and found the phone number belonged to his mother, Delia Ryan. It seemed odd, particularly since she didn't care for Carlotta. Why would those two women be communicating so much on the phone? Of course, it could be Tiffany calling her grandmother. Something to check into, he thought.

He circled the phone numbers on his copy to check out tomorrow. Folding the original bills, he shoved them back into their envelopes, then into his pocket. He'd run them by Paul's place on his way home. After taking care of some unfinished business, he checked the time and figured he better head out or it would get too late to drop by Paul's. The man probably hit work at sunrise and more than likely hit the sack early. He must make good money, since he could afford to take care of

Carlotta's bills, plus pay for a two bedroom apartment of his own.

Hawkman shut down the computer, and locked up the office. He arrived at Paul's complex, and remembered when the construction of these new buildings went up. They couldn't be much over a two years old and were very lavish. One weekend during their grand opening, he and Jennifer had gone through some of them for fun. She'd gotten a lot of expensive ideas from the decorative displays and came home jabbering about the beautiful interiors. He had a time talking her out of buying new stuff for their own home. Smiling to himself, he climbed out of the 4X4 and made his way to unit 102.

A soft light glowed through the draped window. He knocked lightly as not to disturb the neighbors. Paul opened the door as far as the safeguard would allow. "Mr. Casey," he said, hurrying to undo the chain. "Have you found Carlotta?"

"No. Sorry to get up your hopes." Hawkman held out the envelopes. "I just wanted to return these bills so you wouldn't be delinquent."

"Come in, please." Paul took the invoices and gestured toward the luxurious living room. "Have a seat and I'll fix you a cocktail."

Hawkman stepped inside, and sank down on the soft leather sofa. "No thanks on the drink. Don't think it'd be too wise. I have a ways to drive. I'll only stay a moment, but there are a couple things I'd like to ask."

Paul picked up a half-full drink sitting on the bar, and took a swig. "Sure, go ahead."

"First of all, did you have a joint checking account with your wife?"

He strolled to the overstuffed chair opposite Hawkman and plopped down. "Used to, but when she kicked me out, I took her name off everything. I didn't want her skipping town leaving me high and dry."

"Wise move."

"This way at least I know where the money is. Otherwise I wouldn't have a clue."

"The other thing, I noticed on the phone bill that there are several calls to your mother's house. Did Tiffany call her grandmother everyday?"

"Yeah, Mom insisted she call when she got home from school. She worried because Carlotta left Tiffany alone a lot. It really griped Carlotta and she told me to tell Mother not to instill so much fear into our daughter."

"What did your mom say about it?"

"She didn't pay any attention and told me there's too much going on with little girls nowadays. It didn't hurt Tiffany to pay heed to what's happening around her. And I had to agree. You can't turn on the news without hearing about a pedophile raping and murdering some little girl. It certainly didn't harm her to be aware."

Hawkman pointed to the envelopes Paul had placed on the counter. "There are several long-distant phone calls to the same number. Would you check and tell me if you recognize it."

Paul unfolded the bill and studied the numbers, then frowned. "Have no idea who that is."

"Okay, I'll check it out tomorrow." Hawkman stood. "Won't keep you any longer. It's getting late and I need to get home. I'll touch base with you later in the week, and probably talk to your mother sometime within the next two days. Hopefully, I can time it so Tiffany's still in school."

"Thanks. I'll let her know."

Hawkman climbed into his SUV and headed for Copco Lake. By the time he arrived, he noted it was close to eleven and the lights were out, except for the one on the front porch Jennifer always left on for him. When he went into the kitchen, he found a note on the cabinet.

"Please don't wake me, not feeling real well.

Have doctor appointment tomorrow.

Love ya, Jen"

He felt an uneasiness wash over him as he reread the message. She's never ill, he thought, as he glanced toward the bedroom. Nothing other than a cold. She doesn't even like doctors, but obviously something had happened to make her worried enough to see one. He'd definitely let her rest tonight, but he wouldn't leave in the morning until he knew more.

Hawkman spent a restless night. Concerned his flopping around in bed would keep Jennifer from getting a good rest, he got up and went into the living room where he curled up on the couch. It didn't seem long, before he felt a soft hand touch his arm.

"Honey, what are you doing in here?"

He awoke with a start and sat up straight. "Are you all right?"

"Yes, I'm fine."

"But your note said you didn't feel good. I tossed and turned so much, I thought I might wake you."

She smiled. "I just felt extremely tired last night."

"Something else must be troubling you, if you think you should see a doctor."

"I'm pretty sure I've got a urinary tract infection."

"How serious is that?"

"I'll probably need an antibiotic, and I can't buy it over the counter. I'll have to get a prescription. It'll take care of it within a week."

"That's a relief. Your note had me a bit upset."

"I'm sorry. I felt so wiped out yesterday, all I wanted to do was go to bed and sleep. I feel much better this morning."

"Good. What time's your appointment?"

"Not until one o'clock."

"You want me to go with you?"

She grinned. "No, dear, I can handle it. I'm sure you've got things to do."

"Yeah, this new case is proving to be quite a bit different."

Her eyes glistened with interest. "Oh, good, come in the kitchen and I'll fix us some breakfast while you tell me about it."

Hawkman got out the plates and silverware as he told her about Paul and Tiffany. I haven't met his mother yet. Her name is Delia. I get the impression she might be a little overbearing, especially to Carlotta. But according to Paul, she's crazy about her granddaughter."

"Where'd you get the impression she's domineering toward the wife?"

"Guess Carlotta dresses like a bombshell, and doesn't restrict Tiffany's dress code, which doesn't meet with grandma's approval. This I could see with my own eyes. You wouldn't believe this ten year old in her hip-hugger jeans, a belly button ring, a cropped top and make-up."

Jennifer held the egg in midair, her eyes wide. "You're kidding. A ten year old wearing make-up with a belly button ring?"

Hawkman nodded. "Yep. Saw her with my own eyes. She's a beautiful child, long brown hair, big saucy brown eyes, but definitely isn't ready for that type of dress. For crying out loud, she doesn't even have a waistline yet. But what I don't understand is, if dad or grandma don't approve, why do they let the girl get by with wearing these garbs when she's with them?"

Jennifer sighed. "I think kids rule their parents nowadays."

"I believe it." He snuck a piece of bacon off the plate. "Today, I'm going to try and talk to Delia, then I'm going to see about finding these two clods that Tiffany said her mother brought home."

"Do you suspect foul play?"

"Hard to say. Not a word has been heard from the missing woman. It does make me suspicious. On the other hand, she could be with girlfriends, since her car is parked in the garage. But I didn't find a clue at the house indicating where she might have gone."

"That's odd. Not letting anyone know where you're going. Especially, when you've got a child to worry about. You'd think she'd want to leave a number where she could be reached in case of an emergency. Surely she's got a cell phone."

Hawkman snapped his fingers. "Good thinking. I forgot to ask Paul if she had one. Didn't notice a bill on her phone invoice, but sometimes those are separate. In fact, I'm going to call him as soon as we finish breakfast. It surprises me now when I think back on it, Tiffany didn't have one stuck to her ear either."

Jennifer handed him a plate of food. "It seems most kids have one, regardless of their age."

After breakfast, Hawkman gave Paul a call at work. When he hung up, he turned to Jennifer. "He said, Carlotta didn't have a cell phone as far as he knew, and she showed no interest in having a computer. Said she didn't want Tiffany discovering porn on the web."

"Sounds like a mixed up woman if you ask me," Jennifer said. "She lets her ten year old daughter wear far out clothes and make-up, yet doesn't want her to have a cell or computer. Quirky."

"If you're sure you don't want me to go with you to the doctor, then I think I'll take off. See if I can catch Delia Ryan at home before Tiffany gets out of school."

"Why don't you give her a call first?"

"Sometimes a surprise interview gets better results."

"That's true. I'll be anxious to hear what this grandma has to say."

CHAPTER FOUR

Hawkman drove into an older area of town and slowed down, as he observed the lovely landscaped lawns. He finally spotted Delia Ryan's house sitting back from the road with a curved driveway that led to the attached garage, and continued to circle the full length of the front yard. Large trees shaded the roof and rose bushes guarded the front sidewalk and manicured lawn. Very striking he thought. Either Mrs. Ryan had a green thumb or an excellent gardener.

In the center of the open two car garage sat a new large white Cadillac sedan. Looked like widow Ryan had a good supply of money. He parked in the street, climbed out, and straightened his jeans jacket, then made his way to the front door. When he pushed the doorbell, he could hear a strange minor melody of chimes echoing throughout the house.

"Coming," a voice called.

When a woman opened the door, it took Hawkman a moment to speak. He didn't expect to be greeted by a tall, slender, tanned female dressed in a long white terry bathrobe with a towel wrapped around her head.

"Uh, I'm looking for a Ms. Delia Ryan. Am I at the right address?"

"You sure are," she said, smiling and holding out her hand. "You're Mr. Tom Casey, aren't you?"

"Yep, that's me."

Paul told me I could expect you within the next couple of days. Please come in. I just went for a swim. Give me a few minutes to change and I'll be right with you." She led him into the living room and motioned for him to have a seat. "Can I get you a cup of coffee? I have some made."

"Sure, that'll be great."

"Cream or sugar?"

"No, black's fine, thanks."

She set a mug of the steaming brew on the coffee table. "Make yourself comfortable. I'll be right back."

Hawkman picked up the cup and strolled over to the picture window overlooking a huge glistening pool in the back yard. Then his gaze traveled to the sides. Strange, he thought. This is not your typical grandmother. No flower pots or fancy little chairs, but grotesque statues of dragons and demons. Then he observed the interior of the living room more closely. Sipping on the hot coffee, he walked over to the tall bookcase on the far wall and noticed her taste in reading consisted of fantasy, science fiction and the horror genre. Why did he expect to meet a round grand motherly type with a taste for romance? Because she didn't want her granddaughter wearing sexy clothes at ten years of age? Hawkman, you need to adjust your thinking.

He observed oriental statues of dragons stashed in the darkened corners, along with pictures on the walls of space ships and well endowed alien women. Horror books lay scattered across the end tables and coffee table. This is going to prove to be a very interesting interview, he thought.

Delia Ryan entered the room. "Sorry it took me so long. Had a time fixing my hair."

Hawkman spun around to face a sexy woman with long dyed blond hair, dressed in designer jeans, silk white shirt, and demonstrating the figure of a thirty year old. She'd obviously had a face lift or else she wasn't Paul's biological mother. "No problem, you have a very interesting hobby. Looks like you're a real science fiction fan."

"Oh, yes," she said, waving a hand toward the bookcase. "I love this stuff. Takes me into another world."

He nodded. "Yep, it sure would."

"Sit down, let me get a cup of java and we can talk," she said, pointing toward the sofa.

She soon returned and took a chair opposite him. "I'm anxious to know if you've learned anything about where Carlotta might be."

"No, so far I have no leads. I was hoping you'd have information that might help."

She placed her mug on the coffee table. "I wish I could. That woman is such an air head and is not responsible. Can you imagine leaving a ten year old child to fend for herself when all this horrible stuff is going on in the world?" She slapped her hands against her thighs. "Oh, it just makes me crazy. She doesn't let Tiffany be a little girl who would like to play with dolls. No, she has her dressed in hip huggers and has her wearing make-up like a whore." She jumped up and paced the floor. "Making her grow up way too fast without encouraging the child to have any kind of an imagination."

"What does Tiffany think of the demons and dragons you have displayed?"

Delia laughed. "I wouldn't approve of her reading any of my books. I tell her they're something she can look forward to when she grows up. We go to the library and check out literature for her age level. Then we sit around the pool and read together. Sometimes, I'll even read to her. She loves it."

"How does Carlotta take your hobby?"

Delia twisted her mouth into a scowl. "I don't really care. That woman doesn't appear to have a brain cell working. I'd like to adopt Tiffany and keep her away from her mother, but I have to think about my son. After all, he is her father."

"I must admit you don't look old enough to be Paul's mother. But wouldn't a young child be difficult to raise?"

Her eyes lit up as she sat back down on the chair. "Thank you. I work hard at keeping fit. I like challenges and get along with Tiffany fabulously well. We laugh a lot and do fun things, like shopping and getting ice cream. And the child needs someone to pay attention to her achievements. She's a very talented little artist, but I doubt Carlotta even recognizes it. One day, when Tiffany called me, she was crying. Said her mother had ripped one of her drawings in two and threw it on the floor. Made me furious."

"Getting back to Carlotta. Do you know any of her friends or acquaintances?"

"I've never met many of female friends, but there was a woman she introduced me to at her house several months ago."

"Do you remember her name?"

Delia rubbed her temples with her forefingers. "Oh, geez, I can't remember and she appeared a little more levelheaded than Carlotta. I think it was Beth something." She squinted her eyes, then pointed a finger at him. "Beth Matthews."

Hawkman jotted down the name. "Did she mention her line of work?"

"No. I don't recall her mentioning what she did. And Carlotta didn't say."

"Anyone else?"

"Tulip Withers. She's the daughter of Hank Withers who owns the butcher shop in town. A strange girl and gives the appearance of a wilted flower. Very plain with stringy dishwater blond hair, and has dark circles under her eyes. You'd imagine her a very sick person or one on drugs. Hard to tell."

"Do you know where she works?"

"She's a waitress at Mom's Cafe off Main street. She and this other woman, Beth, were at Carlotta's when I got worried about Tiffany and drove over to check on her."

"Have you found Tiffany home alone often?"

"Oh, yes. And if her mother isn't there within an hour, I go pick her up."

"Have you ever thought about calling Child Services?"

"Yes, but Paul won't hear of it. He says if they get involved, then it would hurt his chances of ever getting Tiffany if he and Carlotta divorced."

"Do you think that might happen?"

She pushed strands of hair behind her ears. "I really doubt it, Mr. Casey. My crazy son is still madly in love with the woman. I can't see why, as she doesn't offer him a thing but pain and agony. The only way it would happen would be she divorces him. Maybe she'll find some truck driver who'll promise her the moon, then whisk her away to some far off land." She sighed. "I'm afraid though, she does have enough brains to realize the mighty dollar is nice to have. She's never has to want for anything."

"I get the impression you don't care for your daughter-in-law."

"That's an understatement, Mr. Casey. I've never been able to tolerate her very well. From the day Paul and Carlotta got engaged, I tried to discourage him from marrying the girl, but he'd fallen head over heels. Nothing I said discouraged him. To tell you the truth, I think the little bitch got pregnant to make sure he married her, but I can't verify that as Tiffany came right at nine months after they tied the knot." She took a sip of coffee. "And they seemed fairly happy until about two years ago and then it appeared their marriage fell apart."

"Could you spot a cause?"

"Not really. Of course, Paul worked long hours and they didn't have much of a social life. He tried to get Carlotta involved in a hobby, or with Tiffany's life, but she didn't seem interested. One time I heard them arguing about school events. Carlotta told him she didn't want to be around a bunch of snotty nosed kids with mothers who talked about nothing but cooking meals and kids. The girl hadn't matured and Paul took the brunt of her ravings."

"You said you don't approve of your granddaughter's dress code, but yet, it appears you let her wear those clothes when she's with you and Paul does the same. Can you tell me why she gets away with it when she's with you, since you vehemently disapprove?"

Delia curled a long strand of hair around her finger. "Long story. When Tiffany first wore the hip huggers over here and I noticed the belly button ring, I actually had a tantrum. I carried on something dreadful at Carlotta for ever letting the child get her naval pierced. Unfortunately, this argument occurred in front of Tiffany. Carlotta pointed a finger at my nose and told me I had no business telling her how to raise her child. And if I ever interfered with what she did, I'd never see my granddaughter again. Tiffany let out a scream, ran to the room I have for her here and flung herself across the bed, sobbing. No way could I ever let that happen. Carlotta had every legal right to threaten me. So, I decided then and there, I'd never say another thing about how the child dressed."

"Do you think either Carlotta or Paul had an affair, making their marriage go sour?"

"I doubt my son has time for such a thing. Carlotta is another story. Who knows where she goes or what she does during the hours Tiffany's in school. Her getting shot by an irate wife wouldn't be a surprise." A cynical grin curved her lips. "In fact, I think it might please me."

Hawkman set his mug on the table. "Mrs. Ryan, I've taken enough of your time. Thanks for the coffee, and I appreciate what you've told me. I'll see about talking to both those women you mentioned. Maybe they can shed some light on Carlotta's disappearance."

Delia showed him to the door. "It's been a pleasure visiting with you. But you know, Mr. Casey, it really won't disappoint me if you never find her."

CHAPTER FIVE

Traveling back to his office, Hawkman found himself puzzling over the conversation with Ms. Delia Ryan. On one hand, she seemed genuinely concerned over her granddaughter. On the other, she appeared to have a streak of meanness he couldn't quite decipher. He decided to have a chat with Paul and see if he could gain more insight of the inner workings of this woman's mind.

At his desk, he studied the list of names received from Tiffany and Ms. Ryan. The guy who fixed the overflowing toilet could have been a local handyman Carlotta found in one of those toss away flyers, but he'd try the local plumbing companies first. Plopping the phone book onto his desktop, he flipped to the yellow pages and jotted down numbers. Then he looked up the common name of Jack Smith. It would take several calls to find this guy, if it turned out to be his real name, which Tiffany doubted and so did he.

Next he searched for the two women Delia mentioned; Beth Matthews and Tulip Withers. Not finding either name, he dialed information and discovered they both had unlisted numbers. At least they were still in the area. Before going into an extensive search on these people, he decided to dial the long-distance number repeatedly called from Carlotta's house. An answering machine picked up. "You've reached the Divorce and Family Law Specialist of Phillips and Crammer in Grants Pass, Oregon. Our offices will be closed until next Monday due to some extensive remodeling. Your call is important, so please leave your name, phone number and short message after the beep and we'll return your call. Thank you."

That's interesting, Hawkman thought, as he replaced the receiver. Appears Ms. Carlotta had something on her mind besides staying in an unhappy marriage. Divorce could limit the amount of money coming in for personal use. Right now, Paul appeared willing to supply whatever was needed to make sure Carlotta and Tiffany were comfortable. Why would she seek out a divorce lawyer? Unless there's another man involved.

He'd take a trip to Grant's Pass next week if Carlotta didn't make an appearance. It'd be interesting to see how much information he could obtain from the lawyer without having to seek Detective Williams' help. Who knows, by then, this case could develop into more than a missing person.

Turning to the computer, he punched in the code for the special program he belonged to that revealed unlisted information. Once he located the two women, he jotted down their phone numbers and addresses. Later, he'd drive by their residences and see if they'd talk to him. He felt it a better method than calling on the phone. The surprise factor had paid off more than once.

He glanced up at the computer clock and it read four o'clock. Jennifer should be home from the doctor by now, so he called.

"Hi, Hon, what's the diagnosis?"

"He gave me a strong antibiotic for three days."

"Good. I hope you've started it."

She chuckled. "Don't worry, dear, first dose is down."

"I'll talk to you tonight. Love ya." He hung up, feeling much better. His attention then went to the plumbing companies. After he exhausted the list in the area and found no one employed called Derrick, with a strange last name, he decided he'd better pick up one of those little flyers of handymen. They were usually distributed at the grocery stores or put on top of the newspaper bins.

After going through all the Smiths in the phone book, he decided the name Jack Smith would forever hang in limbo. A ploy Carlotta and the boyfriend contrived to throw Tiffany off guard, just as the child suspected. He'd hit a dead end as far as the two men were concerned. Borrowing an artist from the police department to sketch out their descriptions given by Tiffany might be his best approach. Then he could go through the mug shots at the police station.

He picked up the notes from his desk and shoved them into his pocket. The apartment houses where the two women lived weren't far away, and unless they had unusual working hours, he'd probably catch them home. He assumed the girls were single, since the phone bills were in their names.

Leaving the office, he drove toward Beth Matthews' address, as she lived closest. This group of apartments tended to be quite popular with the younger set and the parking spaces were almost filled. He drove through the three building complex, each supporting several stories, and searched for an indication where number seventy-two might be located. When he reached the last structure, he spotted the apartment on the ground floor.

The parking space in front of her unit was occupied, but off to the side he noticed a thirty minute visitor area. He pulled into a vacant slot and strolled to the entry. A light glared through a crack in the drapes and Hawkman punched the doorbell several times before a feminine voice called out.

"Who's there?"

Removing his Private Investigator badge from his billfold, he held it up in front of the peep hole. "I'm Tom Casey, Private Investigator, and I'm looking for Beth Matthews."

"That's me."

"I'd like to ask you some questions about Carlotta Ryan."

A young woman, approximately five foot three, in her early thirties, and still dressed in her tailored beige business suit, opened the door. She placed a hand on her chest, when she saw Hawkman. He'd discovered women were seldom ready for a six foot man with a patch over his eye and sporting a cowboy hat to be standing at their front door.

"What about Carlotta?" she asked.

"She seems to have disappeared and the family hired me

to help locate her. Since you're her friend, I hoped maybe you could shed some light on where she might have gone."

Beth frowned. "Disappeared?"

"Yes. May I come in?"

"Let me see your identification again."

He handed it to her and watched as she studied the picture, glancing at his face several times. She finally opened the door wider and invited him to enter.

Hawkman shoved the badge into his pocket and stepped into the living room. She gestured toward the couch. "Have a seat. I just put on a pot of coffee; it should be done. I'll get us a cup. Hope you like it black."

"That's perfect"

He observed the casual, but expensive upholstered furniture decorating the small living room as he sat on the end of a comfortable couch. The only thing out of place was a bouquet of wilted roses that sat in the center of an oak rectangular coffee table. Dried petals littered the polished surface around the bottom of the vase.

Beth carried in two mugs and placed one in front of Hawkman as she took the overstuffed chair opposite him. She appeared concerned as she took a sip of the hot brew. "Now, what's this about Carlotta? But first, let's get one thing straight. I'm not a good friend. You might classify me as a business acquaintance. I've only seen the woman a couple of times."

"So what's your association with her?"

"I met her through Tulip Withers, a client of mine."

"What do you do?"

"I'm a real estate lawyer. But she was looking for one to write up a divorce. Tulip thought I might be able to direct her to a good one. Carlotta wanted someone outside of Medford, so I researched a few names at my office. Then we met for lunch. I suggested a Divorce and Family Law Specialist in Grants Pass. And that's been the extent of my association with her."

So far, that part of the story fit, Hawkman thought. "Did you meet her mother-in-law, Delia Ryan?"

"Yes, she came by Carlotta's home while we were there at

the initial meeting and picked up the young daughter. I don't remember the child's name."

Hawkman placed the partially filled mug on the coffee table and stood. "Ms. Matthews, it doesn't look like you can help me. But if you hear anything about Ms. Ryan, I'd really appreciate you contacting me." He handed her one of his business cards.

"Sure. Be glad to. Sorry, I couldn't be more help."

"Do you know if Tulip Withers is a close friend of Carlotta's?"

"I just assumed they were friends, how close I can't say. Maybe she can help you. I have her address in my files. If you'd like, I can get it for you."

"No, thanks. I already have it."

"By the way, how'd you find me? I'm unlisted."

He grinned. "Private investigators have all sorts of little tricks on finding people. If I told you, I'd give away my secret."

Beth snickered. "Okay, I won't probe. But I certainly hope Carlotta's just taken a trip and hasn't met with foul play."

"Me, too," Hawkman said, as he headed for the door.

CHAPTER SIX

Hawkman had forgotten about this apartment complex outside the city limits. Age had taken its toll on the site. The buildings needed new roofs and the parking area concrete needed repair. At least the structures had a new paint job, plus mature trees surrounding the place helped its looks. The grounds were clean and manicured, giving an old, but quaint appearance. A sign propped on the front lawn stated, 'Available Apartment, see office at rear of building #1'.

He followed the drive toward the back, looking for number three twenty-four, and finally spotted it on the second floor of the last building. Several empty parking spaces were available, but no section specified visitors, so he pulled into a vacant spot closest to the stairwell.

Taking the stairs two at a time, he hesitated in front of the entry, pulled his badge from his pocket, then knocked. A woman pushed back the drape at the window beside the door.

"Yes, can I help you," she said.

Hawkman stepped over and placed his identification against the glass. "I'm looking for Tulip Withers. Is that you?"

"Yes."

I'm Tom Casey, a private investigator. I'd like to ask you some questions about Carlotta Ryan."

She furrowed her brows. "Carlotta Ryan?"

"Isn't she a friend?"

"Well, sort of. Hold on a minute."

He stepped back as she opened the door.

"Come in."

"Is this a bad time?"

"I'm due for work in about an hour, so I have a few minutes. Have a seat."

The living room was furnished in an array of thrift shop or garage sale furnishings, a far cry from what he'd just left. Tulip, a tall, stocky woman wore a white waitress uniform. It appeared she'd attempted to tie her hair into a pony tail, but loose stands hung in disarray around her neck and shoulders. Her face had a pasty appearance and dark rings encircled her eyes. She might not look so plain, Hawkman thought, if she'd put on a touch of lipstick. He sat in one of the straight back chairs against the wall.

Tulip let out a sigh and plopped her big frame down on the couch. "Now, what about Carlotta?"

Hawkman explained she'd disappeared. "Would you have any idea where she might have gone or if she went with someone?"

Tulip shook her head. "Not the vaguest. I've known her for years, but we were never really the buddy-buddy type. We usually got together for lunch once a month or so."

"Did she ever mention her marriage to you?"

She smirked. "Carlotta said it bored her silly and advised me never to get hitched." She tossed her hands up and let them drop. "As if I'd ever have the opportunity."

"You knew she and Paul separated?"

"Oh, yeah, they haven't been living together for some time."

"Did Carlotta have a boyfriend?"

"Not that I know of. She never spoke of another man, only Paul. And she berated him continuously."

"Why? Did he abuse her?"

She flashed him a wide-eyed look. "Oh, no! In fact, I thought it stupid of her to kick him out. My gosh, she had everything she wanted. He spoiled her rotten. But Carlotta called him tiring and dull. He worked long hours, but she didn't view it as his making money so she could have a wonderful life style. She thought he was neglecting her." Tulip moaned. "A very immature attitude on her part."

"When did you last see Carlotta?"

She tapped her finger on her chin. "Let me think. It must have been at least two months ago. She'd called and asked if I knew a divorce lawyer. I told her no, but knew someone that might be able to help. I thought it a stupid idea." She shrugged. "But it wasn't any of my business. She asked me to invite the person to her house and she'd serve us a catered lunch. We set a date and I introduced her to my friend who is a real estate attorney. I figured she'd be able to give Carlotta a name or two."

"Did she?"

"Yes, I think she later recommended a firm in Grants Pass, but I don't remember the name. Sorry, I can't be of more help."

Hawkman stood. "I appreciate what you've told me."

"Do you think something terrible has happened to Carlotta?"

"Hard to say, since no one has heard from her. If she happens to contact you, would you call me at this number?" He handed her his card.

"Oh, sure. You know Carlotta is sort of flaky. Maybe she just took off for a break."

"Let's hope that's all it amounts to."

Hawkman left Tulip's place disappointed. So far, he'd found no help from anyone in locating the missing woman. The most valuable information he'd received came from Tiffany about the two men. He might have to talk to her again. Kids of that age tend to know more than they let on. They do a lot of eavesdropping. He remembered Jennifer warning him when Sam was that age and they were making love, 'little elephants have big ears'. He chuckled at the memory as he climbed into his SUV.

He glanced at the clock on the dashboard and read six forty-five. Turning on the ignition, he pulled out of the parking lot and thought he might drop by Paul's place to see if he could enlighten him on his mother's personality. He'd have to be careful. Sure didn't want to offend the man. Also, he'd like to talk to Tiffany again. On his way, he swung by Carlotta's house and it shocked him to see the white Cadillac parked in the driveway.

He stopped at the curb and made his way to the front door. When he heard Delia's voice in the side yard, he detoured to the gate and found Tiffany with her grandmother on their hands and knees trying to coach an animal from under the house. "What's the problem?" he asked, stepping up to the two crouched females.

"Oh, hi, Mr. Casey," Delia said. "Tiffany got worried about a stray cat she'd tried to befriend and it concerned her that the food she'd put out wouldn't be enough. So we came to check. Sure enough, the kitten is still here, but scared spit less."

"We can't get it to come out from under the house," Tiffany said, pouting as she leaned back on her haunches. "Grandma said I could take it to her house, but I think the little thing is too scared, and it's going to be dark soon."

Hawkman picked up a small branch with a few leaves on the end. "Let me try." He knelt down and flipped the stick around just inside the crawl space opening. Pretty soon, a little white paw reached out and batted at it. Hawkman purred softly and the animal inched out of the opening as it played and launched at the twig. He soon lured the little creature out far enough to pick it up, and gently rubbed its head, then handed the cat to Tiffany. "Sit on the step with the kitten for a few minutes and let her get used to you. She's just frightened. You probably startled her when you came searching and she dashed for cover." He smiled. "However, you'll notice she didn't go far."

Tiffany displayed a big smile. "Thank you."

Even though this might be an opportune time to talk to the young girl, Hawkman gave it a second thought and decided it best to let her learn to trust him. Then she might open up more.

"So what brings you over here?" Delia asked.

"Just doing my job and keeping an eye on things. Surprised me to see your car here this late."

"I'm glad you stopped. We probably wouldn't have been able to entice the cat from its hiding place. Oh, by the way, there's a pet carrier in the garage and maybe you can reach it without me having to get a ladder."

"Sure, be glad to help."

Delia led Hawkman through the side door, flipped on the light and pointed to the cage on the top shelf. He reached up and brought it down in a cloud of dust. Fanning his hand in front of his face, he set it on the floor. "Whew, don't think its been used in awhile."

Delia picked it up by the handle. "It's been stored a few years. I'll hose it off." Hawkman followed her out onto the lawn. "One of the neighbors had it stacked with their garbage and Paul rescued it, figuring they'd have a use for it one day. Carlotta had a fit. Said, she never wanted an animal to smell up the house." She set the cage on the grass, turned on the hose, then sprayed off the dirt inside and out. "You know, kids need a pet, especially an only child. But Carlotta couldn't see past her own nose. Very selfish woman." Turning off the water, she went back into the garage, came out with an old raggedy towel and dried off the plastic carrier. "There, that should do it," she said, standing back and inspecting her work.

"Looks like you ladies have everything under control, so I'll take off."

Delia waved. "Thanks for your help."

Hawkman drove off and headed for Paul's apartment. He thought about Delia and felt baffled by the woman. She almost seemed like two different personalities. Today, the doting grandmother clad in jeans and tee shirt, where at their first meeting, she reminded him of a middle-aged sexy woman turned on by demons and dragons.

He reached Paul's apartment and found him home.

"Good evening, Mr. Casey. Anything new to report?"

Hawkman told him about the two women his mother had mentioned. "Did you know either of them?"

"I don't know Beth Matthews, but I've known Tulip for years. Her father, Hank owns the butcher shop in town. We all went to high school together and she followed me around like a little puppy dog." He smiled. "However, she never impressed me, dowdy as they come, and always reminded me of a football player. Didn't have much personality or get up and go. I never could figure what Carlotta saw in her."

"Were they together much?"

Paul shook his head. "Not really, Carlotta had lunch with her occasionally. I think she felt sorry for her."

"Tell me about Delia? I met her and she's quite different than what I expected."

Chuckling, Paul mixed himself a drink. "Can I fix you something?"

"You got a beer?"

"Sure." He handed Hawkman a cold bottle of Corona from the bar refrigerator. "Need a glass?"

"No, this is fine. Thanks."

Paul joined Hawkman on the couch and a grin tickled the corners of his mouth. "So you find my Mother rather interesting?"

"I'd say that's an understatement. For some odd reason, I expected to meet a grand motherly type of woman, only to find a slim, attractive lady, who reads science fiction and horror."

He laughed. "That's my Mom."

"Has she always been interested in the far out?"

"As long as I can remember. But she never pushed it on me and discourages Tiffany from getting infatuated with those genres. She tells her it's something grown ups like, but it might scare kids."

"Does Tiffany show any inclination to want to read them?"

"No, because Mom keeps her supplied with books at her own age level."

"I went by Carlotta's house. Found your mother and Tiffany trying to coach a kitten from under the house."

"Really. That's why I couldn't reach them this afternoon." He stared at him in disbelief. "Did you say, a cat?"

Hawkman smiled, and told him the story.

"Well, I'll be damned," he slapped his hand against his thigh. "I knew that pet carrier would come in handy one day. Tiffany will now have her pet, even if she has to keep it at Mom's."

"You don't think your mother will mind having a feline who might possibly scratch her lovely furniture?"

"Naw, she has a way with animals and will train it beautifully. She and Tiffany will end up with a wonder cat."

"Back to the case of Carlotta. I can't find either of the men Tiffany described. If you don't mind, I'd like to have a police artist interview her and see if he can get enough detail to sketch the men's faces. Do you think it would upset her?"

"I doubt it; she'd probably think it pretty cool. Something she could brag about at school."

"Okay, I'll set up an appointment. More than likely it will be in the evening. I want to move on this case as quickly as possible, since Carlotta has been missing several days. There's been no news from or about her, and I don't like it."

Paul's expression turned to concern. "You suspect foul play, don't you?"

"It's crossed my mind. What I can't figure out is why she dropped Tiffany off at your mom's, then came back home, leaving her car in the garage. It seems out of character, as she knew your mother would come and pick up your daughter as soon as she discovered the child home alone."

"That's true, but if Carlotta planned on being gone for a few days, she might have wanted Mom to know Tiffany's schedule for the weekend."

"Did your mother mention what Carlotta wore? Was she dressed up, or in casual clothes?

"I never thought to ask."

"Someone either picked her up, or she took a cab. I need to find a person who might have witnessed this or had contact with Carlotta the day she disappeared, or even the day before. So far all I have is you, Delia and Tiffany. Do you think she'd have asked a neighbor to keep an eye on the place?"

"I doubt it. She knew Mom or I would come by. But I'll be happy to call around and find out if anyone saw anything unusual on that Friday."

"I think it'd be a good idea. Be sure and inquire if anyone spotted a strange car at the house."

CHAPTER SEVEN

When Hawkman returned home, he found Jennifer lying on the couch with her feet propped up on pillows, watching television instead of working at her computer.

"Hey, sweetheart, you okay?"

"I'm not sure."

He hurried over and knelt by her side. "What do you mean?"

"I've had two doses of the Cipro and I thought the symptoms would have subsided, but they're still with me."

"Are you in any pain?"

"No, just tired. Of course, an infection will do that."

"If there isn't any improvement by tomorrow afternoon, I want you to call the doctor. That stuff is potent and should knock that infection fast."

She reached up and patted him on the cheek. "Don't worry, honey, I will."

The next morning Hawkman sneaked out of bed so as not to disturb Jennifer. He felt anxious about her not feeling well, but yet, these infections were sometimes stubborn and not always eradicated by a three day dose of antibiotics, regardless of its strength.

His objective today would be to set up an appointment with the police artist to sketch the two men Tiffany had told him about. One of them could be responsible for Carlotta's disappearance. If the child gave a good description, he'd at least have something to go by. He knew it'd be more expensive to set up an evening appointment with the artist at Delia's house, but Paul had the money and it would probably be worth the effort.

Hawkman left the house and headed for Medford. He drove straight to the police station and slipped into a vacated visitor's slot. Spotting the detective's car parked in his designated area, meant the man might just be in.

Strolling down the hallway, he poked his head around the door jamb of William's office, then knocked lightly on the wood. "You're always in the same position in this cubby hole when I come for a visit. Bent over a bunch of papers, pen in your hand, and signing away."

Williams jerked up his head and laughed. "Hawkman, good to see you. Come in. What brings you to this humble establishment?"

Hawkman guffawed. "Boy, that's a new one."

"Well, it's been a while since you've graced my modest abode. Thought maybe you'd found bigger and better places to carry on your business."

"Is that a wish?"

Williams pointed at the chair in front of his desk. "Sit down, you big lug. What's going on?"

"Did Paul Ryan file a missing person report on his wife, Carlotta?"

"Yeah, have it right here. So you're the investigator?"

Hawkman slapped the desk top. "Yep, and no clues to what's happened to the woman. It's strange, she doesn't appear to have any close friends and has vanished into thin air."

The detective screwed up his mouth. "I don't have anything for you either. No murders, accidents or corpses come close to her description."

"The only leads I have are a couple of men the young daughter told me visited the house. But she didn't know their full names, so I thought maybe I'd borrow your police artist. If she could give a good enough description for a sketch, then it might give me some advantage."

"We have a couple of guys we call in when needed. They aren't on our payroll. We pay them by the job. I can give you their names and phone numbers."

"Great. I'd appreciate it."

The detective took a black leather book from his desk drawer and flipped it open. He jotted down the information, then tore off the sheet and handed it to him.

Hawkman read aloud. "Jack Franklin and Kent Langley."

"Yes, those are the two men we normally use. They're both extremely good artists and we've had good luck with their drawings."

"Thanks. I'll probably try to get in touch with one of them today." He folded the paper and put it into his pocket.

"They both have day jobs, so you might not be able to reach them until this evening."

"That'll be fine." Hawkman patted the desk. "Good seeing you. Looks like you're still holding down the fort. If anything comes up on Carlotta Ryan, would you give me a call?"

The detective gave him a salute. "Will do."

Once Hawkman climbed back into his 4X4, he made a call to Jack Franklin. The answering machine picked up, so he left his cell phone number and a short message.

Just as he hung up, the phone rang before he had a chance to clip it to his belt. "Tom Casey"

"Paul Ryan here. I made some calls last night to the neighbors. Only one saw anything. The woman told me she'd seen my mother's white Cadillac. But then she retracted her statement saying she wasn't sure it was Friday or the day before. I don't think her statement holds much water."

"I agree. How many did you call?

"The families on each side and the one across the street. I didn't figure any of the others would have noticed unless they happened to be out in their yard. You want me to call a few more?"

"No, that's probably sufficient. And no one spotted any unusual cars?"

"I asked, but no one saw any strange vehicles. I'm sure they'd have noticed a taxi or limousine."

"Looks like we struck out. Thanks for trying."

"No problem. Anything new on your end?"

"I'm working on a couple of things. I'll keep you informed."

Hawkman finally drove out of the station parking lot and headed for his office. He didn't like the feeling in his gut about the disappearance of Carlotta Ryan. Each passing day made things worse and tomorrow, Friday, marked a week since her disappearance.

Behind his desk, with a fresh eclair from the donut shop and a cup of coffee, he looked through Carlotta's phone bill again. There were several calls to Paul's apartment and a few to his office. These could be from Carlotta or Tiffany. He pulled a calendar in front of him and noted the date and times. Most came during the week when Tiffany was in school. A couple occurred in the evenings. Odd, Paul never mentioned how often he talked to Carlotta. Maybe he should ask him. Occasionally, one overlooks what's right in front of his nose.

He studied Carlotta's credit card bill again and noticed several purchases were made at a dress shop the month before. He'd drop by and ask what type of clothing she'd bought. It might give him a clue if she'd pre planned a trip and whether she'd headed for the beach or the mountains.

Hawkman made a quick call to Jennifer before leaving, but got the answering machine. Either she felt better or went to the doctor's. He'd call later.

Sticking the photo copy of Carlotta and Tiffany into his pocket, he took off for the clothes store. When he reached the ladies' department, he asked several clerks if they recognized the females in the picture. Finally, one came forward.

"Yes, that's Carlotta Ryan and her daughter. They like to shop here and I've waited on her several times. Is there a problem?"

"We're not sure." Hawkman showed his badge to the woman. "I'm a private investigator hired by her husband. Carlotta's been missing a week and I'm trying to track down her movements before she disappeared. Knowing about her purchases might give me a clue. Do you remember what she bought the last time she visited the store?"

The woman's eyes widened. "Oh, my. Let me go to the computer. I might be able to tell you in more detail."

Hawkman followed the clerk to a desk in the corner of the room. She sat down and he watched her fingers fly over the keyboard. Let's see, I have several purchases listed for two weeks ago from last Thursday, which probably won't show up on her bill until this coming month." She glanced up at him. "Would you be interested in those?"

"Very much."

She studied the monitor. "It looks like she bought only for herself." Tapping her chin with a finger, she gnawed her lower lip. "You know I probably shouldn't do this. But if you think it might help in finding her, I could make a copy of these purchases since it's quite extensive, ,"

"I'd really appreciate it."

"Promise you won't tell on me."

He raised his hand in a boy scout salute. "My lips are sealed."

She hit the print button, then handed him the sheet of paper. When she stood, Hawkman slipped a twenty dollar bill into her hand.

A big smile creased her face. "Gee, thanks."

He left the store and sat in the truck studying the items Carlotta had bought. It definitely appeared this trip had been planned.

CHAPTER EIGHT

Hawkman left the mall, and swung by Carlotta's place. No cars were parked in the driveway today. Even though Paul had talked to the neighbors, he decided to ask a few questions. He liked to speak to people face to face; body language told him a lot.

He noticed the woman next door watering her front flower bed while watching a young child play. She watched him as he stopped in front of Carlotta's house, climbed out of the vehicle and ambled toward her. "Hi, my name's Tom Casey," he said, flashing his badge. "I'm a private investigator hired by Mr. Ryan and making a few inquiries around the neighborhood"

She reached over and turned off the water spigot. "What's going on? Paul called last night asking a bunch of questions about when I'd last talked with Carlotta and if I'd seen any strange cars in the area."

"Didn't he mention she's been missing since last Friday?"

Putting a hand to her mouth, she flopped down on the porch step. "Oh, my God! No, he didn't tell me. I figured since those two were having problems, he just wanted to know what she'd been up to. I didn't know it involved something so serious."

"There's been no word from her in almost a week and the family's getting concerned."

She frowned. "I can see why."

"Have you noticed any strange activity around the house?"

"No, just the usual traffic. The grandmother's coming and going, Paul's car on occasion." She looked thoughtful. "Now, a couple of months ago, I did see a plumber's truck stop at their place, then a couple of weeks later, another van. I figured they were repairmen."

"Do you know that for a fact?"

"Not really, but each time the man carried a box of tools into the house."

"Did you notice any signs on the sides of the vehicles?

"Only on the first one. It said something about plumbing repairs. I don't recall the name of the company. The other was just a plain white truck."

"When did you last see Carlotta?"

She rubbed her fingers against her temples. "Like I told Paul, I'm in and out so much running with the kids and their activities, I don't even know what day it is. I couldn't even give him any information when we talked, but now that I think about it, I'd just picked up my little girl, Amy from her Brownie meeting. So it had to be on a Thursday. Carlotta and I pulled into our driveways at the same time. I waved and yelled something about her heavy shopping as she lugged a bunch of sacks into the house. She just laughed and went on inside. I don't recall seeing her again."

"You said the grandmother came by often. Do you recollect the last time you saw her car here?"

"Just the other day. She and Tiffany came by, probably to pick up mail or do something."

"What about the week before?"

"Oh, gee, I can't remember, but it seems like Grandma Ryan came by everyday. I know Carlotta got awfully aggravated by her just popping in."

"She mentioned these visits to you?"

"Several times. Said Delia tried to interfere with the way she raised Tiffany and she'd grown to hate the woman more and more with each passing hour."

"I see. What about Paul? Did he come by often?"

"Not as much as his mother. He'd drop by maybe two or three times a week to pick up Tiffany, but seldom got out of the car. He'd give a couple of beeps on the horn and she'd run out. They'd be gone several hours, and when they returned, he never went inside. Tiffany would hop out of the car and run into the house."

Hawkman put out his hand. "Thanks for talking with me. By the way, I didn't catch your name."

"Sue Alexander." She stood and picked up the child playing at her feet. "I sure wish I'd been more help. Do you think something horrible has happened?"

"We certainly hope not."

Touching the brim of his hat, Hawkman turned and headed for his vehicle. After going to several of the other neighbors on the block, he finally gave up on the idea of getting any new information. The families were busy and couldn't tell him much more than Sue had already revealed.

Before driving away from the area, he contacted Paul and inquired about the numerous phone calls coming from Carlotta's place. "Why did she want to talk to you so often?"

"Most of the time it was to take Tiffany to a school function. As I told you, she didn't want to get involved in any of our daughter's activities, but Tiffany liked the social life. So I'd take her wherever she wanted to go."

"Does your daughter have many friends?"

"Hard to say, as Carlotta seldom lets her have anyone over, giving excuses about not going to be home or she didn't feel like hassling with a bunch of snotty nosed kids."

"How about Tiffany's visiting her peers?"

"On rare occasions she'd be invited to a birthday party or a sleep over. I usually took and picked her up. Carlotta didn't even want to meet the mothers."

"That seems rather odd behavior."

"I thought so too. My wife is very possessive in one way, but in another, very selfish. People don't trust her and I feel because of her attitude, parents keep their girls away from Tiffany." He let out a sigh. "And since she dresses like a teenager, a lot of mothers don't approve. They're not ready for that type of change in their daughters yet."

"Why didn't you have more of a say on Tiffany's clothes selections?"

"God knows I tried. But once I left for work, Carlotta took over."

"What about now? She's not around. You and your mother could control what the child wears."

"Yeah, but once Carlotta returns, it would fall right back into the same old routine. I don't want to confuse my daughter any more than necessary. It's hard enough on her right now without her mother around. Children are affected by their parents' breakup and Tiffany's no different. Mom seems to help bridge the gap in the problem."

"How? She told me about Tiffany hearing her and Carlotta disagreeing over her mode of dress."

"True, but Mom never speaks negatively about Carlotta to Tiffany. She knows it would backfire and she doesn't want any thing to interfere with the relationship with her granddaughter. I don't know if she told you, but Carlotta threatened her over the argument about Tiffany's belly button ring."

"Yes, she did."

"So you can see how Carlotta could be quite effective in getting her way."

"I'm beginning to get a much clearer picture of your wife."

"Not too pretty, I'm afraid."

"Let's just say, interesting."

After Hawkman hung up from Paul, and before he could leave, a call came in from the artist Jack Franklin.

"Yes, Mr. Franklin, Detective Williams gave me your name. I need a couple of sketches. The descriptions would come from a ten year old girl. Do you have good luck with children?"

"I find them pretty accurate, that is, if it hasn't been too long since they saw the person."

"How about a couple of months."

"That should be okay. Usually with a few questions, I can draw out the details."

"Excellent. When's a good time for you?"

"How about this weekend? I'm free Saturday or Sunday afternoon."

"Let me get back to you. Are you home now?"

"Yes."

"I'll give you a call as soon as I can."

"Very good."

Hawkman telephoned the grandmother.

"Hello, Mrs. Ryan. Tom Casey."

"Please call me Delia."

"Okay, Delia. Did Paul inform you I wanted to have Tiffany give an artist the description of the two men who visited Carlotta?"

"Yes, he did. I approached Tiffany about it and she thinks it would really be neat."

"The man is free Saturday or Sunday afternoon. What's a good time?"

"Make it Saturday. We're going to a concert in the park on Sunday."

"Say around two."

"That's perfect."

"Okay, see you then."

Hawkman called Franklin back and set up the time. "What's your fee for two sketches? And should I meet you at the house or would you prefer I pick you up?"

He quoted a price. "Why don't I just meet you there. It's easier. Normally, I can finish the sketches on the spot, but if I feel I need to touch them up a bit, you can pick them up later and pay me."

After giving him Delia's address, Hawkman called Mrs. Ryan back and verified the appointment.

He decided to give Jennifer a call before starting home. "Hi hon, tried to call you earlier but didn't catch you. How are you feeling?"

"The doctor wanted to see me as soon as possible and he had an opening this afternoon, so I ran in."

"I'm listening."

"He suspects a kidney stone."

"Those things are painful when you try to pass them. What's his suggestion?"

"He wants to do a intravenous pyelogram."

"What the hell is that?"

CHAPTER NINE

Jennifer laughed. "It's only a x-ray, but the twenty-four hour prep will be the bugger."

"What if he finds a kidney stone?"

"There are methods available where they can crush it before the thing travels down the ureter causing horrible pain."

"When is this going to be done?"

"Boy, you have your nerve teasing me about asking a lot of questions," she chortled. "It's set up for Monday. Let's hope the stone doesn't start moving beforehand."

"What if it does?"

"I'll head for the hospital."

Hawkman felt his throat constrict. "From what I understand, stones are no fun and a person is in too much pain to drive. I have an appointment Saturday afternoon. Should I cancel it?"

"No. I'll be fine. If you're not here and I run into trouble, I'll call an ambulance."

"I hope you're serious, and promise you won't try to deal with it by yourself."

"Hawkman, will you quit worrying. We'll talk when you get home."

"I'm on my way now. I'll see you in a couple of hours."

He put his cell phone in the compartment next to the gear shift and pulled away from the curb. It bothered him not knowing what the procedure entailed for Jennifer. And this thing about a possible kidney stone concerned him even more. If it started moving, and she tried to drive herself to the hospital, it could mean big trouble. He'd wait until after he talked to her tonight before canceling the artist.

Driving toward Copco Lake, he caught himself exceeding the speed limit several times. He didn't need a ticket, so threw on the cruise control when traffic allowed. Finally, the bridge passing over the Klamath River came into sight and he could see his house. He exhaled a breath of relief as he pulled into the garage. Before jumping out of the vehicle, he grabbed his cell phone from the console and stuck it into his pocket. When he entered the kitchen, he noticed a raft of prescriptions lined up on the kitchen bar. Jennifer sat at her computer and glanced up with a sly grin.

"My goodness, you made it home in record time."

"I'm worried about you. Other than a cold, you've never been sick since we've been married."

"I don't think there's anything to be troubled about. My doctor's going to find out what's happening and he'll take care of the problem."

Hawkman picked up a blue paper on the counter titled 'Patient Page', and walked toward Jennifer. "They're calling this an in-depth x-ray. I've never heard of an intravenous pyelogram. It says it's over an hour long and involves an examination of the urinary tract, including the kidneys, ureters and bladder, often done when a patient complains of pain in those areas. But you said you hadn't experienced pain."

"I've only had a slight show of blood in the urine."

He frowned. "You never told me."

She rested her chin on the palm of her hand. "It sounded too scary."

"You said you have a twenty-four hour preparation before this test. What does it involve?

"I have to completely clean out my intestinal tract on Sunday. I don't do well with laxatives, so I have a feeling it's not going to be pleasant."

"I'll be here with you. And we'll see how things go tomorrow and Saturday morning. If no problems arise, I'll keep the appointment. It shouldn't take too long and I'll have my cell phone charged to the hilt. If anything happens, promise you'll call me immediately."

She moved around her computer terminal and put her arms around his waist. "Honey, I love you. Everything's going to be fine. Now, let's talk about something else."

He let out a sigh and hugged her close. Stroking her long brown hair cascading down her back, he closed his eyes and kissed the top of her head. "You'll never know how much I love you."

Her hazel eyes glistened with moisture, she gently pushed away and smiled. "Tell me about your day."

He removed a folded paper from his pocket and handed it to her. "I need your input on something. I found a clothing store where Carlotta shopped the day before she disappeared. The clerk made me a copy of the items she'd purchased. I want you to look them over and tell me what you think."

"Still no word from Carlotta?"

"Nothing. And not a clue to where she's gone. It's a real baffler."

Jennifer sat down at the kitchen bar, unfolded the sheet and read the list aloud. "Bathing suit with matching jacket, seven pairs of bikini panties, four lace uplift brassieres, silk robe with matching negligee and scuffs, three sets of shorts, a pair of designer jeans, three packages of hose, two silk blouses, and two pairs of shoes." She raised a brow and glanced at Hawkman. "Judging from these items, I'd gather this woman had a jaunt planned with a man."

"Why do you say that?"

"Because of the sexy nightgown and underwear."

"Even if this is her normal attire, would those purchases still indicate a trip?"

"I think so, because she's practically replenished her wardrobe. My guess is she's taking a cruise or going to a warm place because of the bathing suit and shorts."

"Hmm. Interesting. I found no airline or cruise ticket purchases on her credit card."

Jennifer placed the list on the counter. "Of course not, a man probably invited her and the vacation's already set up."

Hawkman tapped the top of the bar with his finger tips. "Now to find the man. The two clowns Tiffany described, don't sound like they'd have the money. But one never knows."

"Have you located either of them?"

"No. The names she supplied didn't pan out. The appointment I have set up on Saturday is with one of the artists from the police department. He's to meet me at Delia's place around two in the afternoon. I'm hoping Tiffany can give good enough descriptions so I'll have something to go on."

"Good idea. I'll be interested in seeing those drawings."

***

Hawkman hung around the house Friday, not letting Jennifer out of his sight for more than a few minutes. Saturday morning, he paced the floor wondering if he'd made the right decision to leave. Finally, she came up behind him and poked him on the shoulder.

"Honey, you better get going. You want to be there when the artist arrives at Delia's."

"Are you going to be all right?"

"So far, I'm fine. So don't worry, I'll call you if there's any change."

Reluctantly, Hawkman left the house and headed for Medford. He parked in front of Delia's house about fifteen minutes before the scheduled appointment. Tiffany ran out of the door, toting the new kitten over her arm. He also noticed she had on a pair of normal cut jeans along with a colorful tee shirt that covered her midriff.

"Hi, Mr. Casey."

"Well, hello, Tiffany. How's the new kitten doing?"

"I really like her and Grandma says she's really a smart kitty. And she's so funny when she plays. Makes me laugh a lot.

"I'm happy she's turning out to be a good pet. Have you named her?"

"I call her Princess." She pointed at the cat's white ears. "See this little gray circle of hair? It looks like a small crown."

"Yes, I see it. You picked a good title. Tell me, are you nervous about talking to the artist?"

She rubbed her nose against the cat's head. "No, I think it'll be great."

"Good, he should be here any moment."

About that time, an older Honda Accord pulled up and a man in his early thirties got out carrying a large sketch book. He had twinkling blue eyes with a short trimmed beard and neat mustache.

"Hi, there. I'm Jack Franklin." He came forward with his hand extended. "You must be Tom Casey."

They shook and Hawkman turned toward Tiffany. "This is Ms. Tiffany Ryan. She's looking forward to talking with you."

He smiled and petted the feline's head. "Hey, I may have to take time to sketch this beautiful kitten, too."

Tiffany's eyes opened wide. "Really?"

Delia opened the front door. "You guys coming inside or are you going to stand out there all afternoon."

"We're coming, Grandma." She grabbed Jack's hand and practically dragged him toward the entry. They were both laughing by the time they entered the house.

Hawkman followed and smiled to himself. The man definitely knew how to handle children.

When they all arrived inside, Delia led the artist and Tiffany into the dining room overlooking the pool. She'd put a pitcher of lemonade and a plate of cookies on the table, then motioned for Hawkman to go into the kitchen. "I don't think we want to bother them," she whispered.

He nodded. "You're absolutely right. We want no distraction from the business at hand." He tried to concentrate on his conversation with Delia, but his attention wandered to the male voice in the other room. He heard Tiffany laugh a couple of times, then their conversation lowered to soft and serious.

Hawkman excused himself and exited to the front yard where he phoned Jennifer. "Hi, hon, how are you doing?"

"Fine, no problems. Is your artist doing the sketches?"

"Yes. And he's definitely got a way with kids. He's even had Tiffany laughing. I'm anxious to see the drawings. He should be through shortly and I'll get home."

"Okay, no hurry. I'm doing okay."

Hawkman strolled back into the house just as Tiffany jumped up and took the sheet of paper Jack handed her.

"Oh, this is perfect," she exclaimed, her eyes sparkling. "Look at this, Mr. Casey." She turned the sheet toward him showing a very accurate picture of her holding Princess.

"It almost looks like a photograph," Hawkman said.

Delia studied the picture and beamed. "We'll get this framed immediately. Mr. Franklin really caught your sweet expression, Tiffany. And it appears Princess is going to jump right out of your arms." She smiled at Jack. "You're excellent."

He shrugged and grinned. "Thank you."

The two men walked to the car, where he showed Hawkman the sketches of the men Tiffany described.

He held up the first drawing. "This one Tiffany called 'Derrick' and said he had a funny last name she couldn't remember." He flipped the page over. "She called this man 'Jack Smith', but doubted that's his real name. He handed them to Hawkman. I've sprayed the drawings so they won't smudge."

"Did she have any trouble remembering the men?"

"No. But she did say the man with the scar on his cheek had mean eyes. I got the impression he scared her."

"Yes, I had the same feeling." Hawkman handed the artist a check. "Thanks for your time. I really appreciate it."

"It's great doing the things you love. I hope these work out."

"So do I."

CHAPTER TEN

Hawkman gently placed the two sketches on the middle seat of his 4X4. He'd study them closer when he got home, then later encase them in plastic for protection. It took the artist a little longer than two hours to get the drawings done, but he did an excellent job and had a way of making his young subject relax. Hawkman glanced toward the house. He still had a few questions only Tiffany could answer, but they'd have to wait until he didn't have so much on his mind. These positive events would only make things easier when the time came.

His concern over Jennifer made him edgy. He hopped into his vehicle, waved to Jack and took off. It seemed like the trip home took forever, but soon he passed over the bridge and parked in the garage. He carefully carried the portraits into the house.

Jennifer looked up from her computer and smiled. "Hi."

It relieved him to see her in her normal spot. "You look mighty perky."

"I feel just fine. Still have symptoms, but hopefully we'll know what they are by Monday."

"No pain?"

"None."

"That's good." He placed the drawings on the dining room table.

She got up and moved next to him. "Very interesting. The artist is good. These almost look like black and white photographs. But these guys certainly don't look meek and mild. They're pretty rugged looking characters."

Hawkman pointed to the one where the artist had written

'Jack Smith' in the corner. Mr. Franklin told me Tiffany appeared frightened of this one."

"I can understand why. He's definitely not good looking with that jagged scary scar on his cheek below those scornful eyes. Is he the plumber?"

"No. Not sure what he does. Tiffany had no idea and didn't think her mother called him by his correct name. The neighbor, Sue, suspected both were handymen of some sort as they carried tools when she saw them enter the house. I figure she spotted them on their first visit, because Tiffany implied they both returned at later dates. However, I got the impression they only visited a few times before Carlotta gave them the boot or at least didn't continue any sort of relationship in front of her daughter"

"Then why are you interested in these men?"

"Because, one never knows what lurks in the minds of a jilted lover."

"Well, if anyone's gotten a dirty deal, how about her husband, Paul?"

"I haven't ruled him out either."

She frowned. "But he hired you to find Carlotta."

"Doesn't matter. It's a good cover-up."

Hawkman stared at the pictures. "Have you ever seen either one of these men?"

"No, but wouldn't you imagine they'd roam around Medford instead of our area?"

"Probably." He held up one of the drawings. "By the way, do you have something I could back these with? I don't want to tear them."

"Sure." Jennifer went into the kitchen and came back carrying a couple pieces of cardboard and a box of plastic wrap. She helped Hawkman secure and cover the sketches.

"Thanks. Now they don't feel quite as fragile."

"How are you going to find these men?"

"I don't know. Sure didn't have any luck with the plumbing companies or the phone listings, so thought I'd see if they're in the mug books at the police station. If I don't find them there, I'll have to do some leg work."

She picked up one of the drawings and studied it. "I hate to say it, but if looks have anything to do with it, I'd suspect these men of taking or dealing drugs. Both have shallow looking eyes, with long and unkempt hair." She pointed to Jack Smith. "His beard and mustache are really scraggy and the scar doesn't help his appearance." Placing them back on the table, she put a hand on her hip and scowled. "Why in the world would Carlotta be interested in this type of man, when she has a good looking guy who can supply her every desire? Do you think she's into drugs?"

"Anything's possible. Tulip said she'd complained about what a boring life she had with Paul."

Jennifer folded her arms. "Well, she might find she's bitten off more than she can chew if she's going to attempt to handle the likes of these creatures."

"Very true. One of the reasons I'm interested in talking with them is to find out what they thought of Carlotta and when they saw her last. Let's hope they're still in the area so I can locate them."

***

The next day, Jennifer started the laxative regimen and it hit her immediately. She spent most of the day in the bathroom. Since she couldn't eat any solid foods, Hawkman made her Jell-O and gave her liquids, which soon made her gag.

"Oh, my, I'll be glad when tomorrow is here," she said, flopping onto the bed and holding her stomach. "I'm so miserable."

By nightfall, Hawkman felt relieved when she finally went to sleep. The next morning, he took her to the hospital for the intravenous pyelogram. He tried reading a magazine in the waiting room, but couldn't sit still, so he paced and prayed if they found a stone they'd be able to crush it right away.

An hour and a half passed before Jennifer left the x-ray room looking pale. The doctor followed her out.

"Mrs. Casey, don't leave. I'm going to check with the radiologist and see if they discovered anything."

He left the room only to return shortly, motioning for Jennifer and Hawkman to come into his office. Once they were all seated, he glanced at the report in front of him and took a deep breath. "Mrs. Casey, the technician found no stone. However, there's something pressing against the ureter where it joins the bladder. I'm going to set you up for a CAT scan, also an appointment with a kidney specialist so we can see what's going on. Your urine specimens have been erratic. One time they showed a high white cell count, but the last one was normal. It doesn't make sense."

Jennifer gnawed her lower lip. "How soon will you set these up?"

"I'm putting a 'stat' on the requests, which means immediate attention, so hopefully within the next day or two. I'm hoping to get the CAT scan before your appointment with the urologist, but we'll take what we can get. Someone will call and make arrangements for the time."

Hawkman listened with concern. "Doctor, is this serious?"

"We won't know until we get more tests done."

They left the building in silence. Hawkman held onto Jennifer's arm and helped her into the SUV. As he walked around the rear of the vehicle, he placed a toothpick between his teeth and clamped down hard, then climbed into the driver's side. "You comfortable?"

She nodded and let out a sigh. "I so hoped they'd find something we could fix today."

"Yeah, me too. Do you feel like getting a bite to eat?"

"No," she said, hugging herself. "I just want to go home."

CHAPTER ELEVEN

That night, Hawkman stayed up and watched the late news so Jennifer would have time to relax and fall asleep before he hit the bed. When he finally went into their room, he stood for several minutes gazing at her, his heart heavy at the thought of what she'd gone through yesterday, only to come home today with no answers. And the doctor hadn't given them much of an explanation about the problem either. He hoped the other tests she had to undergo wouldn't be as hard on her system.

He undressed, placed his eye-patch on the bedside table, then slipped between the sheets. His arms ached to pull her close, but not wanting to disturb her, turned away. Suddenly, his ears perked when she let out a loud sigh. He sat straight up and stared at his wife. She rolled over, and tugged at the covers until she had them wrapped around her shoulders. He wondered if she'd experienced a chill. Since she'd had nothing to eat but liquids the day before and only a bowl of chicken noodle soup tonight, it sounded reasonable. Maybe he should get the afghan off the couch. He observed her for several more minutes until her breathing became deep and regular. Satisfied she appeared warm enough, he eased down onto the pillow and closed his eyes.

Arising early the next morning, Hawkman put on the coffee pot, then sauntered into the living room where he stared out over the lake, trying to decide if he should go into the office. He knew Jennifer wouldn't want him hovering over her all day, but that's what he wanted to do. The Carlotta case could wait. In fact, he debated whether he should return Paul's check and tell him to find another investigator. His mind kept jumping back and forth from Jennifer's problem to the missing woman.

He drifted back into the kitchen and took his mug off the top of the refrigerator and poured a cup of the hot brew. As he turned around, his heart squeezed. Jennifer stood at the edge of the counter smiling.

"Good morning, sweetheart," she said. "That coffee smells delicious and I'm starved."

He grinned. "Sounds like good news. I'll get you a cup." He tied a baker's apron around his waist. "And what would madam like to order this morning?"

"Oh, what a treat," she said, slipping onto one of the kitchen stools. "I'll have bacon, eggs and toast."

He placed the big skillet on the burner. "Coming right up."

***

After breakfast, Jennifer sat at the kitchen bar and watched Hawkman clean up the mess. "Honey, I want you to stop worrying about me."

He leaned across the counter and cupped her chin in his hand. "That's asking a lot."

She entwined her fingers around his. "I'm going to be fine. The doctors will find the problem and correct it."

"I don't like all the mystery. Your primary doctor doesn't seem to have a clue about what's going on."

"He's only an M.D., not a specialist. At least he's not sitting on it and is referring me to someone who might be able to diagnose my problem."

"Yeah, you're right. But you've always been healthy."

"I still am. So a little problem has occurred. I don't want you hanging around here moping. Get on with your case and we'll take one step at a time."

"When you read my mind, you scare me."

She grinned. "Why?"

"Because, I'd about decided to give Paul back his check and tell him to hire another investigator."

Jennifer shook her head vehemently. "No way. You'd drive me crazy hanging around here. I don't want us changing our life style because of some minor health problem. You keep working on the case and I'll keep writing my books."

He reached over and touched her cheek. "It's a deal."

After he hung around observing Jennifer for an hour, he felt it would be safe to leave her. He placed the sketches in a binder and took off for Medford. Stopping by the police station, he showed Detective Williams the drawings.

After Williams studied the portraits, he folded his arms and leaned back in his chair. "This one looks familiar." He pointed at the one of Derrick. "But right off the top of my head, I don't recognize these two. You certainly might find them in the mug book. They definitely don't have the appeal of upstanding citizens."

"My impression exactly."

"Let me know."

"Will do."

Hawkman found a vacant computer room where he could study the mug book without being interrupted. He had the pictures of the two men pretty much in his mind, but placed the sketches on the table so he could compare the shots. He booted up the computer and clicked on the mug book icon. Meticulously studying each picture, it didn't take long before he spotted the photo of the so-called Jack Smith. His real name appeared to be Alfonso Gomez. He quickly went to the data file and discovered the man had been arrested a year ago on a felony drug charge, but then released for lack of evidence. He'd also been hauled in for involvement in a bar brawl, but again the charges were dismissed. After printing out the file, Hawkman continued his search for Derrick.

Several minutes later, he found a clean shaven man resembling the sketch. Hawkman played with the computer until he had a mustache and small beard placed on the face. The photo fit. The man's name was Derrick Altbusser. No wonder Tiffany didn't catch the German last name. He pulled up the data on this man and found similar charges, also dismissed.

Both men had associated with drugs. No biggies, but they were connected with the drug world and obviously knew dealers to supply their habits. Could it be Carlotta decided to get a few kicks and experiment? This might put a whole new approach on investigating her disappearance.

He rubbed a hand across his face and fingered his own mustache. The thought of dropping such a bomb on Paul would probably put him into shock, but he'd have to find out if he ever suspected Carlotta of doing drugs. It might explain her uncaring attitude toward her daughter's school activities, along with her unusual behavior toward Tiffany's friends and their parents. He'd talk to Paul first, then approach Delia.

He gathered up the printed materials, put them into the folder and strolled back to Detective Williams' office.

"You busy?"

"I'm always busy. But have a seat and tell me what you found."

Hawkman placed the printouts of the two men in front of the detective. "The data file had fairly recent addresses, so they may still live in the same places. Anyway, this is where I'll start my search."

Williams tapped his pen on the desk top as he looked over the information. "Appears our little lady may have gotten involved with the wrong crowd."

"Yes, and it bothers me. I have a feeling she's very naive. Could have easily been swept along with the crowd and who knows where she's ended up. Maybe in a shallow grave."

The detective turned a sharp eye toward Hawkman. "You don't usually go for the negative."

Hawkman swept up the files and stowed them back into his folder. Pushing back his cowboy hat, he sighed. "Yeah, I know. But my gut tells me there's something terribly wrong here. And it's bugging the hell out of me because I can't put my finger on it."

"You will. The case is young."

"The lady's been missing over a week. Not a good sign."

Williams fiddled with some papers on his desk. "You've got a point. But things will come together."

Picking up the binder, Hawkman stood. "Won't keep you any longer. I'll let you know if anything breaks."

The detective gave a salute. "Same here. Good luck."

Hawkman left the station and climbed into his 4X4, leaving the door open while he called Jennifer. "Hi, hon, any news?"

"Yes, both appointments are set up. However, the CAT scan is the day after the appointment with the kidney doctor. But I spoke with my primary physician and he said it won't make any difference. The kidney doctor plans on doing a cystoscopy."

"A what?"

Jennifer laughed. "You definitely don't understand medical terms."

"No. I've never dealt with many doctors except for my eye and few injuries. But I've never heard of all these test they're doing on you. So what's this one about?"

"I'll explain it more in detail when you get home. It's no big deal."

"Give me some sort of a hint."

She chuckled. "It involves inserting a narrow telescope and inspecting my bladder."

"Good Lord, I hope they'll put you under."

"No. It's not painful. In fact, I've researched it on the internet. I'll be able to watch a monitor and see what I look like inside."

"You actually want to see it?"

"Sure, it'll be interesting."

"When is this test?"

"Thursday and the CAT scan will be on Friday. You know what that is, don't you?"

"Yes, they put a dye in your arm, then run the big machine over your body and take layered pictures."

"Very good. So I probably won't get the results until Monday."

"So we're playing the waiting game again. How are you feeling?"

"Fine. At least we know there isn't a kidney stone waiting to make it's appearance."

"I guess that's good news."

"Did you find those guys in the mug book?"

"Yes. I'm leaving the police station now and going to their last known addresses."

"Good luck. I'll talk to you later."

Hawkman hung up and shut the vehicle door. He took the data file from the binder and checked the addresses. Alfonso Gomez's dwelling sounded familiar. He also recognized the hotel address given as Derrick's residence. He'd hit there first, since it was closer. He removed his shoulder holster and gun from under the seat and slipped it on. After shrugging back into his jacket, he glanced at the sheet and checked the room number, then placed the papers on the passenger seat. He turned on the ignition and drove into the street.

When he arrived at the hotel, he pulled into their lot but hated to park among all the junker cars. At least the sun hadn't gone down and it would probably be safe. He set the alarm and locked up.

Straightening his jacket and adjusting his hat down above his brows, he made his way to the entry. The old place had been somewhat transformed. A new coat of paint enhanced the outside and plants graced the flower boxes going up the steps. He figured it had either changed hands or a couple of women had moved in. When he tugged open the heavy front door, it didn't squeak and his boots sunk into new carpeting at the entry. With all this up grading, Derrick might not have been able to afford the rent and moved out. He'd better check the registry at the desk first.

A small sign tacked on the wall had 'office' with an arrow pointing to his right. He moved into the room and approached the tall bar like structure located at the far end. A poster stating the services available rested on the counter top and a young woman sat on a bar stool behind it reading a romance novel. Hawkman stood for a moment waiting for her to look up, but she seemed so engrossed, he finally cleared his throat. She almost jumped off the chair and her hand went to her heart.

"Oh, you scared me half to death."

Hawkman snickered. "That must be a pretty good book."

She blushed. "Yeah, it is. Can I help you?"

"I'm looking for a Derrick Altbusser. This is the last address I have of my old buddy, but wanted to make sure he still lived here before I ran up and down the hall banging on doors."

"Sure doesn't sound familiar," she said, looking thoughtful. "But let me check." She thumbed through a ledger on the desk. "No, we don't have anyone here by that name."

"Do you by any chance have a record about a year ago. Maybe you could see if he left a forwarding address?"

"Sure, hold on a minute." She left the room and returned with another large black bound book and plopped it on the counter. Flipping through the pages, she ran her finger down a line of names. "Here he is. He moved out about eight months ago. The only forwarding address he left is a Post Office Box number. You want it?"

"It might help. Maybe I can track him down."

"One, five, four, six."

He jotted the digits on a slip of paper and slipped it into his pocket. "Thanks, appreciate your help."

Hawkman left the hotel and drove toward the other address, when he rounded the corner, he remembered Tulip Withers lived in this same complex.

CHAPTER TWELVE

Hawkman had Alfonso's apartment number, but decided to stop and check with management to see if he still lived in the complex. He parked and a thought flashed through his mind. He quickly jotted on the note pad he kept in the vehicle; call Phillips and Cramer law specialist in Grants Pass and find out if they were back in their building this week.

He left his vehicle and strolled into the small dingy room, but found no one manning the desk. A small bell sat on the top of a stack of papers, so he hit it a couple of times. Shortly, a man about five foot four, his shirt straining at the buttons over a fat beer belly, came slowly out of the back through a curtained doorway. A cheap cigar hung from his lips and the odor permeated the area.

"Yeah, can I help ya?"

Hawkman flashed his badge. "I'm looking for Alfonso Gomez, wanted to check and see if he still lives here."

"Got his room number?"

"Two forty-four."

When the man opened a large black ledger, a big ash fell off his cigar onto the pages. He brushed it aside and adjusted his reading glasses. Running his finger down the margin, he glanced up. "Yep. He still lives in the same place."

"Do you have his employment record?"

The fellow let out a wheeze and rested the cigar in a filthy ashtray. "I'll have to check his folder. Is this guy in some kind of trouble?"

"Not sure."

"I'm usually not required to give out personal information. But I don't want no problems at my place. Hold on a second."

He turned to a tall filing cabinet and pulled open a drawer. After a few moments, he took out a small folder and thumbed through the sheets. "The last employment I have listed is six months old."

"Who's it with?"

"Group called, 'Handyman for Hire'."

"Has he always paid his rent on time."

"Yep, first of every month."

"Ever had any issues with him?"

He shook is head. "Nope."

"Okay. You've answered my questions. Thanks for your help."

Hawkman left the vile smelling room and climbed into his 4X4. He drove around building two and spotted the apartment on the lower floor. No working van was apparent in the parking area, but the company possibly supplied the vehicles which the employees weren't allowed to bring home. He pulled to a stop and went to the door. After knocking for several seconds with no answer, he turned to leave just as a man in the next unit stepped outside and glanced in his direction.

"You looking for Alfonso?"

"Yes."

"He's gone most every day of the week doing odd jobs."

"Does he still work for "Handyman for Hire"?

"Yeah."

"What time does he get home? I might have some work for him?"

"All depends on what he's doing. But he's normally here around six o'clock or a little later."

"Thanks, I'll check back this evening."

Before pulling away from the apartment, Hawkman punched in the phone number of the law offices in Grants Pass. "This is Tom Casey, private investigator. I'd like to speak with the lawyer handling Carlotta Ryan's case."

"Hold on a minute."

"Jessica Phillips."

Hawkman hesitated a moment when the heard the woman's voice, but then repeated his spiel and asked when she'd last seen Carlotta.

"I'm sorry sir, but I'm not allowed to divulge that type of information."

"The woman's been missing for over a week and the family is quite concerned. Have you seen or talked to her?"

"Oh, my. No, I haven't seen her for over two weeks," she said, her voice sounding a bit flustered.

"Did she approach you about a divorce?"

"Sir, could we set up an appointment? I don't like to discuss these things over the phone."

"Sure. When's a good time?"

"How about Wednesday afternoon at three o'clock"

"I'll be there."

"Could I have your name again?"

After hanging up, Hawkman figured she'd check him out, which suited him fine. The appointment time was perfect, as Jennifer didn't go for her tests until Thursday and Friday.

He drove away from the complex and headed for the post office. Inside, he walked up and down the row of small boxes set into the wall until he finally found number one five four six. Shading the glass with his hand, he squinted into the small door. He could make out the name Derrick Althusser on the top letter. So the man still collected his mail from a P.O. box. He'd go into the computer and do a search; maybe he'd have some luck in finding a recent address.

Dropping by a fast food place, he grabbed a hamburger, fries and soda to go. He parked in the alley behind his office, then walked around to the donut shop and bought a cream filled eclair. He plopped down at his desk and hit the answering machine. His stomach turned a flip flop when Jennifer's voice came through on the first message.

"Hi, hon. Just wanted you to know I'm running into Yreka to do some shopping. Didn't want you to worry. I'm feeling fine. Love ya, Jen."

Hawkman breathed a sigh of relief and unwrapped his food. After he ate, he wiped off the desk with a napkin, and threw the debris into the trash can, then phoned Paul. "Tom Casey, here. Am I calling at a bad time?"

"No, I'm on a break. What's happening?"

"Not a lot, but I'm moving on some leads. I need you to do me a favor. I want you to check Carlotta's credit card bill and see if she's made any purchases since she's been gone. If she has, check the store and the town."

"That'll be easy enough, I can go onto the computer and get the latest update."

"Great, get back to me as soon as you can."

Paul returned the call within an hour. "Mr. Casey. there's no new charges on her card since the date she disappeared."

"That's interesting."

"Have you kept a vigilant watch on the phone messages at the house?"

"Yes, one or two for Tiffany. And a couple of tele marketers. Nothing personal for Carlotta. Not even a hang-up."

"Keep an eye on the credit card usage and report back to me if anything shows up, also on any strange calls that might come in."

"Will do."

Hawkman booted up the computer and clicked on the program he'd purchased to help him search for missing persons. He entered Medford, Oregon, into the search square along with Derrick Althusser's name. The computer hummed for a few seconds, then popped up with a recent address and phone number. He jotted down the information, then punched in the digits on his portable phone. After four rings, an answering machine came on. "You've reached Derrick, leave a message and I'll get back to you as soon as I can."

He dropped the receiver on the cradle. Glancing at his watch, he decided he'd have time to check out the address before he hit Alfonso's pad. Rereading the street and number, he realized he hadn't been in that area for a long time, so took his

GPS receiver and mapped it out. He shut down the computer, unplugged the coffee pot and headed out the door.

Arriving at the address, he discovered what appeared to be an old motel turned into apartments. Not too shabby, but nothing one could brag about. He drove down the long driveway and found number eleven. It surprised him to find the place draped in yellow police tape across the entry and front lawn.

This didn't look good, so he phoned Detective Williams on his cell. "Hey Williams," he gave Derrick Althusser's address. "What gives?"

Hawkman could hear the detective rustling papers. "Appears the man overdosed. Got a call this morning from a neighbor. Said he couldn't rouse his buddy, and they were due on a job."

"Did the guy find him inside?"

"No, said he couldn't get Derrick to answer the door. It worried him, because he knew he messed with drugs, so he went back to his place and called us from there. Sure enough, we broke open the door and found him on the living room floor dead. Why are you interested?"

"He's one of the men in the sketches I showed you."

"I thought one of them looked familiar, but I couldn't place him at the moment. And I didn't have the report in front of me. The artist did an excellent job. Now that I think about it, looked just like the guy."

"You sure he died of an overdose?"

"Haven't gotten the autopsy report back, but his body had all the earmarks."

"Find anything in his room that might connect him to Carlotta Ryan?"

"Haven't finished investigating the scene yet, but so far, nothing."

"Let me know, if you do."

"Sure thing."

Hawkman made a U-turn and headed out of the complex.

He could mark Derrick off the list. But it did indicate Carlotta might have used drugs. He'd talk to Paul about any suspicions he had about his wife using narcotics.

CHAPTER THIRTEEN

Hawkman drove toward Alfonso's place. *When he came* within sight of the man's apartment, he noticed a white van in front with one of those magnetic signs on the side that read "Handyman for Hire". Easy to remove if you're doing a drug run, he thought, as he parked alongside.

He reached inside his jacket and released the velcro catch off his shoulder holster. "Can't be too cautious," he muttered. Buttoning his jeans jacket at the waist, he climbed out of the 4X4. On the way to the entry, he flipped on the voice activated recorder in his pocket.

Alfonso opened the door on the second knock. A towel hung around his neck, and his hair dripped with water as though he'd just stepped out of the shower. He gave Hawkman a questioning look. "Yeah?"

Interesting, Hawkman thought, as he noted the man had a fresh haircut and had shaved off his beard and mustache. The scar down his cheek stood out like a piece of shiny silk. "You Alfonso Gomez?"

"If you want a job done, you need to call and set up an appointment."

Hawkman flashed his badge. "No, I'm a private investigator and need to talk to you about Carlotta Ryan."

The man's face paled for a split second, then recovered quickly. "Don't know her."

He started to close the door, but Hawkman blocked it with his foot. "Yeah, you do. Carlotta's daughter identified you as Jack Smith."

The man's eyes narrowed. "Oh, yeah? Well, I ain't Jack Smith either."

"The mug shots at the police station proved you're Alfonso Gomez. And you've been in trouble with the law a couple of times."

"So have a lot of other guys in this town."

"Look, Alfonso, we can banter back and forth or I can call the police and let them question you. I thought maybe you'd be a little more cooperative. Not too good for business to have a bunch of cop cars sitting in front of your place."

He let out a grunt. "Okay, so what's the deal about Carlotta?"

"She's been missing for over a week. The family's concerned and we're trying to find her."

The man's eyes opened wide with a hint of fear. "Hey, I had a short fling with the woman a few months ago. It didn't work out and I haven't seen her since."

"How'd you meet her?"

"She set up an appointment to have her garbage disposal fixed. I went over and repaired the damn thing and before I could get out the door, she came on to me like a hot potato." A smug grin lit his lips. "Hey, she's got a beautiful body and showed most of it in her short skirt and sexy top. Boobs hanging out all over the place." He gestured with his hands in front of his chest. "Man, I got real interested, and made a date to see her later. I could just taste getting a handful of those." He rolled his eyes. "Wowee!"

"Okay, Gomez, I got the picture. So you set up a date. Did you pick her up at the house?"

"Yeah. But we couldn't leave until she made sure the nosey kid got home from school."

"Why was that?"

"Beats me. I couldn't figure it. Guess she just wanted to make sure the brat was locked in the house."

"How long did this affair go on?"

He shrugged. "A couple of weeks. Then she told me to stop comin' around."

"Did she give a reason?"

Alfonso grimaced. "Naw. Probably thought she could do better than a handyman."

"I see. Did she ever take drugs while with you?"

Alfonso shifted his position. "Huh, whatta ya mean?"

"Smoke a joint, sniff cocaine."

"What difference does it make if she's missin'?"

"I need to cover all the bases. Did she?" Hawkman watched the man's face and noted he'd averted his eyes.

"Don't remember."

"When did you see her last?"

Fiddling with the towel around his neck, he frowned. "Hey, man, I already told ya. It's been a few months." Alfonso reached for the door knob, and turned to go back inside. "I've had enough of your questions."

"Do you know Tulip Withers?"

He whipped his head around. "Who? You talkin' about a person or a flower?"

"A woman. She lives in this same complex."

Alfonso scratched his chin. " Nope, don't know no one around here. I come home from work, eat, flop into bed, and get up in the morning to go to my next job."

Hawkman turned to leave. "Thanks for your time. I may want to ask you more questions."

"Don't know what else I can tell ya. I've told ya everything I know about Carlotta." Alfonso stepped backwards into his apartment and shut the door.

Hawkman stood for a moment surveying the area. When he climbed into his vehicle, he jotted down the license plate of the Handyman's van and flipped off the recorder in his pocket. He noted it was only eight o'clock. He still had time to run by Paul's place and talk to him about his wife.

When he drove by the front of the apartment, he noted the unit sat shrouded in darkness and he didn't see the Lexus. Turning around, he headed out, but as he approached the exit, the black car swerved into the lot. Since I'm here, might as well go see him, he thought. He made a U-turn and parked next to Paul's car.

"Mr. Casey, how's it going?"

"Okay."

As the men walked toward the entry, Paul continued. "I'm concerned about my daughter. Stopped by Mom's this evening and they were out by the pool. Tiffany sat off to the side with the cat in her arms. When I tried to involve her in the conversation, she just stared off into space. It bothers me, she's just not her happy self. I think she's worried about her mother. And I don't know what to tell her."

"Not much you can say, other than be truthful. She'll see right through a lie and her trust would vanish. Tiffany's smart enough to figure something has happened."

"That's what I'm afraid of and she's imagining the worst." Paul moved around behind the bar. "Want a drink?"

"Beer's fine." Hawkman sat down on one of the stools as Paul mixed himself a cocktail. "I need to ask a few more questions about Carlotta."

"Sure."

"Was she into drugs?"

Paul looked shocked. "No. Why are you asking?"

"I suspect she might have fooled around with a few."

"Oh my God," Paul said, bringing his fist down on the bar top. "What makes you think so?"

"I became leery when you told me about her nonchalant attitude toward Tiffany's school activities and involvement with other mothers. Didn't sound natural. Plus, the men Tiffany told me about have been arrested at one time or another on drug related charges." Hawkman waved a hand. "Don't get too excited yet. It may be no more than prescription drugs. Did she ever have a reason for pain pills?"

"She hurt her back lifting stuff out of her car a few months ago, and I think the doctor gave her some, but I have no idea what kind."

Paul crossed into the living room and flopped down on the couch. "If she got into drugs of any kind, she did it after I moved out. Truthfully, I have no way of knowing what she did with herself after I left. She pretty much cut me out of her life."

Hawkman shifted from the bar stool to a chair facing Paul. "Mind if I talk to your mother?"

"No, not at all." He leaned forward placing his forearms on his knees, rotating his drink between his fingers. "She's seen more of Carlotta these past few months than I have. Her concern about Tiffany being left alone might have stemmed from her uncertainty about my wife's behavior. Even though she never mentioned it."

"It could be Delia may not have realized what she witnessed, but knew something wasn't right."

Paul placed his drink on the coffee table and rubbed the back of his neck. "I sure don't like the way things are coming down. If drugs are involved, she could be buried in some shallow grave out in the woods." He shivered. "I can just see her back talking some drug lord about the price of cocaine."

"I doubt she ever got that far in her experimenting. But it doesn't take a higher up to put her in a grave. The little guy can do it about as well."

CHAPTER FOURTEEN

The next morning, Hawkman decided to leave early and stop by Delia's before the lawyer's appointment. Tiffany would be at school, and the child didn't need to hear negative stuff about her mother at this point. Things were already making an impact on her. It made Hawkman sick to his stomach when parents didn't consider how a divorce or separation affects the children in a family. They're too interested in their own selfish wants, he thought, as he drove toward Medford.

He'd called Delia to make sure she'd be home, and she sounded pleased he wanted her involved. When he arrived, she opened the door dressed in jeans and a tee shirt, with a pan of freshly baked chocolate chip cookies in her gloved hand. The aroma swirled around Hawkman's nose.

He sniffed the air. "Oh man, those smell delicious."

She laughed. "There's plenty for you. Come into the kitchen while I put these into the cookie jar. I've got a pot of coffee brewing so we can munch and talk."

A smudge of flour rested on the tip of her nose as she busied herself. She finally washed her hands, removed her apron, set a plate of cookies on the table, and poured them each a cup of java, then she flopped into the chair. "Whew. I'd forgotten how long it took to bake cookies."

Hawkman couldn't stand the temptation and helped himself to one of the warm delicacies. Holding up half a cookie, he nodded. "Excellent."

"Thanks," she said. "They're Tiffany's favorite. Poor little thing is really in a slump. Paul and I are beside ourselves about what to do."

"Not much you can say to ease her pain. We're all in the dark right now."

An expression of concern crossed her face. "What did you want to talk about?"

"You and Paul have both discussed Carlotta's strange behavior in regard to Tiffany's activities and how she reacted to other families. Did you see a pattern develop or were those actions always there."

Delia scooted her finger around some crumbs on the table. "I'm trying to remember how she reacted when Tiffany came along. She seemed pleased and took good care of her. Not until the last couple of years did Carlotta react with displeasure when people called her to volunteer at the school. So I think the pattern developed later. She lost the sense of responsibility for taking care of her child. The things she wanted became more important than Tiffany's needs."

"Can you pinpoint anything which might have caused the change?"

"I'm sure her and Paul's marital problems didn't help."

"True. What about drugs?"

Delia shot him a look. "Are you insinuating Carlotta had a drug problem?"

"I don't know. They do alter people's minds. I'm just trying to hit all angles."

She rubbed her eyes. "I hate to admit it, but it entered my mind. I kept pushing it back, praying she had more sense."

"What made you suspicious?"

"At first, I didn't think a lot about it because she'd twisted her back and the doctor had given her some pain pills. So I figured it would be natural for her to be a little out of it during the healing process. However, several weeks passed and her demeanor became more erratic."

"How?"

"For instance, one day she left a message on my machine telling me she wouldn't be home when Tiffany got out of school and if I didn't want her there alone I better go get her. I thought it a little presumptuous as I could have had other plans. She did this several times and I finally approached her about leaving those types of messages and explained why it upset me."

"How did she respond?"

"She shrugged it off and said, Tiffany's old enough to stay by herself."

"Did you ever see Carlotta when you suspected she might be high?"

Delia sighed. "Yes. I had to take Tiffany home early one night because I had a meeting. I went inside to make sure Carlotta was there. She came staggering into the living room and almost fell. Her eyes were glassy, and she looked a mess. I asked her if she was all right and she said, "Hell yes, couldn't feel better." Shoving some loose strands of hair behind her ear, she continued. "Believe me, it sure made me hesitate about leaving my granddaughter."

"Did you witness this on more than one occasion?"

She refilled their coffee cups and sat back down. "Unfortunately, yes. Several times."

"What did Paul think of her actions?"

"I know this sounds strange, but I never told him."

Hawkman leaned forward. "Why?"

"He'd have never believed it of his beautiful Carlotta."

They spent a few minutes discussing Tiffany's change in behavior and hoped time would heal her wounds. If not, she would encourage Paul to seek professional help.

Checking his watch, Hawkman rose. "I've got an out-of-town appointment, so I better get on the road. Thanks for your time."

"Good seeing you again."

He left Delia's, baffled by the information. Why had she not confided in her son with Tiffany's welfare at stake? Did she feel she alone had the power to protect her granddaughter from whatever evil lurked? Maybe she's read too many weird books. But now he could see why Delia had been so obsessed with not letting Tiffany be by herself. What bothered him the most, was the thought of the child unaccompanied with a drugged mother. Tiffany could have been in more danger than being left alone in an empty house.

Delia pretty much confirmed his suspicions about her daughter-in-law's possible drug use. Maybe a more thorough search of Carlotta's house would turn up something.

As he drove toward Grants Pass, his mind drifted to the questions he'd ask the lawyer, Jessica Phillips. He wondered how much she'd answer without being subpoenaed? She seemed rattled on the phone when he admitted Carlotta had been missing for over a week, and it might act in his favor.

He arrived at the complex address and spotted the lawyers' offices on the ground floor. After parking, he walked into the waiting room with ten minutes to spare. The receptionist at the front desk glanced up and gave him a wary smile. It always amused him when young people saw him for the first time. They usually backed off from a man wearing an eye-patch.

"May I help you?" she asked.

"Tom Casey. I have an appointment with Jessica Phillips."

She checked the black bound book on the desk. "Have a seat. I'll let her know you're here." Leaving the chair, she headed down a small hallway, then disappeared around the corner. She soon emerged, and motioned for him to follow. "Ms. Phillips will see you now."

He trailed her down the corridor to a door with, 'Law Office of Jessica Phillips' written in white letters across the frosted glass window. The woman behind the desk rose as he entered and extended her hand. She wore an expensive blue suit with a matching cowl neck silk blouse. Eyes of the same hue glistened as she studied him.

She smiled "Hello, Mr. Casey. Nice meeting you. As you can imagine, I did a little investigation of my own before your arrival. Read and heard nothing but good things."

Hawkman chuckled. "Thank you. I didn't think you'd want to talk to me about any important details unless you were sure I was legit."

She gestured toward the chair in front of her desk. "Have

a seat. You've got me worried about Carlotta Ryan. I've tried to reach her the last few days and she hasn't returned my calls."

He frowned. "You've called her at home?"

"Yes. Is there something wrong?"

"You said you left messages."

She glanced at her ledger. "I've called three times in the last two days and asked Carlotta to call me."

"That's odd, I have someone monitoring the answering machine and I never got the report of those messages." He noticed her worried expression. "Don't worry. He might not have checked for several days."

Jessica rattled off a phone number. "Is that the same one you have for Carlotta?"

"Yes."

She let out a sigh. "You told me when we spoke on the phone she'd been missing for over a week. Has there still been no word from her?"

"Nothing."

"This doesn't sound good," she said, leaning back in her chair and looking hard at him. "I assume since you're a private investigator you don't like the way it's going either."

"No, I don't. So tell me, how long has Carlotta been your client?"

"I normally wouldn't talk about a client-lawyer relationship. It's against all our rules. But with her missing, I'm going to bend them."

"Appreciate it. I need all the information I can get if I'm going to find her."

"Do you have any clues?"

"Very few."

She opened a thin file on her desk. "I've only had two appointments with Mrs. Ryan."

"I'm assuming they were on the subject of divorce, since that's your firm's specialty along with family law."

Jessica nodded. "At our first meeting, I recommended she and her husband attend marriage counseling. This is usually my first step before starting divorce proceedings."

"How did she respond to your suggestion?"

Picking up a pencil from the desk, she tapped the eraser on the file. "Not too receptive. She felt the marriage had hit a brick wall without a chance of survival. I tried to point out the breaking up of the marriage would only harm her daughter and markedly reduce her accustomed life style."

"How did she react?"

"She swore her husband would never let it happen."

Hawkman wiped his forehead. "Boy, she had a lot of brass if she expected him to let her live like she wanted while he paid the bills."

"I thought she was very naive, and tried to explain how divorce did strange things to relationships, changing people drastically."

"After the first meeting, then what?"

"I asked her to think about my suggestion and call me when she'd made a decision. Within a week, she contacted me and wanted to proceed with the divorce. So we set up another appointment."

"How'd that go?"

"Sort of odd. I had trouble holding her attention trying to explain about certain papers we needed, like the legal stuff that goes into preparing a divorce. She never took a note and I kept catching her gazing out the window."

Hawkman stared at her. "Did she appear to be drugged?"

"Yes and no. I asked her if she was okay. She told me she'd taken a pain pill for her back and her mind seemed to be floating. So I figured she wasn't with it. I made a list of the items and gave it to her. She was supposed to have them collected by our next meeting."

"What did she think she'd gain by divorcing Paul?"

Jessica let out a small groan. "Everything. I tried to explain divorce didn't work that way. Usually the state split mutual property down the middle, then the bread winner would more than likely pay child support and possibly alimony. I told her if she could get Paul to agree on certain items, then she'd make out better."

"How'd she respond?"

"She informed me she didn't intend to tell him what she planned on doing, and just wanted him served the papers. I warned her she'd regret surprising him and a judge wouldn't go for it. Especially when her husband hadn't committed adultery or been abusive."

"Interesting. Did she ever comment on what motivated her wanting a divorce and why not continue in the present arrangement?"

"No. I assumed there was another man and she wanted to be free."

CHAPTER FIFTEEN

Hawkman tapped his fingers on Ms. Phillips desktop. "Did she ever mention another man?

"No, and I felt it too early in our discussion to ask. I probably would have eventually. More out of my own curiosity than anything, because it really had no bearing on the divorce, unless Mr. Ryan had filed."

He stood. "Did Carlotta ever suggest Paul had a girlfriend?"

"Not at all. I had the feeling he appeared like clean fallen snow. I don't know why she wanted to divorce him."

"I appreciate your candidness. You've helped a lot. One more quick question. Has she paid her bill?"

She glanced down at her ledger. "Yes, she put down enough for the first three meetings. So she still has a credit. We hadn't started filing the papers yet."

"I won't take any more of your time."

She rose from her chair. "Please, let me know if you find her."

"I will." He handed her his card. "Give me a call if Carlotta gets in touch."

Hawkman left the law office and sat in his vehicle for a moment, pondering the interview. Jessica Phillips had given him much more than required and he admired her honesty. He doubted she'd left much out. Normally he didn't care for law offices that dealt in divorce, but they served a purpose. This woman appeared to have scruples.

He turned the ignition and headed back to Medford. He wanted to search Carlotta's house and needed Paul's approval.

He also wanted to find out why he hadn't reported Jessica's calls. With time marching on and no word from Carlotta, the scenario turned more grim and made his gut tighten.

Approaching the city limits, he punched in Paul's number on the cell phone. "Tom Casey here. Wondered if you could meet me at Carlotta's house in about thirty minutes?"

When Hawkman turned into the cul-de-sac, the Lexus was already in the driveway. He parked in the street and hopped out. Paul climbed out of the car and looked at Hawkman with concern.

"What's happening?" he asked.

"I need to search through Carlotta's personal belongings and take a closer look at any notes or appointments she might have jotted down."

"Sure, no problem."

Paul unlocked the door and gestured for Hawkman to go ahead.

"Have you been here, since our last visit?" Hawkman asked.

"No, it makes me nervous."

"Doesn't Tiffany want to come over and take more things to her grandmother's?"

"Mom brings her if she needs to come."

Hawkman stepped into the kitchen. "Why don't you check and see if there are any messages on the answering machine."

Paul went into the den and punched the button. Jessica's voice echoed through the room three times with the same message. "This is Jessica, please give me a call."

Hawkman stood at the doorway. "Who's that?"

Paul shrugged. "I don't know."

He didn't want to tell Paul about the pending divorce just yet, so he left it alone. "I'll need you with me while I go through Carlotta's things."

Paul followed him into the bedroom and sat on the overstuffed chair by the vanity. "This room gives me the creeps."

Hawkman shot him a look. "Why? You used to share it with your wife."

"I guess that's the reason. There's no telling how many other men have slept in the bed besides me."

Going into the bathroom, Hawkman opened the medicine cabinet. Immediately, he discovered the prescription for the pain pills, along with Valium and a couple of others for anxiety, also a container of birth control pills nestled among the rest. Odd, he thought, why didn't she take those? He assembled the drugs on the back of the toilet, then checked the physician's name and discovered each one had been prescribed by a different doctor. He poked his head around the door. "Paul, did your family belong to an HMO?"

"No, Carlotta didn't like them. So we had our own doctors and just paid through the nose."

Hawkman gathered up the medicine bottles, and dumped them onto the bed. "Mind if I take these with me?"

Paul reached over and fingered the array of pill containers. "My Lord, looks like she was teetering on the edge."

"Appears so." Hawkman then approached the dresser and methodically went through every drawer. It took him over an hour to thoroughly search the room which revealed nothing more of importance. He moved into the den and pointed at the large oak desk. "Did Carlotta use this?"

"Yes, one of her favorite pieces of furniture." Paul flopped down on the small couch. "Looking for anything in particular?"

Hawkman sat down in the chair and opened one of the drawers. "Clues about people your wife knew. Someone she might have had contact with the week before she disappeared or even earlier." He turned in the chair and faced Paul. "I need to question Tiffany again. I know you might not want me to right now, but the child may be the only one who can help. It might even be good for her to talk to someone outside the family."

Paul squirmed. "I hate to see her upset."

"I'll try to keep it on a light key."

"If you feel it's important. You've got to do what you deem necessary to get to the bottom of this." Paul slapped his hand against the arm rest. "Damn Carlotta. She's really upset us all by pulling this stunt." He got up and paced the room. "Why'd she up and leave without telling anyone?"

Hawkman thumbed through some papers. "Did you two have an argument before she disappeared?"

He lifted his arms, dropped them to his side and exhaled loudly. "We disagreed about stuff all the time. I'd gotten to the point I hated to come over here, because anything would set her off."

"For instance?"

"She blamed me for the toilet running over, a drippy faucet, the garbage disposal going out and any other broken appliance. I told her to hire a handyman and get the stuff repaired. She not only wanted me to fix it, but to do the calling. I kept telling her I didn't have time. And if those items didn't get my dander up, she'd start on something about Tiffany."

While Paul talked, Hawkman continued going through the desk and found a small diary. He flipped through the pages and raised a brow as he noticed scheduled appointments and notes. "I'd like to take this with me, too."

Paul squinted at the book Hawkman held up. "What is it?"

"A calendar of sorts."

"Sure, take it."

"I'll return all these things when I'm through."

"I'm not worried."

"Sorry about keeping you so long. I'm almost done."

Paul stared out the window. "I really liked this area. I miss it a lot. Maybe I'll be able to move back soon."

Hawkman glanced at him, wondering what he meant. He soon closed the desk, and moved into the kitchen where he checked the cabinets for anything suspicious and then the drawers under the phone for any sort of scribbled notes. Not finding any, he finally turned to Paul. "Okay, I think that's about it."

Finding a small plastic sack in the pantry, Hawkman slipped the prescribed drugs and small book inside. "I'll see what I can find out from these items. It may give me a clue or two about Carlotta's disappearance."

Paul silently walked out the front door.

***

Hawkman returned home to find Jennifer asleep on the couch. She held the television control in her hand, with the sound on mute. This worried him. She never took naps. This ailment appeared to be sapping every ounce of her energy. He hoped those doctors found something soon. Maybe the next two days of tests would end this mystery.

He went back to his computer room and closed the door so as not to disturb her. He placed the items from Carlotta's house on his desk and turned on the light. The booklet interested him the most. The prescriptions could wait. He'd have to contact each doctor, and he hadn't decided if it would be worth the effort. It seemed pretty apparent Carlotta had a drug problem. It might have started with pain pills, but had escalated out of hand.

He opened the small book. Working backwards on the calendar, he noted several entries where Carlotta commented on how disgusted she'd gotten with Paul. Several memos caught his attention; 'Paul doesn't trust me.' Others mentioned 'the flower called' or 'lunch with the flower'. "Did she mean Tulip?" he mumbled aloud. He pulled a yellow legal pad toward him and made some notes. Maybe Paul would know if she referred to Tulip as 'the flower'? He also wanted to mention her to Tiffany.

Delia didn't act like she knew Tulip real well when she mentioned the two women at the house. Which seemed natural enough. Even though they'd all went to high school together, Delia having no daughters might not have close contact with many of the girls unless Paul brought them home or introduced them to the family at a function.

Engrossed in his note taking, he didn't hear his office door open. But he definitely felt the soft arms wrapping around his neck.

CHAPTER SIXTEEN

Hawkman swiveled his chair around and pulled Jennifer into his lap. "Hi, sweetheart, how are you doing?"

"I feel all tuckered out."

"I'll sure be glad when tomorrow and Friday get here. Maybe we'll get some answers as to what's going on with you."

"Hope so, I'm beginning to think this is all in my head."

He gave her a squeeze. "You're not the type to imagine stuff to make you sick. By the way, what time's your appointment?"

"We have to be there by nine thirty."

"Good, glad it's early. I know we won't know anything until next week, but at least we're on the way of finding out something."

She picked up the book. "What's this? Looks like a diary."

"I guess that's the proper name for it, but it appears Carlotta used it like a calendar where she made appointments and wrote comments. I've found some interesting tidbits in it so far. Haven't gone through the whole thing yet."

"Like what?"

He opened to one of the pages where he'd placed a marker and pointed. "Like right here, she refers to a person quite often as 'the flower'. I'm wondering if this isn't Tulip?"

"Sounds logical."

"If so, it's odd because I got the impression from Ms. Withers, she and Carlotta weren't close buddies."

"Depends on how you classify close." She placed a finger on the entry. "The reference here could be no more than setting up lunch dates or canceling them. You really can't judge whether they were close from this, unless you heard their conversations."

He turned to another area. "Here she makes some very derogatory remarks about Paul. They definitely weren't getting along."

"If she kicked him out, I'd say it's pretty obvious."

"Of course, they had the child to consider, but you'd have thought with him not around Carlottas' emotions would have simmered down."

Jennifer read through some of the passages. "It appears she expects him to keep everything up and running. Here she mentions the drippy faucet and he told her to get a handyman. From what she wrote, it sounds like she met his response with a furious retort, instead of any sense of responsibility."

"Paul told me about some of her requests while I searched the house. He said she demanded a lot. He told her he didn't have time to do the repairs and even offered to pay for the handyman. She didn't want to search for one, but wanted him to do the dirty work. I get the feeling Carlotta expects a lot out of people."

"Certainly sounds like it. But she doesn't want to give anything in return. I wonder if she treats her little girl the same way?" Jennifer scooted out of his lap. "I'm hungry. Want me to fix you a sandwich, too?"

"You feel like it?"

"Yes. I've got to do something or go out of my mind."

He smiled and gave her a pat on the butt. "I'll be there in a few minutes."

***

The next morning, they arrived at the urologist's office. After Jennifer registered, they took a seat. When the nurse called to take her into the area where the doctor would perform the cystoscopy, Hawkman stood.

Jennifer placed a hand on his arm. "No, you can't go in there with me. Wait out here, I'm sure it won't take long."

He didn't like the idea of his wife on a table with instruments going inside her body without him there to hold her hand. The minute she walked down the short hallway, he started pacing. He took a toothpick from his pocket and chewed it until it became soft. Taking a vacant chair, he picked up a magazine and thumbed through it without even noticing the pictures. He kept eyeing the passageway where Jennifer disappeared. The minutes dragged, and even though less than an hour had gone by, he swore a half a day had passed before she finally appeared in the corridor. He jumped up and met her before she made it into the waiting room. "Are you okay? You look like nothing happened?"

She laughed. "I'm fine. It didn't hurt and I watched on a monitor as he took a tiny telescope and examined my bladder." She tossed her head back in an arrogant manner. "I'll have you know I have a very nice, clean looking organ there. Everything appeared in excellent condition."

He patted her shoulder and grinned. "That's good news."

"However, the doctor said there's something going on. The pyelogram showed my right kidney is slightly swollen. He'll know more after he examines the CAT scan results."

Hawkman scowled. "I don't like the sound of that."

Jennifer looped an arm around his. "Honey, let's just take a step at a time. I'm trying not to worry, because stress isn't good."

He grasped her hand. "You're right. Let's go for lunch."

She smiled up at him. "Great idea."

***

The next morning, Hawkman woke up early, his body dripping with sweat. He'd spent a restless night fighting a nightmare about Jennifer. A huge thing resembling a bladder, with a telescope dangling from it's side, had chased him down a hillside. When he stumbled and fell, the monster flattened on top of his body and practically suffocated him from it's weight.

He climbed out of bed, slipped on his eye-patch and went to the kitchen in his underwear. The cool air in the house felt good against his damp skin. After plugging in the coffee pot, he went to the main bathroom and took a quick shower. He toweled his hair, wrapped the terry around his waist, adjusted the eye-patch, then returned to the kitchen for a mug of java. When he glanced out the window, he watched the sun's rays play across the sky and over the hills as daylight entered the new day.

He sighed, turned around and almost spilled his coffee. "Sweetheart, did I wake you?"

A smile tickled the corners of her mouth. "No, but it sure looks like your nerves are on edge."

"I did have a little trouble sleeping. I had a nightmare about a bladder monster."

She bent over in laughter. "Oh, my. That's funny. You were definitely doing a lot of tossing and turning. Did it finally get you?"

He cackled. "Almost, but I woke up before it asphyxiated me."

She glanced up at the wall clock. "Fortunately, I can have a cup of coffee. It's early enough. Can't have any food and no liquid for an hour before the test."

"So what does this one entail?"

"We'll have to kill some time while I sip the chalky fruit flavored drink. After I finish it off, I go in for the test. They have me lie on this portable contraption, then inject a dye into my arm which outlines the organs. They turn on the machine and it runs my body back and forth taking layered pictures."

"I've heard about these. Pretty complicated and intricate machine."

"Great invention though. Years ago they'd have to do exploratory surgery to see what's going on. This makes things so nonintrusive. And so much safer for the patient."

"And it doesn't hurt, right?"

"No. Except for the needle in the arm. I understand I might feel a warm sensation surge through me from the iodine, but it only lasts a few minutes." She blew across her cup. "I've never had one before, so I'll tell you more about it later. And you really don't have to go with me. I can manage just fine. I'm sure you'll find everything rather boring and you need to work on the Carlotta case."

He snapped up his head. "Are you kidding. It can wait. They're going to put my sweetheart through a big ugly machine. There's no way I'd let you go alone."

As soon as they arrived at the hospital, the girl behind the counter gave Jennifer two cold berry flavored drinks in bigger than pint size plastic containers, and instructed her to report back to the desk after she'd downed the last drop. She and Hawkman strolled around outside as she slurped the liquid through a straw, shuttering after each swallow.

"This is horrible stuff. I can tell you right now, the flavoring doesn't help."

He gave her a pat on the back. "You're almost finished."

She finally tossed the empty into the trash can. "Now I've got to dash to the bathroom before going in for the test."

When Jennifer returned to the registration area, an attendant led her to a big enclosed truck sitting in the parking lot. Hawkman followed and stood outside as they entered and closed the door. He trod up and down the sidewalk for close to an hour before she came out. Hurrying to her side, he put an arm around her shoulders. "How'd it go?"

"No big deal. I did feel a sensation of heat flash through my body. It really felt strange, but only lasted a minute or so."

"Did they mention what they saw?"

She shook her head as they ambled toward the SUV. "No, the technician said the radiologist would send the results to my doctor and he'd contact me. So I don't expect to hear anything until Monday. Probably late afternoon."

"Dang. We're on hold again."

"Yes, it does try us. But I have to remember I'm not the only patient in this hospital. Many in worse condition than me."

"You're right, but I'm selfish. As far as I'm concerned you're the only one."

She playfully tapped him on the cheek. "Hawkman be nice."

***

Saturday morning found Hawkman restless and not able to keep his gaze off of Jennifer's every move. Even while reading the paper, he kept glancing over the top as she sat at her computer.

She finally let out a long sigh. "Why don't you go to the office? You're driving me crazy. I can't stand the idea of you not letting me out of your sight for the next two days."

He folded the paper and placed it on the coffee table. "I'm sorry, you're right. You're definitely on my mind. I have things I need to do and I'm sure working will help me keep from worrying."

"Please go do them," she pleaded.

He grinned. "You're feeling okay?"

"I'm fine."

He went to the Hawkman corner, plopped on his hat, took his shoulder holster from the hook and placed it on the counter. Feeling his belt for his cell phone, he remembered he had it charging in his office and hurried back to retrieve it. When he returned, he glanced at Jennifer who had her gaze fixed on the computer monitor. "Okay, hon, I'm outta here. I'll see you this evening."

She raised a hand and waved. "Love ya."

He slipped his gun and holster under the driver's seat and backed out of the garage. On the way to Medford, Hawkman phoned Delia. "I spoke with Paul about my talking with Tiffany again. He said it would be fine. I wanted to check and see if she might be available this afternoon?"

"Yes. In fact, I think she'd welcome the visit."

"Would she go for me taking her to lunch?"

"She'd love it."

"Say I'll pick her up about twelve-thirty."

"Sounds great."

When Hawkman arrived at Delia's house, it relieved him to see Tiffany in jeans that hit her waist and a cute flowered tee-shirt that covered her middle.

She'd pulled her hair back in a pony tail with a little butterfly clip and didn't have on make-up. The child actually looked like a cute little ten year old.

"Where would you like to go eat?" he asked, as they walked toward the 4X4.

"McDonald's", she said with a twinkle in her eye.

"Are you sure?" he asked, while opening the passenger side door. "I'd be more than happy to take you to a nice walk-in restaurant."

"I love their hamburgers and I don't get them very often."

He laughed. "McDonald's it is." Then closed the door.

When they reached the fast-food restaurant, Hawkman pulled into the parking lot. "Do you want to go inside, or eat in the car?"

"Inside, maybe some of my friends are there and I want them to see me with the big man with the eye-patch. None of the kids believed me when I told them I knew a private investigator who looked like a cowboy and a pirate all wrapped into one."

Hawkman guffawed. "Okay, good enough." She had a reason for her request, he thought, pulling into a parking space.

As they sat at the table, Tiffany eyed the room of people. "Darn, I don't see anyone I know."

"We'll eat slow and chat, maybe one of your friends will wander in."

"So what do you want to talk about?" she asked, taking a bite of french fries.

"Tell me about the day your mother disappeared after taking you to your grandmother's."

"Oh, Mom didn't take me over. When I got home from school, she'd already left. There was a note on the table telling me to call Grandma, because she didn't plan on coming home for several days."

Hawkman stared at her. "Really? Do you still have the note?"

She nodded through bites. "Yeah, it's at Grandma's in my jewelry box."

CHAPTER SEVENTEEN

It took Hawkman a moment to digest what Tiffany had just told him. He'd never doubted Paul's word about Carlotta taking the child to her grandmother's. Did he intentionally lie? He took several bites of his hamburger before continuing. "Tell me a little about your mom."

Tiffany cocked her head. "Not much to tell. She didn't like me having kids over or me going to visit anyone at their house. I had the feeling Mom didn't like little people. The only reason she paid any attention to me was because I belonged to her. She hoped to make me more grown up, I guess. I really didn't like wearing make-up or showing my belly button. Made me feel funny. And none of my friends wore clothes like she wanted me to wear. But I did it because she thought they were great."

"What about your mom's buddies?"

"She doesn't have many friends."

"Doesn't she see Tulip often?"

Tiffany threw back her head, covering her mouth as she laughed. "Oh, the flower."

"Is that what you call her?"

"Yeah, more as a joke. Tulip's okay, but Mom calls her dowdy, because she doesn't know how to dress or fix her hair."

"Do they visit a lot?"

"I'm not sure what Mom does when I'm in school. But I do know when she has a fight with Dad, she invites the withered flower over just to aggravate him."

"Does your dad like Tulip?"

"He's always nice, but I think it's because he feels sorry

for her. Mom said they'd all been friends since high school and Tulip always had a crush on my Dad"

"I guess he knows she likes him?"

Tiffany giggled. "It's pretty obvious. When she's around him, she really gushes."

"What do you mean?"

"She tells him what a wonderful man he is by making enough money so Mom and I can have anything we want. If she had a man like him, she'd be in heaven." Tiffany laughed out loud again. "Tulip really carries on until it makes Mom sick."

Hawkman stifled a smile. "I'm surprised your dad puts up with it."

She made a funny face. "He just brushes it off."

"So, tell me how your mom has been these past few months. Did she ever yell at you?"

Tiffany wiped her mouth with a napkin and the corners of her mouth turned down into a pout. "Yeah, she got kinda mean just before she left."

"How?"

"One day she slapped me real hard and made me cry."

"Had you done something wrong?"

"I told her she'd been acting funny."

"And she hit you for saying so?"

"I guess. It's the only thing I could figure out."

"What do you mean by her acting funny?"

Tiffany's chin quivered. "Oh, like a drunk person. Almost falling into stuff. And she'd quit putting on her make-up or dressing up. She looked sick. I know she hurt her back real bad a long time ago and she told me the pills made her act strange. But that didn't make sense, because she'd healed."

Hawkman decided not to pursue the medication bit. He'd already gotten the picture. And Tiffany had figured out quite a bit on her own. No need for him to add wood to the fire. "Did you see your mother pack a suitcase?"

"No."

"Did she mention going on a trip?"

Tears welled in the youngster's eyes. "No."

He felt he better stay off that topic, too. It certainly didn't make the child happy to talk about it. "Tell me about Princess. How's she doing?"

"She's just fine." Then her mouth broke into a big grin and she whispered, "Some of my friends just came in the door."

He straightened. "What should I do?"

"Nothing, just slurp on your soda."

Three little girls bounded to the table and stared at Hawkman.

Tiffany gestured toward him with a dainty flip of her hand. "This is Mr. Tom Casey, the private investigator I told you about."

"Nice meeting you, Mr. Casey," they said in unison, then scurried off to their own table, whispering and giggling as they looked over their shoulders.

Tiffany's eyes glowed as she wadded up the food wrappers. "We can go now."

"How do you like staying with your grandmother?" Hawkman asked, as they drove back toward Delia's.

"It's fun. She's really sweet and we do a lot of neat stuff, plus, I get to see my Dad more often." She ducked her head and a tear slid down her cheek. "But I miss my Mom. I think she's dead."

Hawkman yanked his head around. "What makes you think such a thing?"

She picked at a spot on her jeans. "Mostly because she hasn't called or sent me a postcard."

"Maybe she hasn't had time."

"We always promised, if we were gone from each other for more than two days, we'd be sure to call or write."

"I see. That's a good promise." Hawkman felt her tension and decided to change the subject. "Would you mind if I borrowed the note your mom left. I'll make a duplicate of it and bring it back tomorrow."

She wiped her face with the back of her hand. "Grandma's got a scanner. I can make a copy at her house."

"That's a great idea."

Hawkman parked in front and they strolled toward the front door making small talk. When they entered the house, Delia met them in the hallway.

"Well, now, where did you two eat lunch?"

"McDonald's," Tiffany said, as she raced to her room.

Hawkman held up his hands and shrugged. "I offered to take her any place she wanted to go and that's what she chose."

Delia rolled her eyes and laughed. "I should have known. She loves that place." Then she glanced toward the child's room. "What's she up to in such a hurry?"

"Tiffany told me her mother had left a note the day she went away telling her to call you when she got home from school. She's going to make a copy for me. Paul told me Carlotta dropped Tiffany off here."

Delia looked surprised. "Wonder where he got such an idea? I thought I told him I'd picked her up. Maybe I didn't, under the circumstances."

Tiffany came running back and handed Hawkman a sheet of paper. He glanced at it, then folded and stuck it into his pocket.

She turned to her grandmother, her big brown eyes twinkling. "We had a great time. Joanne, Kathy and Denise all came while we were there. They got to meet Mr. Casey." She folded her arms across her chest. "Now, maybe they'll believe me."

Delia smiled. "Good. Did you thank Mr. Casey for taking you out?"

"Thank you, Mr. Casey. I enjoyed our lunch. I hope we can do it again soon."

"You're more than welcome," he said, touching his hat. He turned to Delia. "Enjoyed the encounter with your granddaughter. She's a very bright and personable little lady."

She winked. "I think so too."

***

Delia stood at the front door, gnawing her lip as she watched Hawkman drive away. She wondered what Tiffany had told him about Carlotta. She decided to talk to Paul and clarify that she'd picked up Tiffany.

Closing the door, she headed toward her granddaughter's bedroom. "Sweetheart, can I see that note your mom left. You never showed it to me."

"Sure." She jumped up from playing with Princess and snatched a crumbled piece of paper off the dresser. "Here it is." After handing it to her, she dropped down onto her knees and moved a small ball on a string across the floor, then burst into giggles when the cat hunched and attacked it.

Delia sat down on the bed and smoothed out the sheet. She read in silence.

"Tiffany, Call Grandma to come and get you.

I'll be gone for several days. Love, Mom"

She furrowed her brow. It didn't even look like Carlotta's handwriting.

.

CHAPTER EIGHTEEN

Hawkman went to his office, reviewed the notes he'd taken on Carlotta's case, then added more about Tiffany and the one she'd copied from her mother. He circled Delia's, Paul's, Tulip's and Alfonso's names. He felt Paul hadn't leveled with him and now he had suspicions about Delia. Also, he'd chat with Tulip again, as she seemed more in the picture than he'd originally thought. Alfonso appeared a toss-up. Even though he felt it a coincidence the man lived in the same complex as Tulip, he didn't want to mark him off the list just yet.

Thumbing through Carlotta's diary, he saw many references to 'the flower'. Tulip left the impression she and Carlotta only had occasional contact. But from the entries, it appeared they talked on the phone or saw each other at least once or twice a week, especially in the past two or three months. He wondered about a drug connection. He added a talk with Tulip to his priority list, along with Paul, since his story didn't jibe with his daughter's. But that could have been a misunderstanding with all the trauma involved. The circle tightened, but didn't come together like Hawkman wanted. Too many gaps.

He leaned back in his chair. His mind drifted to who might have killed Carlotta. So far no evidence indicated foul play. No body had been uncovered, but his gut told him this woman had been murdered. Hawkman figured it wouldn't be long before he'd need to pull Detective Williams into the investigation. He had several suspects in mind who had a motive. He felt the time had come to weed them out and find out which one actually got rid of Tiffany's mother and where they'd disposed of the corpse.

He decided to drive by Carlotta's house again before going home. Something about the place nagged at him, but he couldn't put his finger on it. Maybe walking around the premises would shake up his mind.

When he reached the cul-de-sac, the street lights lit up the area. He parked in the driveway and took the large flashlight from the satchel he had behind the seat. He ambled around one side of the house, then headed toward the back yard. Then it struck him like a swat between the eyes as he swung the light beam along the foundation. Normally crawl spaces going under houses were covered to keep out rodents, but on the day he rescued the cat, he remembered the opening had been wide open.

Hawkman hurried around to the side where he'd found Delia and Tiffany trying to lure out the kitten. The small crawl space had been secured and fastened with a slide latch. Not wanting to disturb any finger prints, he used the butt of the flashlight to tap the bolt away from the fastener, then pried open the door with his pocketknife. Getting down on his haunches, he peered inside and ran the light beam across the dirt. He stopped when he spotted a square shadow behind a concrete pier. He moved the flashlight ray more slowly and could make out what looked like a suitcase. If his memory served him right, it matched the luggage he'd seen in Carlotta's closet.

He stood, and took his cell phone from his belt. "Hey, Williams, I think I need your evidence van over here at Carlotta Ryan's house. Not sure what I've discovered, but I don't want to touch anything until you've seen it." Hawkman gave him the address, then sat on the front porch steps to wait. When the van arrived, followed by the detective's unmarked car, he stood and strolled toward the vehicles.

"So what'd you find?" Williams asked, climbing out.

"I don't think it's a body, as there's no odor. But it appears to be a matching suitcase of Carlotta's. Her husband assumed she'd taken it on her trip."

Hawkman directed them to the area and stood back watching as the crew dusted the outside wall for prints. "Doesn't look like there's anything readable on the outside," one of the men said. He then flashed a large light under the house. He turned toward Hawkman. "Did you go crawl under here?"

"No."

"Good, because there appears to be drag marks. I'm going to take some impressions."

Another technician ventured under the house and made a wide berth around the plaster molds they'd poured. He managed to drag out the suitcase with a hooked apparatus so as not to disturb any evidence that might be on the bag. Once they had it outside the men dusted it with their powder.

"Looks like we have a few prints. You want me to open it?"

Detective Williams nodded. "Yes."

The man unzipped the cover and threw the lid back. Hawkman and Williams squatted on their haunches and studied the contents. The detective took his pen and moved the neatly packed clothes around.

"Looks like some of these items still have tags on them."

Hawkman eyed the new gown, along with several items he recognized on the buying list from the local store. "If my guess is right, most of these were purchased by Carlotta at one of the local shops before she disappeared. I have an itemized list in my files at the office. Want me to go get it?"

Williams shook his head. "Bring a copy by tomorrow. The crew will have to go through the things first. Then we'll check each item individually." He stood, slid the pen back into his pocket, then instructed the technicians to bag and tag the suitcase. He turned his attention back to Hawkman. "What made you look under the house?"

Hawkman rose from his squatting position and told him about the nagging thought causing him to revisit the house. He couldn't put his finger on it until he did a walk-around the premises.

"So, what do you make of it?"

"It seems highly improbable for a woman to take a journey without her wardrobe."

The detective stared at him. "So you're thinking she's dead?"

"Unfortunately, my suspicions are heading that direction fast. If I find a body, you'll be the first to know."

"Thanks. Any suspects in mind?"

Hawkman kicked a pebble with the toe of his cowboy boot. "Several."

A few moments of silence elapsed. "Are you going to enlighten me?"

"Not yet. I need to narrow my list. If I need help though, I'll give you a call."

They walked toward their cars.

"What's your guess as to a motive for killing this young woman?" Williams asked.

"I think she asked for it. The people I've talked to indicate she's a spitfire. She didn't seek approval for any of her actions, even from her husband, as far as I've learned. Did what she wanted in spite of the consequences."

"Sounds like she might have made a few enemies."

"Yep. Now gotta figure out which one got mad enough to kill her."

Williams slid into driver's seat of his car. "I'll talk to you tomorrow and let you know if we find anything unusual on the suitcase."

"I'm going to be interested in those prints."

Hawkman drove away from the house and headed for Paul's apartment. He circled the complex but didn't see the Lexus in front of the unit. Figuring Paul had probably stopped by his mother's, he decided to wait and talk to him on Sunday. He didn't want to question the man in front of Delia.

CHAPTER NINETEEN

Hawkman returned home and found Jennifer in good spirits. She'd prepared steak, a big salad, and baked potatoes for their dinner.

He folded his arms around her waist. "Boy, you sure know the way to a man's heart."

She grinned. "Your weakness for food showed up before we were ever married."

He looked surprised and poked a thumb into his chest. "Me? Like food?"

Waving him off, she laughed. "Sit down and enjoy. Tell me what you did today."

He hung his hat on a hook in the Hawkman corner, then plopped down at the kitchen bar and related the story of finding the suitcase under the house. "Remember me showing you the list of things Carlotta bought before Paul reported her missing?"

"Yes."

"I'm pretty sure those were the items packed in the bag. We'll know more when we compare them to the list I have."

She reached over and patted his arm. "Mighty ingenious of you to realize something amiss at the house."

"Thanks. Now to find out who hid the suitcase under there and why. I'm hoping Williams finds some readable prints on the handle or sides of the bag. They also took some plaster imprints of drag marks in the soil where it'd been scooted into position."

"How would that help?"

"Not sure, unless they find the print of some type of

footwear they could trace and there's the possibility they could estimate the weight of the person."

"This whole scenario is sending shivers down my spine."

"Unfortunately, I'm thinking the same thing." He finished the steak and wiped his mouth with a napkin. "By the way, I'm staying home Monday. I want to be here when the doctor calls. So don't try shoving me out the door, because I won't go."

She winked. "Okay."

***

Sunday morning, Hawkman made a quick call to Detective Williams, then took off for the Medford police station. He stopped by his office and picked up the list the clerk had given him at the clothing store. When he arrived at Williams' office, he found one of the crew members he recognized from Carlotta's house, talking to the detective.

Williams motioned for Hawkman to come in. "Sorry I didn't introduce you last night, but this is Bill Rader, our top lab technician."

After they shook hands, Hawkman noticed the suitcase resting on a table to the side. "You guys find anything of interest?"

Bill scratched the back of his head and made a face. "Yeah, we found a couple of good prints on the handle and one on the metal running down to the wheels. We've run them through the system, but they don't match up with any on file. So, whoever hid this suitcase, doesn't have a record."

"What about those drag marks?"

"We found what we're assuming to be a knee print and were able to estimate the weight of the person to be anywhere from a hundred and thirty to two hundred pounds. We did find an interesting indentation that appeared to come from the toe of a shoe or boot." Shrugging he continued. "Of course, none of those findings are conclusive and would sure as hell be hard to match."

"So we can eliminate a small child from shoving it under there?"

"Yeah, that's about the only thing it might prove."

The detective turned to Hawkman. "Think we could possibly get a print or two of Carlotta's at the house so we can eliminate her? And we're wondering if you could obtain prints of the family and from some of the suspects you have in mind?"

"Let me call Paul and see if he can meet us at the house. You could also get his prints while there." Hawkman rubbed his chin. "Since Alfonso has a police record, his would have showed up on the search, so he can be crossed off the list. I certainly don't want the people I suspect to become suspicious, so I'll have to do a little scheming."

Williams grinned. "I doubt you'll have any problem."

"Have you seen enough to get involved in this case?"

The detective scratched his head. "Not yet, but I'm very interested."

Hawkman contacted Paul, explained they needed to dust for Carlotta's prints at the house and made arrangements to meet him there in an hour. When Hawkman, the detective, and the lab van arrived, Paul stood beside his car in the driveway. He dangled a key in front of Hawkman.

"I had an extra one made. This way you can get into the house anytime, as I might not always be available."

"Thanks," Hawkman said, pocketing it. "Are you going to leave?"

"Do you need me for anything?"

"The detective would like to have your fingerprints too, so he can eliminate them."

Paul looked puzzled. "Eliminate from what?"

"I'm working on the possibility Carlotta might have been abducted. If so, we need the family's prints to distinguish them from any strange ones we might find in the house."

Paul's face turned ashen. "Mr. Casey, why didn't you tell me your suspicions?"

"I'm not sure of anything, and I have to explore every avenue. I've asked for this detective's expertise and the use of his lab."

Hawkman noticed beads of sweat popping out on Paul's brow. "Do you object to letting the police take your prints?"

His mouth twitched. "Uh, no, of course not. But it scares me to think someone might have taken her from the house. Especially with Tiffany so close. Have you found other evidence that might support this theory?"

"Like a struggle or blood?" Hawkman asked.

Paul gulped and nodded.

"No."

"I don't like the sound of all of this," Paul muttered.

Williams walked by him and patted him on the shoulder. "Let's get inside, before your neighbors start giving us curious stares."

Bill Rader and his assistant followed them inside. "Where's the washer and dryer?" Bill asked.

Paul looked at him with a puzzled expression. "The washer?"

"Yes."

"Why would you be interested in it?"

"I'd imagine Mrs. Ryan usually did the laundry. We'd more than likely find a set of good prints on the detergent bottle or measuring cup. Even on the lid of the machine."

"Oh, yeah, that makes sense."

"We'll check other areas of the house to make sure they match." He gestured toward his aid. "Mike will take your prints now."

Bill crossed through the kitchen toward the laundry area, while the other technician opened his kit on the table. "If you'll step over here, Mr. Ryan, we'll get this out of the way."

Afterwards Paul wiped his fingers with an alcohol cloth. "Do you need me any longer?"

"No. You may leave," Williams said. "But, we may want to talk to you later."

"Mr. Casey knows where to find me."

Hawkman accompanied Paul out to his car. "I understand Tulip Withers works in town at Mom's Cafe."

"Yeah. Why are you interested in her?"

"I'm contacting anyone who has known or talked to Carlotta in the past few months."

"She's worked there for years. Need directions?"

"No. I know where it is. Thanks."

When Hawkman strolled back inside, Williams was staring out the window as Paul drove away. "The man seems mighty nervous."

"He's scared his wife is dead," Hawkman said.

"Has he told you this?"

"No, but I've observed it in his face and actions."

"You sure it's not guilt?"

Hawkman pushed back his cowboy hat with his finger. "I'm not positive about anything at this point." He turned toward Mike. "Do you have an extra kit I could borrow. Left mine at home."

"Sure. There's one in the van. I'll get it."

The crew soon finished, and Hawkman locked up the house, then walked out to the vehicles with the detective. "I won't be at the office tomorrow, so I'll call you late afternoon. I'm going to see if I can't secure some prints tonight, but it might be a day or two before I can get them to you."

"No problem," Williams said, as he climbed into the car.

Hawkman drove to Delia's house in hopes of finding her and Tiffany. He parked in front and carried the printing kit under his arm. Delia answered the door with a surprised expression.

"Well, hi. Didn't expect to see you today."

"Didn't have time to call. I've been over at Carlotta's house with the police."

She frowned. "That doesn't sound good."

"We're fingerprinting the area in case someone abducted Carlotta. I want to rule out the family's prints since they could be all over the house. Especially Tiffany's. To do so, I need to get both your fingerprints on file."

"Sure, let me get her."

Hawkman left the house, a job completed with more ease than he expected.

He drove downtown, and turned off Main street where he

found a parking spot near the front of Mom's Cafe. He dug into the bag of stuff he had behind the seat until he found the small duffle bag. Carrying it into the cafe, he slid into a booth, and picked up one of the menus stuck in a rack at the end of the table. Out of the corner of his eye, he spotted Tulip wiping off one of the tables. She soon approached and gave him a weak smile.

"Hello, Mr. Casey. Fancy seeing you here."

"Ms. Withers, I didn't realize you worked at Mom's."

"Been here for years. What can I get for you today?"

"First off, I'd like a canned Pepsi and a glass of ice. Then give me a minute to glance over the menu."

She stuck her small tablet into the pocket of her uniform. "Sure. Be back in a moment."

Within a few minutes, she'd returned carrying the can of soda and glass of ice. "There you go. Had time to make your decision?"

"Yes. I'll go for the number five, braised chicken breast, mashed potatoes and vegetables."

"Good choice," she said, writing out his order. "Be back shortly."

Hawkman watched her disappear to the back. Careful not to smudge her prints, he poured the Pepsi into the glass and quickly slipped the can into a plastic bag then zipped it into the duffle.

***

Monday morning, Hawkman awoke in an empty bed. He jumped up, threw on a pair of jeans and a tee shirt, then hurried to the kitchen where he found Jennifer sitting at the kitchen bar and gazing at the phone.

"Has the doctor already called?"

"No. I'm waiting for it to ring."

He put his hands on her shoulders. "Honey, it could be late this afternoon before he calls. You can't sit here and stare at that thing all day."

Patting his hand, she stood. "You're right. I'll fix breakfast. It will help keep my mind off things."

"Can I help?"

"Why don't you set the table."

After they ate, Hawkman noticed she'd become very quiet. "What's wrong?"

She sighed. "I guess I'm a bit anxious."

Early afternoon, Hawkman sat reading the paper in the living room, and Jennifer sat at her computer. When the phone rang, she jumped up, almost knocking over her chair in her haste to answer.

"Hello."

Hawkman placed the paper aside as he listened.

"And what do you suspect?"

When Hawkman saw her grab the cabinet with her other hand and the color of her cheeks turn white, he bounded to her side. She placed the receiver on the cradle and looked up at him with tears in her eyes.

"There's a possibility I have cancer."

"Oh my God," he said, taking her in his arms as the tears rolled down his cheeks.

CHAPTER TWENTY

Hawkman held Jennifer in his arms for several minutes, his heart pounding so hard, he wondered if she could feel it. Finally, he tilted her tear stained face toward him. "Honey, which doctor called and what exactly did he say."

She reached toward the tissue box on the counter top. After dabbing his cheeks, she wiped away her own tears and took a deep breath. "The urologist. He said he suspected lymphoma cancer and wants to talk to me. But they'd have to take a needle biopsy before they know for sure."

"What's lymphoma?"

"I don't know. But the word cancer is scary enough. Regardless of the kind."

"The big 'C' is definitely hard to swallow. When are they going to do the biopsy?"

"As soon as they can set it up. They'll let me know. It will be done using a CAT scan. Then I assume, once they find out for sure, they'll direct me to an oncologist."

Hawkman guided her toward the living room. "I think we both need to sit down. This is earth shaking news and I need to absorb it a little better."

As they nestled on the couch, Jennifer shoved loose strands of hair behind her ears. "My head is spinning. I can't quite comprehend what I've heard. How am I going to break the news to Sam?" Tears welled in her eyes again.

Hawkman pulled her close and gently kissed the top of her head. "We'll wait until we have all the facts before we tell him or anyone."

***

The next few days passed in a blur for Hawkman and Jennifer. He hated to leave her side, but she insisted he concentrate on the Carlotta case. She seemed to accept the prognosis, much better than he. She'd tried to soften the blow by explaining they wouldn't have any true answers until after the biopsy.

Hawkman had a difficult time trying to focus on Carlotta's disappearance, since Jennifer occupied his every waking moment. The thought of losing the love of his life wrenched at his heart. How could he live without her? Trying to push the morbid thoughts from his mind, he researched lymphoma cancer on the internet and read every article he could find on the subject. The statistics looked better than normal and it amazed him how much progress had been made in the treatment of cancer and the resulting increase in survival rate. Even though it gave him hope, he still couldn't accept the fact that his Jennifer had this horrible disease.

The time approached for the biopsy and Hawkman paced the hospital waiting room and corridor waiting for Jennifer. He chewed at least two toothpicks to mush before they informed him she could leave. He went to the small recovery room and stood outside the door while she dressed. When she greeted him, he held onto her arm, guided her through the main building and into the parking lot where they moseyed toward the SUV.

"How'd it go?" Hawkman asked.

She sighed. "Not too pleasant. It surprised me when he had me turn over onto my stomach and went through my back with a long needle. The nurse told me they'd added a tranquilizer to the IV. Not sure I felt it, but it's bound to have helped or I'd have jumped off the table, screaming."

He gave her a squeeze. "You're giving me the willies."

"Sorry, just telling you what happened. You've been through lots worse stuff."

"Maybe, but that was me, not you."

She gave him a faint smile. "You're sweet, you know."

"I love you, too." He kissed her tenderly, then opened the passenger side door and helped her into the vehicle. "Take it easy. I promise I'll go slow over the speed bumps."

On their way home, he could feel she'd been traumatized by the ordeal, and tried to keep his questions to a minimum. "Did they give you any idea about when you'd hear the results?"

"It could be several days. I think they have to send it out to another lab."

"This waiting game is getting to me."

"Honey, think about it. It's been less than a month since we figured out something strange was going on inside my body. Look how fast they've put me through all these tests. The doctors are moving very quickly trying to solve the problem. I can't complain."

"You're much more patient than I am. I wanted it all done yesterday. In my eyes you're the only person I want the doctors to treat."

She put her hand on his arm. "I know. Things have to be done in order, and it takes time for results."

He felt his jaw working as he ground his teeth.

"For the next few days, I want you to work on Carlotta's case. Get your mind off me."

"You're asking for a big miracle."

"Well, at least try. It won't help to sit around and brood. The answers won't come any sooner. I'm going to work real hard on concentrating on my writing. It's not going to be easy for either of us. But we have to try or lose our minds. We have to keep a positive attitude."

***

The next morning, Jennifer pushed Hawkman out the front door. "Take those fingerprints to Detective Williams. Who knows what they might reveal."

She watched her husband head for the garage, the print kit tucked under his arm and his shoulders slumped. A lump formed in her throat as she realized how much they loved and needed each other. There were times over the years when it seemed his work took priority over her needs, and she'd wondered where she stood on his list. Now she knew. How could she have ever doubted his devotion. Men are different, she thought, they don't show their feely, touchy emotions like women. It makes them special, so there's a balance maintained within the family.

She closed the door as he drove out of the driveway. Walking into the dining room, she gazed out the window as his 4X4 passed over the bridge crossing the Klamath River. "I love you, Hawkman, and I'm going to be all right," she said aloud. Saying a silent prayer, she took a deep breath and sat down at her computer.

As the machine booted up, she stared out the window across the lake and thought about all the beauty she could see from her own little domain. Memories rushed through her mind of all the good times she'd experienced with Hawkman and Sam. Tears filled her eyes and washed down her cheeks. She quickly wiped them away. "Get a grip on yourself. You've got to be strong." Clicking on the folder of her latest book, she focused on the written material.

CHAPTER TWENTY-ONE

After Hawkman contacted Detective Williams to make sure he'd be in the office, he left the house, feeling a large knot in the pit of his stomach. He'd never experienced the dark emotional cloud hovering around him and didn't know for sure if he knew how to cope. Several miles down the road, before driving out of the forested area, he pulled to the side and parked. He jumped out of the 4X4 and climbed up the embankment into a cluster of trees. Walking faster and deeper into the forest, he pulled his gun from his shoulder holster and started firing at the limbs. Tears flowed down his cheeks until he emptied the casing. Depleted, and sobbing, he slumped down on an old fallen redwood trunk. His gun hanging in his limp hand, he wiped his face with the back of his sleeve and stared into space. He sat there for over an hour before he sucked in a deep breath and rose. Shoving his weapon into the holster, he strolled back to his vehicle and continued his journey toward Medford.

When he reached the detective's office, Williams frowned. "Where you been?"

"Did we set a time?"

"No, but you look like you've been in a fight or dragged through the dirt."

Hawkman ran a hand across his face and felt where grit had accumulated on his forehead, cheeks and chin. "Uh, excuse me. I'll be right back." Making a quick trip to the bathroom, he looked at his reflection in the mirror and grimaced. He placed his hat on the end of the counter, removed his eye-patch, filled his hands with cold water several times and splashed it onto his face. Ripping out a couple a paper towel from the holder, he wiped off the drips, replaced his eye-patch and plopped his hat onto his head, then returned to Williams' office with a sheepish grin on his lips. "Did a little target practice before leaving home. Turned out dustier than I thought."

Williams chuckled. "I see." He leaned back in his chair. "So what've you got?"

Placing the fingerprint kit on the desk, along with the paper sack holding the empty can from the restaurant, Hawkman sat down. "I acquired the prints of Delia and Tiffany Ryan, plus Tulip Withers. Your guys got Paul's."

The detective raised a brow. "These are your suspects?"

Hawkman nodded. "They all have a reason for getting rid of Carlotta, except for the little girl, Tiffany. But I thought it a good idea to get her prints for elimination purposes."

"Interesting. Are you going to let me in on how you've come to this conclusion?"

"Soon. I have a few more things to investigate. Once I have some definite answers, then you'll know." He pointed toward the fingerprint kit. "How long will it take to compare these to those on the suitcase?"

Williams tapped the top of the box. "Not long. I'll get the guys on it first thing Monday morning. They should have an answer by the afternoon."

Hawkman stood. "Sounds good. I'll call you."

The detective eyed him. "What's eatin' you?"

"Nothing. Why?"

"You aren't yourself. Everything okay at home?"

"All's fine. I'll talk to you Monday afternoon." Hawkman hurried from the office and made his way to the parking lot. Climbing into the 4X4, he glanced into the rearview mirror. His features looked the same. Nothing appeared written on his forehead. How the hell did Williams detect things weren't right?

He slammed his hand on the steering wheel. The detective took a wild guess and it hit home, that's all, so get a hold of yourself and shape up. You have a case to solve and a wife to look after. Who says you can't do both?

Hawkman jerked the wheel and headed for his office. He detoured down Main street so he could stop at the Chocolate Factory and pick up Jennifer's favorite box of dark chews and nuts. Jumping back into the 4X4, he noticed the small shop across the street tucked between a couple of other businesses. He read the sign, 'Wither's Meats'. Even though he'd picked up steaks there before, as they had a good reputation for their prime cuts, he hadn't given the place much thought. But it piqued his curiosity now, since he'd learned the owner was Tulip's father. He pushed the box of chocolates out of the sun, slipped out of the vehicle, and crossed the street.

A bell jingled above his head as he pushed open the door. The butcher, dressed all in white with a soiled apron around his middle, appeared behind the glass display case. "Yes sir, what can I do for you today?"

Hawkman studied the different portions of beef and pork, then pointed at the filet mignons. "Those look excellent. Think I'll take a couple."

"Good choice," the man said, sliding the door open. He wrapped the two in butcher paper and placed them on the counter. "Will there be anything else?"

"No thanks. Are you the owner?"

"Yes."

"I met your daughter, Tulip."

The man's smile turned into a scowl. "That woman won't help me here. Even though I trained her well as she grew up. After her mother died, I really needed her help, but she chose to work in that flea-bitten joint down the street. Said she had no stomach for cutting up cows and pigs." He grumbled as he handed Hawkman his change.

"I'm sure it's hard finding good help."

"Yeah, all the big grocery stores take over the butchers because they can give them great perks. I can't offer more than a good wage."

"Have a good day." Giving a wave, Hawkman left the store and drove to his office. He stashed the meat and chocolates into the small refrigerator Jennifer insisted he'd find useful when they furnished the office. She proved right as he'd used it on many occasions. He sat at his desk, opened Carlotta's file and studied the notes. Leaning back, he tapped his pencil on his chin. Interesting, he thought, there are several unanswered questions he needed to ask his suspects. But he decided to wait until next week after Williams compared the prints. In addition, he didn't want to interrupt any time Tiffany had with her dad or grandmother. The child didn't need to hear questions that pointed to the murder of her mother.

Paul and Delia didn't know they'd discovered the suitcase, and he wondered if the surprise factor would help in the investigation. Their expressions and body language would show him a lot. He also needed to find out why Paul's story on how Tiffany got to Delia's on the day of Carlotta's disappearance differed from his daughter's and mom's. The note proved Carlotta did not take Tiffany to her grandmother's. Did Paul truly misunderstand, or was he hiding something? Hawkman felt he might've made a mistake in telling Delia how Paul's story varied. A mother might cover for her son, regardless of the circumstances. He'll have to wait and hear Paul's explanation before making any judgment. It ran through his mind these two could be conspirators in the disappearance of Carlotta. If it turned out to be true, Tiffany might end up in a foster home. The thought sent a shiver down his spine.

He picked up the phone and gave Jennifer a call. "Don't worry about dinner tonight. I'm bringing home filet mignon."

"Oh, yummy. That sounds delicious. I'll make a salad and get the baked potatoes ready."

"If you insist, but I'll be glad to fix the whole nine yards."

"No problem. Give me some idea when you'll be home."

"I'll leave here in an hour."

"Okay. I'm looking forward to the meal."

After hanging up, he decided tomorrow he'd take the falcon for a hunt, and Jennifer out in the boat, as she seldom fished anywhere but off the dock. Not that she couldn't drive the Boston Whaler wherever or whenever she wished; it was just fun being together. Satisfied with his plans, he turned his attention back to the file and scribbled some notes.

Hawkman soon left the office with the steaks and chocolates in hand. When he reached the house, Jennifer had finished making the salad, the bakers were ready to pop into the microwave and a loaf of sweet french bread sat on the cutting board ready to be sliced.

That night in bed they lay cuddled in each other's arms. Holding her close, he caressed her hair, wondering if she'd lose those beautiful long locks if she needed chemotherapy? Squeezing his eyes shut, he tried to imagine her with a bald head, but couldn't make the picture materialize.

Jennifer's body relaxed and her breathing fell into a rhythmic pattern. He realized she'd fallen asleep. Kissing her forehead, he savored her sweet smell before gently pulling away and tucking the covers around her shoulders. He positioned his arm tenderly around her waist and closed his eyes.

The next morning, Hawkman quietly slid out of bed, pulled on his jeans and a tee shirt, then padded to the kitchen in his bare feet. He plugged in the coffee maker, then removed a pound of bacon from the refrigerator. Turning on the burner under the big black skillet, he removed several strips and threw them into the pan. Taking out four eggs, he placed them carefully on the counter.

Even with the exhaust fan sucking most of the smell to the outside, the aroma of frying bacon floated through the air. Hawkman checked down the hallway several times wondering how Jennifer could sleep through the wonderful smell of food. He shook his head, musing how women just didn't have the sensory appreciation men did when it came to great grub.

His attention went back to the browning meat when two arms encircled his waist.

"Boy, you sure know the way to a woman's heart."

CHAPTER TWENTY-TWO

Hawkman laughed and gave her a quick peck on the cheek. "I wondered how long it would take to drag you out of bed. My plans today call for us to get an early start."

She stepped back and pointed a finger at her chest. "I'm included?"

"You bet. Bring your camera and we'll take Pretty Girl out for a hunt, then we'll come home and I'll take you out in the boat to do some fishing. I'm in the mood to catch a big bass or trout."

She put a hand on her hip. "My goodness, what brought on all this spoiling, plus you surprising me with the fabulous box of chocolates?"

He handed her a filled plate and ducked his head. "Guilt. I've neglected my beautiful wife too long."

"Hmm," she grinned. "I like your change of heart."

After breakfast, they took the old truck and the falcon up into the hills. While the bird soared above their heads, Jennifer snapped pictures of a big four point buck, a covey of quail and a couple of wild turkeys scurrying across the road. It didn't take long for Pretty Girl to find herself a nice meal of squirrel. They waited for her to eat, then Hawkman whistled. The bird circled high in the sky, then slowly descended, landing on his protected arm.

When they arrived home, Jennifer sat on the deck reviewing the pictures she'd taken with her digital camera while Hawkman filled Pretty Girl's water and food dishes before placing her back into the aviary.

"These pictures are great. I can hardly wait to load them

onto the computer. The one of the buck turned out fantastic. He stood like a king on top of that rock ledge."

"I sent word to the big guy to find a good spot so you could get the perfect shot."

She grinned. "Right. And he minds well."

"Let's gather the fishing gear and give the lake a try. It's been awhile, and I'm wondering if those bass still hang out in those holes where I used to frequent?"

"Nothing like the present to find out." She placed the camera into its case and went inside.

Jennifer fixed a lunch to take, while Hawkman loaded everything into the boat. Several hours later they returned in good spirits with a stringer full of fish. Hawkman noticed she sat quietly as he tied up the craft.

"Hon, you okay?"

"All of a sudden I'm extremely tired."

He helped her from the boat onto the dock. "You go on up to the house and relax. I'll bring the gear and clean the catch." Watching her stroll up the gangplank, he noticed her usual feisty step had lost its pep. This worried him. He hoped he hadn't overextended her energy level and planned to be more careful in the future.

Later that evening, he sealed the last of the perch with the vacuum packer and stored them in the freezer. When he glanced into the living room, Jennifer had stretched out on the couch with an afghan tossed lightly over her body and appeared sound asleep. His stomach wrenched. The cancer seemed to be taking its toll, and he prayed she could conquer the challenge that lay ahead.

***

Monday morning, Hawkman lingered around the house until Jennifer peered over her computer. "Aren't you going into work?"

"I wanted to wait and see if you got a call."

"If I do hear from the doctor today, all he's going to tell me is the biopsy's verified there's cancer and what kind. We have to accept the fact it's churning inside me."

"But won't he tell you the next step?"

"I'll definitely find out, but I can relay the news to you by phone. Nothing else is going to happen today. You don't have to hang out here wasting valuable time you could be spending on the Carlotta case."

"Are you telling me to get out of your hair?"

She sighed. "Yes. You drive me crazy pacing the floor. I can't focus knowing you're so worried."

He nodded. "You're right. I'm heading for Medford. Promise you'll call the minute you hear anything."

"I promise."

When Hawkman reached the city, he drove straight to the police station. He hadn't heard from Williams, but decided he'd stop by in case they'd had time to compare the prints. He found the detective's office locked, so he stopped by the front desk.

"Detective Williams around?"

"He's at a meeting in town and probably won't be back for a couple of hours. Can I give him a message?"

"No, I'll call him later."

Hawkman left and drove to his office. When he unlocked the door, stale air filled his nostrils. He crossed the room and opened the window. Peering up at the dove's ratty nest, he saw the pair had departed their temporary home again. Seemed these two doves had trouble conceiving fertile eggs. No new hatch after three tries.

The days were warming up, and he'd soon have to turn on the air conditioner. Stepping to his desk where he'd left Carlotta's file, he flipped open the folder. He'd memorized everything in it, but he scanned his latest notes. The question marks in the margins reminded him of what he needed to pursue.

He put on the coffee pot, then sat down and listened to the two messages on his answering machine. The first came from an automated tele marketer, which made him frown. He hated receiving those on his business phone. The other came from a previous client who needed an extension on his bill. He'd had a medical emergency and it would be next month before he could pay the balance. This didn't bother Hawkman as he knew the person well and he'd eventually get paid.

Until he heard from Williams about the fingerprints on the suitcase, he couldn't proceed to question his suspects. Waiting made him restless, but he knew he couldn't push the detective who'd call as soon as he had anything to report.

Then the aroma of freshly baked delicacies wafted through the window. Hawkman's stomach growled, even though he'd eaten a hearty breakfast. He'd come to the conclusion this wonderful aroma would forever be a weakness he couldn't control. Trotting down the stairs, he entered the bakery. The old man with flour dusted hair glanced up and grinned, then shoved a long pan filled to the brim with goodies onto the counter.

"I knew you wouldn't last long up there. Take your pick. Today it's on me. We're celebrating our tenth anniversary of business."

Hawkman pointed at a large bear's claw. "Congratulations! I had no idea it'd been so long. Time sure flies. But I can see why you've stayed in business; your products are one of the best and I'm addicted."

The old man stood taller. "Thank you. We take a lot of pride in our baking."

Hawkman carried his choice up the steps and placed it on the desk while he poured himself a cup of coffee. Just as he closed his mouth over the pastry the phone rang. Washing the bite down with a swallow of the hot brew, he punched on the speaker phone.

"Casey, Private Investigator."

"Hi, thought I'd let you know I heard from the doctor."

Hawkman stiffened in his chair. "What'd he say?"

"The biopsy verified it's follicular lymphoma. He's set up an appointment with an oncologist for Thursday."

He swallowed the lump in his throat. "So it really is cancer?"

"Honey, we pretty much knew it. But the doctor assured me they can make it go into remission with treatment. We'll make up a list of questions, so we'll know exactly what to ask when we see him."

"Good idea." He glanced at the bear claw held in his hand and noticed he'd clenched it so tight that his fingers had dug through the dough.

"I'll talk to you more when you get home. Did you find out anything about the prints you gave to Williams?"

He dropped the pastry onto the napkin and sucked on his fingers to get off the sticky. "Uh, no. Williams had a meeting and wouldn't be back for a couple of hours, so I'm waiting for his call."

"What are you doing?"

"Licking sweet stuff off my hands."

"You've been at the bakery again."

"Yeah, you know I can't resist."

"You do have a fondness for sweets," she said, laughing. "We better get off the line in case the detective tries to call. I'll talk to you later."

He punched off the speaker phone and leaned back in the chair. Feeling like he'd been smacked in the jaw by her news, he wiped the back of his hand across his lips expecting to find blood oozing from the corners of his mouth.

When the phone rang, he jumped, the sound bombarding through his brain like a loud firecracker. He grabbed the receiver. "Casey here."

"Don't bite my head off."

"Sorry, detective. Didn't mean to come on so strong. Had my mind focused elsewhere."

"I think you better drop by as soon as you can. Have some interesting results from those prints. I think you'll find the report rather astounding."

CHAPTER TWENTY-THREE

Hawkman pulled himself together and drove to the police station. When he reached the detective's office, he gave a quick knock on the door jamb and stepped inside.

Williams looked up from his desk. "You certainly didn't waste any time getting here."

"I've been waiting for these results before delving deeper."

The detective handed him the report. "I think you'll find this rather interesting. I made you a copy."

Hawkman scooted a chair forward and sat down. Reading through the report he raised his brows. "It looks like several people handled this suitcase."

"Yeah, the lab even found one of the little girl's prints at the bottom of the rail near the rollers."

Pushing his hat back with his forefinger, Hawkman scratched his sideburn. "This is going to be more complicated than I suspected. I'd hoped this would have told us who shoved the bag under the house."

"Nothing's easy. The prints on the handle are the clearest, you might want to pursue those first. There are several of Carlotta's on the metal areas, which we expected."

"It's reasonable for Paul's to be present, since he's the husband. But the most interesting are Tulip's. Why would her fingerprints be on Carlotta's suitcase?" He glanced back at the report. "I see Delia's not mentioned."

"No, nothing matched her prints." Williams picked up a file he had on his desk. "I've decided to open this case as one of ours. The woman's been missing for close to two weeks and you're going to need help. This case is getting more involved by the day. We won't take an active role yet. So go ahead with your investigation. We'll be here to assist."

"Appreciate the work you've already done. Yes, I'm afraid it's getting to the point where I might need a search warrant to do some snooping." Hawkman stood. "Guess I better get myself in gear and do some serious questioning."

Williams cocked his head and stared into Hawkman's face. "Everything okay with you?"

"That's the second time you've asked that question. Do I look like something's bothering me?"

"Yes and no. But I've noticed lately you aren't your witty self. Much too serious."

"Got a lot on my mind."

"Wanna talk about it?"

"Not right now. Maybe down the road." Rolling up the fingerprint paper, he hit it against his other hand. "I'll get back to you when I get some answers."

The detective's gaze followed his friend as went out the door.

***

Hawkman climbed into his vehicle, checked the time and phoned Paul. "Hello, Mr. Ryan, Tom Casey. We need to talk. When will you be home?"

"Have you found Carlotta?"

"No. But I have some important questions."

"I'll meet you at my apartment in fifteen minutes."

"See you then."

Hanging up, Hawkman turned the key in the ignition and headed for Paul's place. Driving into the complex, he noted the black Lexus already parked in front. He pulled alongside and hopped out. As he stepped to the front door, he could hear a muffled male voice. Assuming his client might be on the phone, he knocked softly. The voice became silent and after a few moments, Paul opened the door.

"Come in, Mr. Casey." He gestured toward the living room.

"Have a seat. You sounded so grim on the phone, I hurried right home."

Hawkman chose the chair facing the couch where Paul sat down. "Things are not looking good. Have you checked Carlotta's credit card bill lately?"

"Yes, right after you called in case you asked. Nothing."

Leaning forward, Hawkman placed an arm on his thigh. "I'm concerned we might not find Carlotta alive."

"What do you mean?"

"I found her suitcase filled with newly purchased clothes under the house. I doubt your wife is the type to go on a trip without her new wardrobe."

Paul came forward, his expression somber. "Under the house?"

Hawkman studied the man's face. "Yes, and the bag had your fingerprints on it."

Paul's eyes widened and his coloring turned ashen. "I haven't handled that suitcase in a long time." Then he snapped his fingers. "Wait, I did use it when I took a business trip back east a month ago. I borrowed it from Carlotta."

"Can you prove it?"

"Yes, I'm sure work has an invoice of the trip."

"Good. You're going to need it. Also someone who saw you with that particular suitcase."

Paul's mouth dropped open. "Mr. Casey, you're scaring the hell out of me. I'm not sure I can provide someone who would recognize the bag."

"I think you better try. Maybe a busboy at the place you stayed would remember. The police are getting involved and you better have plenty of proof of your whereabouts for the past three weeks. More than likely you'll become a prime suspect for the murder of your wife."

"Murder!" Paul launched from his seat and walked around the couch. "You haven't found her body, have you?"

"No, but everything is pointing to the fact that your wife didn't leave on any trip. Doesn't that sound mighty suspicious to you?"

"Hell, yes."

"You've already lied to me about Carlotta taking Tiffany to your mother's."

Paul's head drooped forward, his hands clutching the back of the couch. "I just assumed Carlotta had taken Tiffany over. I was very upset and Mother later corrected me."

"Did she set you straight after I talked with Tiffany and she showed me the note Carlotta had left or before?"

Paul lowered his eyes. "After."

"How many other fabrications have you told me?"

He straightened and raised his right hand. "None, I swear. It was just a misunderstanding."

"I'm trying to believe you. Another thing I need to know is, if anyone has driven or been inside Carlotta's car since she disappeared."

"Not that I'm aware, but I could call Mom and find out. She or Tiffany would be the most apt to get into the car for some reason."

"Maybe you should check right now."

Paul stepped into the kitchen. Within a few minutes he returned to his seat across from Hawkman. "No, neither of them have even been near the Camry. Mom didn't think it a good idea for Tiffany to be reminded of her mother's disappearance."

"I'm going to have it dusted for prints. So you better be telling the truth. If we find any evidence you've been in that car, your butt is fried."

"I loved my wife, Mr. Casey, I wouldn't have harmed her."

"They all deny it, Mr. Ryan. It won't hold up, so I'd advise you to answer all my questions truthfully."

"I will."

"How often do you see Tulip Withers."

Paul stared at him. "Tulip?"

"Yes."

"Seldom. Only when Carlotta has her over for lunch or dinner."

"How about phone calls?"

"Mr. Casey, Tulip's had a crush on me since high school.

She calls my office, apartment and leaves messages on all my phones. I've tried to discourage her, but with no luck."

"What kind of messages?"

He shifted his position and stared at the ceiling. "Oh, she tells me what a wonderful living I make for my family. And how Carlotta doesn't appreciate me. Silly high school stuff."

"Do you like the woman?"

Paul ran his fingers along the cushion seam. "She's okay, but I'm certainly not attracted to her if that's what you're implying. I'm courteous for Carlotta's and Tiffany's sake. They both seem to care about Tulip. To tell the truth, I feel pity for her because she has no one but her dad."

"Has she called since Carlotta's disappearance?"

He nodded. "Yeah."

"What did she want?"

"Oh, she wants to bring me dinner. Figures I'm lonely and not eating right. Tells me how worried she is about Carlotta, wonders when she'll return, and can't understand why she left such a precious daughter."

"How do you respond?"

"I don't. I screen my calls and know it's her, so I don't answer."

"When did you hear from her last?"

Paul scratched the back of his neck, and screwed up his mouth. "About two days ago."

Hawkman stood and moved toward the door. "I'd suggest you find yourself a good lawyer."

"Wait." He jumped up and stepped in front of Hawkman. "Will you stay on the case and find Carlotta?" He choked back the tears. "Dead or alive."

"Yes."

CHAPTER TWENTY-FOUR

Hawkman left Paul's apartment, not sure what to think about the man's responses. He played the innocent quite well, and acted genuinely frightened at the prospect of being accused of his wife's murder.

Tiffany's fingerprints on the suitcase didn't bother him. He figured the child could have handled the bag many times. No reason to even question her about it, since he doubted she'd even remember touching it.

He swung by Tulip Withers' place, but found it dark and the old blue Honda he'd seen parked in front missing. On the way through town, he drove by Mom's Cafe and spotted her car in a slot near the restaurant. He would catch Tulip at home tomorrow, before she went to work.

This woman baffled him. If she hid the suitcase under the house, why didn't she wipe off the prints? He couldn't fathom anyone being so naive as to think the bag wouldn't eventually be found and the impressions lifted. Tulip didn't appear super smart, but it didn't mean she couldn't think.

As Hawkman drove toward Copco Lake, his thoughts shifted to his wife. He felt pretty good for staying focused on the Carlotta case most of the day. Jennifer would want to hear the latest, and he hoped she'd been successful in concentrating on her writing. They'd compare notes when he got home.

Then he remembered she'd told him to think about questions for the oncologist on Thursday. Several popped into his mind immediately. He felt his jaw tighten at the thought of a cancer doctor. Now he knew how people felt who said it could never happen to them. "It can," he mumbled and gripped the steering wheel until his knuckles turned white.

When he came in sight of Copco Lake, he took the splintered toothpick from his mouth and dropped it into the ashtray. Driving across the bridge, he rolled down the windows and let the sound of the rushing water soothe his nerves. He took several deep breaths as he turned into the driveway and parked in the garage. As he stepped inside the house, it did his heart good to see Jennifer at her computer. She glanced up and smiled.

"Hi, you're home earlier than I expected. Make any headway on the case?"

"Yep. As a matter of fact, I did."

Her eyes lit up and she left the computer. "I can hardly wait to hear about it."

He grinned. "Let me take a breath or two first."

"You want a drink or a beer?"

"Beer will be fine," he said, hanging his hat and shoulder holster in the Hawkman corner.

She handed him a frosty bottle, then mixed a gin and tonic for herself. He fingered through the envelopes piled on the counter top as he waited. "Lots of junk mail."

"It seems we get more each day."

They settled in the living room and Hawkman told her about the visit with Paul. "I can't quite figure whether the guy's innocent or guilty as hell."

"Did you check out the business trip with his company?"

"Not yet. It's on my list of things to do."

"If he did go on one and used the suitcase, it would definitely be reasonable to expect his prints on it. And from what you've told me about the man, it seems he cared very much for Carlotta, even though they weren't living together. I think he hoped they would eventually patch things up."

"It's possible. But not sure I trust him. There's something about him that rubs me wrong, but I can't put my finger on it."

"What about Tulip Withers?"

"Going to see her first thing in the morning. She'd already gone to work by the time I finished up with Paul."

"And Delia?"

"None of her prints were on the bag."

"I guess she couldn't have wiped them off without taking the others too."

"True. The fact the police found Paul's, Tulip's and Tiffany's prints on the bag baffles me,"

Jennifer frowned. "Tiffany's?"

"Her prints were near the rollers. She could have touched the suitcase anytime. She doesn't worry me. I'm not even going to question her."

"Good."

"So how has your day gone?"

He hazel eyes glowed. "Great, I wrote two chapters on my new book."

"Excellent."

Picking up a clipboard on the end table, she took a pen from beneath the clip. "As much as I hate to bring it up, let's think about some questions for the oncologist on Thursday. We can add to them each day."

"I've already thought of a few."

***

Late Tuesday morning, Hawkman left the house and headed for Medford. If Tulip liked to sleep in, he didn't want to roust her too early and risk uncooperative behavior toward this private investigator. He stopped by his office first to pick up the phone bill in case she denied talking with Carlotta as often as it stated.

When he arrived at the complex, he parked in the vacant slot next to Tulip's Honda. He sat for a minute studying the apartment. Having only been in the living room, he didn't know for sure if she had one or two bedrooms. He scanned the other flats in the building and they all appeared about the same size.

Climbing out of his vehicle, he meandered up to the door

and knocked. The curtain moved at the window and Tulip's face came into view.

"Hi, Mr. Casey. Hold on, I'll be right there."

He heard the chain lock rattle and the click of the dead bolt turn before the door opened.

"Come on in and have a seat. I hope you have good news about Carlotta."

Hawkman sat down in the chair he'd used at his last visit. Tulip's hair hung in a long braid down her back. Wisps had escaped and were clinging to her cheeks. She wore a pair of faded jeans and a sloppy shirt several sizes too big. Flopping down on the couch, she shoved the loose hair behind her ears with her fingers.

"I wish I had favorable news, but unfortunately, I'm here to ask more questions," Hawkman said.

Tulip folded her arms at her waist. "I don't know what else I can tell you."

"You told me you only spoke or saw Carlotta occasionally. Yet her phone bill indicates you talked quite often."

She leaned forward. "I told you, I seldom heard from Carlotta.

Hawkman removed a copy of the bill from his pocket and showed it to her. "I've marked the calls coming to your phone number in red. It appears you talked with someone from her number about twice a week up until Carlotta disappeared. Could you explain those to me?"

Tulip studied the bill, then touched her chin. "Oh, those came from Tiffany."

Hawkman raised a brow. "Tiffany?"

"Yes, if you'll notice all these calls came after school let out." She pointed at the time's listed as she handed him the sheet of paper. "Tiffany liked the food at Mom's and many times Carlotta left money for her grandmother to take her out to eat. Delia usually brought her over to the restaurant because she could get a good meal." Tulip rolled her eyes. "Even though I'm sure the girl would have rather gone to McDonald's. Tiffany would call before I left for work and ask me about the special of the day. If she liked it, she asked me to save her favorite booth for her and her grandmother. Otherwise, I guess they ended up eating at a fast food place."

Hawkman returned the bill to his pocket, then stared into Tulip's face. "We found Carlotta's suitcase."

She avoided his gaze. "What suitcase?"

"The one I presumed she'd be taking on the trip as it had all her latest purchases inside."

"Where'd you find it?"

"Under the house."

"What!"

"That's right. And it had your fingerprints on it."

Tulip stiffened and her face paled. "How could my fingerprints be on her suitcase? I don't even know which one she took. She has a set containing about three or four bags."

"How'd you know?"

"Because about a month ago, when I stopped by for lunch, Carlotta asked me if I could reach one of them in the top of her closet. She said Paul needed it for a trip and would be by to pick it up later that day. I'm quite a bit taller than her, so I gave it a try and managed to haul it down."

"Do you remember how you grabbed it."

"Yes, I took hold of the handle. I remember because it slipped out of the notches and I whacked myself in the shin as it came down off the shelf. Had a good sized bruise for about a week."

"Guess that explains why your prints were on the bag." He let out a sigh, pulled down his hat close to his brow, and stood. Then he pointed at the doorway leading from the living room. "How many bedrooms does this apartment have?"

"Two."

"Isn't it more expensive than having one?"

"Oh, yes, but my dad supplies me with lots of meat, so I had to have an extra room to keep a chest freezer. The money I save on beef and pork pays for the extra cost." She rose from the couch. "I also have a daybed in there in case I ever have company."

"I bought some filets from your dad the other day. He said he'd trained you to be a butcher, but you'd rather be a waitress than help him at his store. How come?"

She shuddered. "I've never liked cutting up dead animals."

CHAPTER TWENTY-FIVE

Hawkman drove away from Tulip's apartment in a quandary. He wouldn't have believed her tale except for the fact she'd mentioned Paul's trip which tied right in with his story. Whoever pushed the bag under the house only touched the cloth portion or wore gloves. Maybe he didn't wipe off the handle or metal parts on purpose hoping any prints left on the suitcase would draw attention away from him.

He felt like he'd slid back to square one. The only other detail he had to go on was the possible weight of the person who did the deed. Shaking his head, he felt like his brain had filled with mush. He had too much to think about and needed to clear the channels so thoughts would run smoothly. Something didn't fit the puzzle, but what?

It bothered him to hear Tiffany made those phone calls. When the young girl spoke of Tulip, he got the impression she thought of her more as a joke than a person she'd confide in. Could the child know more than she's telling?

Strange, neither Tiffany nor Delia mentioned going to Mom's to eat. But since it didn't appear to have anything to do with Carlotta's disappearance, the family probably thought it insignificant. Maybe he should speak with them and emphasize how important it is to tell him every detail leading up to Carlotta's disappearance, regardless of how minor it might seem.

He came to a stop sign, pulled his cell phone from his belt and punched in Delia's number. She may have already left to pick up Tiffany from school. The phone rang four times before the answering machine came on. He decided not to leave a message. He then phoned Detective Williams.

"Hey, Williams, surprised I caught you in the office."

"A nice quiet day. We've just had a few robberies and disturbances of the peace until the phone rang."

"Well, we can't have it so calm at the police station."

"I'm sure you're going to make chaos."

Hawkman chuckled. "I've questioned Paul and Ms. Tulip Withers. They both have good reasons for their prints being on the suitcase. And their stories check out."

"I'd like to hear them. You think those two could be in cahoots?"

"Anything's possible, but I have my doubts. Found out another little tidbit, probably not important, but might have a bearing on the case. I'm going to speak with Tiffany and her grandmother. I'll let you know what I discover."

"Sounds mighty suspicious. Don't tell me you think that kid pushed the suitcase under the house?"

"No. Her weight doesn't match the ground measurements. And as far as her prints being on the bag, she could have touched it anytime. I'm sure our killer wore gloves, but what I find curious is, why the prints weren't smudged. The person must have just handled the cloth area. Why did they do this? Or did they have a motive in the back of their mind?"

"Hmm, you've got a point. Possibly playing a game to throw off the authorities."

"My thoughts exactly," Hawkman said. "By the way, talking about fingerprints, made me think about something else. Why don't you have your lab team go over Carlotta's car. Supposedly, no one has driven it or been inside the vehicle since she vanished. I'd like to know for sure. I've told Ryan to expect you some time soon."

"Good. I'll give him a call and get my group over there this evening or first thing in the morning. Keep me informed on what you find out."

"Will do."

Hawkman signed off and headed toward Delia's house.

He doubted he'd find them home, knowing she and her granddaughter could be shopping or at the ice cream parlor. When he rounded the corner, to his pleasant surprise, the garage door stood open and he could see the big Cadillac parked inside. He pulled to the front curb, climbed out his 4X4 just about the time he heard the two talking and slamming car doors. As they backed out and the garage door rolled down, Delia spotted him and braked. She stared out her window with a curious expression, then rolled down the glass and stuck out her head.

"Hi, Mr. Casey. What brings you here today?"

He stepped up to the car. "I wanted to speak with you and Tiffany."

"Can it wait, she has a school project due and we've been working like crazy to get it completed. Now we need to get to the library and store."

"No problem. Will tomorrow about this time be all right?"

Tiffany gave him a big grin and a little wave from the passenger seat.

"Yes, much better. Thanks. By the way, any news?"

"Nothing." He moved away from the car as she backed out of the driveway.

Some inner feeling drew him toward Tulip Withers' place, even though he assumed she'd already gone to work. As he slowly cruised by her apartment, it surprised him to see Alfonso's van parked in front of her place. Hawkman pulled into an empty slot on the opposite side and killed the engine. Figuring Alfonso wouldn't pay much attention to his vehicle unless he recognized him, so he slipped on a pair of sunglasses, removed his cowboy hat, and slapped on a ball cap. He then adjusted the rear mirror so he could get a good view of the front door. Not seeing Tulip's car anywhere, made him wonder what the handyman was doing there. She didn't seem the type to allow anyone inside without her being present.

Hawkman picked the clipboard off the passenger seat, and placed it on the steering wheel. He noted the time and jotted it down along with the license plate number of the van, then waited. A faint glow glistened through the curtained window of her apartment in the area of the kitchen, but he couldn't see any shadows or silhouettes.

Thirty minutes passed before the light flickered out and the front door slowly opened. He slid lower in the seat as Alfonso stepped outside with a tray of tools, placed them in his van and drove away without ever glancing across the parking lot. Hawkman waited a few moments, then drove by the intersection where Alfonso lived, and spotted the man going into his apartment.

If the two didn't know each other, what was he doing repairing something inside her place? Hawkman drove to Mom's Cafe. The evening crowd hadn't hit yet and he found Tulip refilling the salt shakers.

"Good evening, Ms. Withers."

Her head snapped up and she forced a smile. "Hello, Mr. Casey. I see you've returned for more of Mom's cooking."

"No, I just came from your apartment, hoping to catch you before you left and instead found a man inside."

She spilled salt across the table. "In my apartment?"

"Yes, looked like a handyman."

"Oh, whew. You scared me for a moment." She cleaned up the scattered salt, then scooted the shaker to the end of the table and gave the surface a final swipe. "It's about time they fixed that leaky faucet. The complex said they'd send a repairman as soon as they found a new guy to replace the one who'd retired." Then she furrowed her brow and gazed at him. "Why did you want to see me?"

"I wondered if Tiffany had called you since her mother disappeared?"

"No. And I miss her. She's such a sweet little girl. I guess Delia cooks her meals now. Carlotta sent Tiffany out a lot, which I personally didn't think a healthy habit. But she hated to cook." She sighed. "Poor Paul, guess he never ate a good home-cooked meal while living with her. That woman definitely didn't know how to treat a man."

Hawkman touched his hat and turned toward the exit. "Thanks for the information. Have a good evening."

As he drove toward the office, he mulled over what Tulip had said about the apartment complex hiring Alfonso as their handyman. He obviously carries a master key and has access to all the units. It made Hawkman wonder how close they'd checked the man's record. He could just hear the calls coming into their main office when items of value started disappearing from the renters.

He parked in the alley and took the stairs two at a time. Jennifer would be proud of him for resisting the wonderful aroma of doughnuts coming from the bakery. The afternoons were getting warm and the office felt stuffy. He left the door ajar and opened the window, letting a nice breeze blow through. He noticed the red light on the message machine blinking and sat down. Picking up a pencil and placing a yellow legal tablet in front of him, he punched the play button.

The first dispatch hung up. The second communication came from Delia asking him to hold off coming by tomorrow until four as she needed to talk with Tiffany's teacher before coming home from school.

The third made him stare at the machine as a muffled voice came across the line. "Drop the Carlotta case or Tiffany will be hurt."

CHAPTER TWENTY-SIX

Hawkman saved the message, then listened to it several times trying to recognize the muffled voice, but to no avail. He stuck a toothpick in his mouth and leaned back. The situation with Tiffany bothered him. He punched in Williams' number.

"Detective Williams."

"Hawkman here. Just received a call threatening Tiffany's welfare if I continued to pursue the Carlotta case."

"Par for the course. Did you get the I.D.?"

"Pay phone downtown."

"Figures."

Hawkman picked up a pencil and tapped it on the desk. "I don't like the child being involved. Worries me. Maybe protection should be provided until we get to the bottom of this."

"Don't have the manpower right now. Have a big drug sting in progress. You might have to hire one of your guys. The problem with Carlotta's case is we have no proof there's been any foul play. No body, blood or anything."

"Maybe I haven't been looking in the right places. I have a gut feeling that woman's corpse is close."

"You find it and my department will get serious."

"You're a lot of help."

"Sorry, I'm strung out like a tight rubber band. And unfortunately, the Ryan case has slipped to the back burner. But before it did, I received the report from our lab on the prints in the car. All we found were Carlotta's and Tiffany's."

"Thanks, appreciate the information."

After hanging up, Hawkman called Paul.

"Mr. Ryan, could you drop by my office on your way home from work? I have something very important to discuss."

Within the hour, Hawkman glanced up at the tap on his door. "Come in."

Paul entered, his expression strained with worry. He crossed the room to the front of the desk. "It makes me very nervous when I get these types of calls from you."

"You should be. I want you to listen to something."

Hawkman punched on the machine and played the message. Paul dropped down in the chair, his face pale. "My God. Who would want to hurt Tiffany?"

"Do you recognize the voice?"

He shook his head. "No, it's so muted, it's even hard to understand."

"I feel someone is playing a game. But to be on the safe side, I want close surveillance of your daughter. Don't let her out of your sight. Note any strange car or person in the neighborhood. I also think you better keep her home from school for the next few days."

Paul furrowed his brow. "She isn't going to be happy." His eyes wide, he glanced up at Hawkman. "What reason am I going to give her?"

"I think you better tell the truth. If she realizes the danger, it will make her more aware of her surroundings."

"Yeah, but at her age, it could cause nightmares."

"It might, but it's a risk you're going to have to take. Better than having her kidnapped or hurt. In fact, it might be a good idea if you stayed at Delia's for the rest of the week. Don't take off work, but be there at night. I imagine your mom can handle anything during the day."

Paul stared at the floor. "What's someone trying to do, other than put the fear of God into us?"

"I wish I knew, but they obviously think we're getting close to something or they wouldn't have made the call."

"Would you mind dropping by my Mom's with me, so I can prepare her for this. I could use your moral support."

"Sure. I'll take the recording, so she can hear it." Hawkman slid the CD into his pocket and the two men left the office.

***

Delia heard the car pull into the driveway and peered out the window. When she saw Paul and Mr. Casey coming up the sidewalk, she could tell by her son's expression and rapid walk there'd been a breakthrough in the case. She took a quick look down the hallway toward Tiffany's bedroom and could hear the computer game playing.

Gnawing on her lower lip, she opened the front door and studied both men's solemn expressions. "What's wrong?"

"Mom, we need to talk in private, then we'll speak with Tiffany."

She led the two men into the den off the kitchen and closed the door. "Okay, what's going on?"

Hawkman walked over to the computer and booted it up, then inserted the CD. After the message played, Delia's face expressed horror. "What the hell? Who would hurt Tiffany?"

Paul put an arm around his mother. "We don't know. Mr. Casey received this on his answering machine today and feels we should take every precaution to protect her. Which means keeping Tiffany home from school for the next few days."

She gaped at Hawkman. "How will we explain it to her and the school?"

"School's no problem," Paul said. "You call and tell them she's sick. As far as Tiffany, Mr. Casey suggests we tell her the truth."

Delia raised her arms in disbelief. "You can't tell a ten year old child her life might be in danger from some idiot. She won't know how to handle it. News such as this could affect her the rest of her life."

"That's true," Hawkman said. "How would you deal with it?"

She put her hands on each side of her face and paced. "I don't know."

"Sit down, Delia," Hawkman instructed. "The child has

accepted the fact her mother has disappeared. And I have a feeling she pretty well knows she's dead."

Delia plopped down in a chair. "I think you're right."

Hawkman observed the two adults. "Then why not involve her in the truth, instead of trying to skirt around it. The child's smart enough to figure things out for herself. The minute you keep her home from school and she catches you watching her every move, she'll put it together."

"How serious is this warning?" Delia asked.

"I'm not sure. It could be a scare tactic with no action following. But I don't think we want to chance it."

"No, we can't," Paul said. "Mom, why don't you get Tiffany in here. We might as well get this over with."

Delia left the room and soon returned with her granddaughter in tow. The young girl stared at each person, then sidled up to her dad. "No one looks very happy. Is something wrong?"

Paul took Tiffany's hands. "We need to talk."

"What about?"

When they'd finished explaining the danger, Tiffany turned to her dad. "Will you stay with us?"

"Yes."

Then she went to her grandmother. "Can he sleep in my room?"

"Of course, darling. There's plenty of space to move in the daybed."

Tiffany smiled. "It's really comfortable, Dad. I've slept on it before."

He took her in his arms and gave her a hug. "It'll be fine."

Hawkman removed the CD from the computer. "While I'm here, I might as well talk to you about another problem. Then we can cancel tomorrow's visit."

"Sure," Delia said.

He turned toward Tiffany. "I understand you made several phone calls to Tulip Withers when you were at the other house. Is this true?"

"Yeah. Mom would leave me money to go eat and when

Grandma came to pick me up, she figured I'd get a better meal if she took me to Mom's Cafe. So before we left, I'd call Tulip and find out what specials they had for the day, because some things I didn't like."

Delia smiled. "Carlotta left food money for Tiffany all the time and I didn't think it a healthy habit for her to have a hamburger and french fries so often. But I didn't dare go against Carlotta's wishes, so we worked out this method. Tiffany would at least get a well-balanced meal a couple of times a week." She laughed and winked at her granddaughter. "But when they didn't have what she liked, off we went to the hamburger joint."

"You hadn't told me this before," Hawkman said. "And I'd like to impress upon all of you to inform me about everything, even if it seems minute and insignificant. It might lead to a clue toward finding Carlotta."

Tiffany looked down at the floor and scuffed her feet against the carpet. "You're probably going to find my Mom buried in a dirt grave." She threw her arms around Paul, buried her head in his neck and sobbed. "I'm sorry, Dad, but I think Mom's dead."

Paul squeezed his eyes shut and held his daughter.

CHAPTER TWENTY-SEVEN

When Hawkman left Delia's, he circled the block and cruised through the surrounding areas. Figuring most people would be home from work and errand running, he made a mental note of the cars parked on the streets. Not seeing anything suspicious, he turned toward home.

Jennifer reacted in disgust upon hearing the recording. "That's horrible. Who would threaten a child?"

"A very sick person."

"How did Tiffany react to the news?"

"Very grown-up. But she believes her mother's dead. I think she came to the realization sooner than her father."

Jennifer sat down in the chair and hugged her knees. "Children seem to have an uncanny sense about such things. I hope being threatened doesn't leave a lasting impression and make her frightened of people forever."

Hawkman slumped down on the ottoman in front of her. "I think Delia and Paul are aware of the dangers and will watch her closely. If necessary they can seek professional help. I felt she needed the truth, regardless of the circumstances."

"I agree with you. At least she won't feel betrayed by the only two people she has left. My heart tells me she fears her mother let her down and now she's dead, so no restoration can be made." She rested her chin on her knees. "Do you have any idea who might have left such a message?"

"None. I feel like I've slid back to square one."

She reached over and touched his shoulder. "Honey, I can tell you've got me on your mind too much. You need to think clearly and it's interfering."

He took her hand and kissed her fingers. "It's a little hard not to think about what you're going through."

"Granted, it's hard. But lay it aside." She gave him a kiss on the cheek, then leaned back in the chair. "You know, there's the chance you're searching in the wrong direction. Go back over every soul you've talked to about Carlotta. That person could be the key."

"You're right. Tomorrow, I'm going to the office and concentrate on the file. I've felt all along I've missed an important factor, but haven't been able to put my finger on it."

"It's because your mind is cluttered."

He patted her knee and stood. "I think I'll hit the sack. How are you doing?"

"Tired, but okay. I'm right behind you."

Helping her out of the chair, he put an arm around her and they headed for the bedroom. "Another day, then we'll find out what the oncologist has to say."

She nodded and forced a smile.

***

The next morning, Hawkman sat at his desk in his Medford office with Carlotta's file spread out on the surface. He'd decided to go over each tidbit and reevaluate what needed further investigation. Several hours passed as he read through his notes of observations, questions and answers of everyone he'd interrogated. He finally leaned back, stretched his arms, flipped up his eye-patch and rubbed his eyes. Adjusting the patch back over his eye, he got up and poured himself a cup of coffee, then sat down and picked up the phone. He needed to touch base with Jessica Phillips, the lawyer Carlotta had hired to handle the divorce.

"Jessica Phillips, please."

"May I ask who's calling?"

"Tom Casey, private investigator."

After a few moments, a female voice came across the line. "Hello, Mr. Casey. Good hearing from you again. I hope you have some good news about Carlotta."

"Wish it were true, but I wanted to check and see if by some chance you've had any communication with her."

"I'm sorry. Not a word, telephone or otherwise."

"Thank you. That's all I needed to know."

Hawkman hung up with a sigh and again glanced at the papers strewn across his desk. Then his gaze fell upon a notation he'd made in the margin of one of the sheets of notes. He raised his brows, grabbed a pencil and circled the words. Hoping to catch Ms. Withers before she left for work, he jumped up, ran his fingers through his hair, plopped on his cowboy hat and left the office.

When he reached her apartment, he saw her through the same routine of peeking out the window before letting him in.

"Hello, Mr. Casey." She motioned toward the living room. "Have a seat. Your visits are getting rather frequent. Is there a reason?"

"I'm investigating a missing person and have to cover every avenue."

"Carlotta's been gone a long time without any word. I have this feeling in the pit of my stomach she's met with foul play."

Hawkman sat down on the same hardback chair. "Do you know for a fact she hasn't contacted anyone?"

Tulip shrugged. "Well, no. But I have this impression you think I know where she is."

"Do you?"

She wrinkled her forehead into a frown. "No."

"Tell me a little bit about your family."

"Why my family?" she scowled, sitting down on the couch.

"Do you have brothers or sisters?"

"No. I'm an only child."

"Your father mentioned your mother died. How long has she been gone?"

"About eight years."

"Why didn't you leave the area, since you weren't going into business with your father?"

"Because he wanted me to stay in town. Otherwise, he

wouldn't be able to see me much, as he wouldn't close the shop any length of time for a visit."

"Sounds a little selfish."

Her gaze drifted to the floor. "Dad's very possessive."

"Where does he live?"

"In a beautiful home on the west side, near the foothills. He wanted me to share it with him, but I knew I couldn't stand to be under the same roof with all his ranting."

"Oh? What does he carry on about?"

"Me, mostly. How I've screwed up my life. Never got married. That sort of thing."

"Do you see him often?"

She took a deep breath and exhaled. "Yes, at least two or three times a week. He stops by after I get off work."

"What does he do during the time he closes shop and you get off?"

"He cuts up the meat, then scrubs that butcher shop down until it sparkles. No germ could live there when he's through. It takes him several hours to prepare for the following day. If he finishes early, he comes by the cafe and has a cup of coffee."

"You sound as if you resent his attention."

"It gets a bit old," she said, bitterly. "I wish he'd leave me alone and get a life of his own."

Hawkman noticed she had her hands clenched tightly in her lap. "Does your dad know the Ryan family?"

She rolled her eyes. "He's lived here most of his life and knows everyone in this town." Then she glared at Hawkman. "Why are you asking me such questions? Do you think my Dad had something to do with Carlotta's disappearance?"

He placed his hands on his thighs. "I'm doing my job."

Tulip stood and put her fists on her hips. "Well, I think you're way out of line and I'm not going to answer any more."

"That's your prerogative, but the police are getting involved and they will probably question you and your dad."

A flash of fear crossed her face. "So be it."

Hawkman arose and crossed the room to the front door.

With his hand on the knob, he turned back to Tulip. "You might even consider getting a lawyer."

Her mouth dropped open. "Am I a suspect?"

"Everyone who knew Carlotta is under investigation. The woman's been missing for over two weeks and it doesn't look good."

Hawkman left the apartment and climbed into his vehicle as she watched from the entry.

***

Tulip stood in the doorway for several minutes after Hawkman left the premises, the questions referring to her father ricocheting through her mind. She slowly closed and locked the door, then headed for the phone.

Her fingers trembling, she punched in the number. "Dad, I need to talk to you as soon as possible."

CHAPTER TWENTY-EIGHT

When Hawkman drove out of the apartment complex, he figured Tulip would head straight for the phone. Her show of fear gave him reason to question Mr. Withers.

He headed downtown, found a parking spot in front of the butcher shop and meandered inside. There were a couple of customers at the counter and Hank raised his head and smiled.

"Be right with you."

"No hurry, take your time," Hawkman said, watching the man's calm demeanor as he wrapped the peoples' choices in white paper. The area finally cleared and Hank wiped his hands on a towel hanging off the counter.

"Now, what can I get you?"

"Nothing today. I want to talk to you about Carlotta Ryan."

"Oh. Tulip told me the girl has been missing for some time now."

"Yes. How well did you know her?"

"I didn't see much of the little lady, but her husband, Paul, bought meat here often. Gave me the feeling he did most of the cooking in the backyard." He chuckled. "You can pretty well tell by the cuts they buy. He's a nice guy. I've always liked him."

"Did you ever meet Carlotta?"

He waddled his head. "Oh, sure. She grew up here. I know about every soul in this town. Pretty sad when her folks were killed in a horrible head-on car crash. Some drunk clobbered them."

"Yes, terrible tragedy. What do you think of Carlotta?"

Hank shrugged. "Not sure what you mean. I don't know her well, but run across her here and there in town. In high school, she appeared to be, what would you call it, sort of an air head? Tulip ran with the same gang of kids. But how Carlotta ever latched onto Paul Ryan, I'll never know. He could have done so much better."

"What do you mean?"

"Tulip tells me Carlotta kicked him out of the house. Stupid move if you ask me. Wonder what she thought that would accomplish? Plenty of women in this town would give their eye teeth for his attention." He pulled a paper towel from a roll hanging on the wall, sprayed the counter with ammonia and wiped it down. Stopping in the middle of a swipe, he peered at Hawkman and let out a sigh. "How I'd love to have that pretty little Tiffany as my granddaughter. Looks like I'll never be a grandpa. Tulip has no prospects for marriage and looks like she's going to be an old maid. And her child bearing years are almost over."

"I've heard she's always had a crush on Paul Ryan."

Withers nodded. "Yep and I tried to encourage her to fix herself up. Put on a little make-up and do something with her mane. She has pretty hair, but never does anything to it. Just braids it and let's it hang. That won't catch a man." He sighed and threw the debris into a bag hanging on the counter edge.

"Do you know Delia Ryan?

"Oh, yeah, she's been a regular customer for years. Fine woman." He laughed. "Except for her attraction to fantasy and horror books. She does have some strange furnishings in her house. It would give me nightmares to wake up and see some of those statutes or pictures staring me in the face."

"So, you've been in her house?"

Hank rubbed a hand over his chin. "Yeah, being we've both been widowed, I tried to court her some years back. Didn't work. I'm not her type, and the truth be known, she's too independent for me."

"You like to have control?"

"I guess you'd say I like to have some say in how my household's run. But that woman is in full command and won't tolerate interference. She has Paul under her fingertips and I think that's one of the reason Carlotta kicked him out. She didn't like the competition."

"That's an interesting perspective. What gave you such an idea?"

Hank moved down the counter and checked his meat supply. "Guess by some of the things Tulip told me. Delia was very much against the marriage from the beginning. But Paul bucked her and the wedding took place. Carlotta gave birth to Tiffany exactly nine months later so they say. So you can come to your own conclusion there."

"Did Tulip ever mention how Carlotta and Paul got along?"

"She said they fought a lot, and thought the woman had lost her mind when she told him to get out. Tulip tried to talk her out of taking such a drastic move, but Carlotta said she'd fallen out of love and wanted a divorce."

"Is there another man involved?"

"I don't rightly know. But it's possible. She may have run off with some loner and you may never find her."

"You think she'd just up and leave Tiffany without so much as a word?"

"Hard to say. To hear Tulip talk about the situation, Carlotta seemed more interested in her own life rather than her daughter's. She had the child dress like a teenager instead of letting her grow up in her own time."

"When did you last see Carlotta?"

The butcher reached inside one of the refrigerated counters and rearranged the display. Hawkman noticed a tic in the man's left cheek. "Hmm, hard to say. I don't recall seeing her for a long time. I'm pretty much stuck in my shop, so I'm not tooling around town."

"Have you encouraged Tulip to be attentive to Paul since Carlotta threw him out?"

Hank stepped back and raised his bushy eyebrows. "Why not? He's the catch of the town with Carlotta out of the picture. It sure as hell can't hurt."

"Why do you say Carlotta's out of the picture."

The man's face flushed. "Well, she's up and vanished. No one's seen her for weeks."

"True, but she might show up out of the blue."

"Well, I wouldn't bet any money on it."

About that time the bell above the door jingled and a customer walked in.

"I've got work to do, and I have nothing more to say."

Hawkman touched his hat. "Thanks for your time."

Back in the confines of his SUV, Hawkman thought about the dialog he'd shared with Hank Withers. The butcher knew a lot about the Ryan family, but he felt the man had lied about when he'd last seen Carlotta.

***

Tulip reached her father, only to be turned off by his telling her he had a store full of customers. She quickly told him the private investigator had been there asking pointed questions.

"Don't worry, I'll handle the son-of-a-bitch," he'd hissed.

Tulip paced the floor, then jumped into the shower. Letting the hot water beat against her back, she closed her eyes and tried to relax. She felt guilty for wasting energy, but at the moment she felt her sanity might be more important.

She finally stepped out of the stall into the steamy bathroom and toweled dry. After wrapping the large terry around her body, she peeked out, never knowing for sure whether her father might have let himself in with his key and be standing at her bedroom door. He'd never touched her, but she'd caught him staring at her with a look that sent chills down her spine.

Pulling a fresh uniform from the closet, she dressed for work, then glanced at herself in the mirror and groaned. One of these days, I'm going to try some make-up, she thought, as she rebraided her hair, wrapped it around her head, then secured it with two butterfly pins. She grabbed a clean apron from the dresser drawer and tied it around her waist as she headed for the kitchen. Snatching her purse off the counter, she hurried out the front door. Tonight her dad would surely come over and maybe they could discuss this whole debacle about Carlotta and Paul.

***

Hawkman decided he'd drop by Delia's and talk to Paul before he went home. Tomorrow would be taken up with Jennifer's doctor's appointment and it would be Friday before he could follow up. As he cruised through Delia's neighborhood, he noted the vehicles and saw nothing strange or out of order. When he arrived at the house, Paul's car sat in the driveway and he answered the door.

"Mr. Casey, is every thing all right?"

"I'd like to talk to you out here in the yard, if that's okay."

"Yeah, hold on a minute. I don't want Mom and Tiffany to be alarmed when I don't come back inside."

He returned in a few moments and the two men stepped away from the house. Hawkman stood in the grass, his thumbs hooked in his jeans front pockets.

"Are you good friends with Hank Withers?"

Paul's expression turned pensive. "I don't know how good, but we're friends. I've traded at his butcher shop for years, along with my parents. Mom still shops there too. Why?"

"Did you ever talk to him about Carlotta?"

"No more than the normal chitchat. He used to tease me about never seeing my wife buy meat. I guess in time, he figured out Carlotta didn't do much cooking."

"Did you ever confide in him about your marriage situation?"

"I might have told him we were separated. I don't really remember."

"Tiffany ever go with you when you went into the shop?"

"Oh, yeah, many times. He always kept a jar of suckers for the kids. He loved to talk to the younger set. Many times I had to rush him on my order, so I could get home and fire up the bar-b-que."

"Do you ever remember him pumping Tiffany for information about her mother?"

Paul frowned. "Boy, I sure don't like this line of questioning. Do you suspect Mr. Withers of having something to do with Carlotta's disappearance?"

"I'm not sure. But I've got to follow every lead. You know, he'd like to see his daughter married to you. And I'm wondering how bad he wants this wish to come true."

Paul stepped back and stared at Hawkman. "My God, surely not enough to murder Carlotta."

CHAPTER TWENTY-NINE

Hawkman raised a hand. "Hold it, Paul. I didn't say anything about murder. I'm just wondering if he ever had any contact with Carlotta. Did he encourage her to leave you? Maybe to set you free so he could push Tulip your way? How much did he know about the friendship between his daughter and your wife? These are some avenues I feel are worth investigating and any light you could shed on this would help.

Paul tread back and forth on the sidewalk, then faced Hawkman. "Man, I don't know the answers to any of those questions. Carlotta pretty much did whatever she pleased. She never confided in me about who she saw or contacted during the day. And once I moved out, I have no idea what she did."

"I doubt Mr. Withers would take the time off from his shop to go by Carlotta's house during the day, but he might have stopped by in the evening. I didn't think much about it at the time. But didn't Tiffany mention the butcher man had been by?"

Paul glanced toward the front door. "I could ask her."

"Don't do it right now. Wait until you have an opening that won't alert her to something suspicious. I don't want her to have any ill feelings toward Mr. Withers if it's not warranted."

Exhaling, Paul nodded. "Okay. I get the picture."

"Call me on my cell as soon as you talk to her."

"I will."

Hawkman started to leave, but then turned. "I hate putting you through this, but it's the only way we're going to get to the bottom of Carlotta's disappearance."

"This whole thing gives me a skull thumping headache, but

I understand." His shoulders slumped, Paul trudged back into the house.

Hawkman climbed into his vehicle and started home. He didn't like the gruesome ideas forming in his head. But he had to explore every lead and prayed his morbid thoughts wouldn't come true.

***

Hawkman felt the bed jiggle as Jennifer arose early. He watched her as she moved toward the bathroom. She left the door open and stood in front of the mirror brushing her long hair. As she fingered the strands, he could see her gnawing her lower lip and could imagine her thoughts. She'd talked about the effects of chemotherapy and the possibility of losing her hair. It would be a shock, but from what he'd read, it would grow back, maybe even prettier than now.

He moaned and stretched, then swung his feet to the floor. "Good morning, my pretty lady."

She glanced at him and snarled. "Wonder how gorgeous I'll look when I'm bald?"

"Let's not worry about that until we talk to the doctor. Who knows what kind of treatments they have today."

"I've pretty well searched the internet for all the information I could find. And they haven't developed any medications without the side effects yet. They're close, but not there. So I have a feeling I'm going to be on chemo. Which means I'd better be prepared to lose my locks."

Not knowing quite what to say, Hawkman decided to change the subject. "You going to shower first?"

"Yes. Why don't you go put on the coffee. Let's just have cold cereal this morning. I'm not in the mood to fix a big breakfast."

"No problem." He slipped on his eye-patch, and stepped into his jeans. Bare chested, he exited to the kitchen. As he waited for the coffee to perk, he examined a wig catalog Jennifer had placed on the counter. This had definitely been on her mind.

A chill traveled up his spine when he considered what she had ahead of her.

They entered the doctor's waiting room and the nurse soon ushered them back to one of the small examination rooms. The attendant handed her a flimsy gown and asked Jennifer to remove her clothes from the waist down. She climbed upon the table with the drape around her body. The doctor soon entered and examined her abdomen, then moved to his computer.

"The diagnosis according to the biopsy report is: Small Lymphocytic Lymphoma. It's in the lymph nodes in your groin."

"And what does that mean?" Jennifer asked.

"It's a low grade non-Hodgkins lymphoma and usually has a relatively slow growth rate. We'll use chemotherapy to treat it."

"Which one are you recommending?"

He eyed her. "Sounds like you've done your homework."

"I did do some research on the internet."

"Good. I plan on using CVP-R, which is a Vincristine injection with Rituxin included in the treatment, along with a five day oral regimen of Cyclophosphamide and Prednisone tablets. The chemotherapy is repeated every three weeks. The total course consists of six treatment cycles. We'll run a CAT scan after the fourth treatment and see how things are progressing."

"Does the chemo start working immediately?"

"Yes."

"What's the prognosis?" Hawkman asked.

"Very good. We can usually knock it into remission and if it comes back, we can hit it again. If she had to develop cancer, this is the one to have. We can treat it very successfully and keep it under control. I'll give you a pamphlet which will help you understand the whole process."

Hawkman nodded. "Good."

"Will I lose my hair?" Jennifer asked.

"Yes."

"How long does it take?"

"Three weeks."

"I guess I better see about ordering a wig."

The doctor smiled. "That's a good idea." Then he moved to her side. "What I want to do now, is get a bone biopsy to see if it's in the marrow. I can extract it from your hip."

Hawkman rose from his chair. "Does that make a difference if it's there?"

"Don't worry, the chemo will take care of it."

Hawkman stared at him. "You're going to put a needle into her bone without deadening it?"

"I'll use a local anesthetic. It's not that painful and it'll only take a few minutes."

Jennifer tugged on Hawkman's arm. "Honey, why don't you go into the waiting room."

He looked into her eyes. "You think I should?"

"Yes. I'll be fine."

Once he left her, he stuck a toothpick into his mouth and paced the floor. Fifteen minutes passed before Jennifer appeared carrying a packet of literature. He went to her side, took the package and placed an arm around her. "Honey, you're pale as a ghost. Are you okay?"

She sucked in her lower lip. "Well, it wasn't fun, but it's over and he'll let me know as soon as he gets the report back." They sauntered slowly down the corridor toward the exit. "Meanwhile, I start chemotherapy this coming Monday."

He stopped her and stared into her face. "You're kidding. So soon?"

She clutched his arm. "It's cancer, hon. You don't fool around with this stuff."

Hawkman bit down on the toothpick and it cracked into two pieces inside his mouth. Spitting the small splinters into his hand, he tossed them into the trash receptacle outside the door. "You're right."

"Also the kidney doctor is setting up an appointment to put in a stent."

"Why?"

When they reached the 4X4, he helped her in and jumped into the driver's side. "Please explain to me about this stent."

"The nodes are pressing against my bladder near the ureter, blocking the free flow of urine, causing my right kidney to swell. He doesn't want any damage done and to make sure, a stent will be placed into the ureter leading from my bladder to my kidney. It will relieve the pressure. Then he'll remove it at the end of the chemo."

"So what does this entail?"

"I'll have to go under anesthesia, but it's really a very minor procedure."

"When did you see this doctor?"

"Yesterday. I didn't think it necessary you go with me. My oncologist isn't real happy about it, but if it will save the kidney, he'll go along."

"What's the date for this procedure?"

"His office will contact me."

Hawkman reached over and grasped her hand. "My sweetheart, I wish it was me going through this and not you."

"Just stick with me and I'll whip the big 'C'."

He squeezed her fingers. "I'll be there. Believe me, I'll be by your side every step of the way."

CHAPTER THIRTY

Friday morning, Hawkman felt reluctant to leave and roamed around the house until Jennifer finally stepped into his path.

"Honey, there's nothing you can do for me today but drive me to distraction. So please go work on the Carlotta case. I'll call if I receive any news. The only thing I ask is that you hold Monday free to take me to the infusion room in Medford."

"Do I stay with you during your treatment?"

She shook her head. "No. I called the nurse and talked to her about the procedure. She said, unless I particularly wanted you present, there wouldn't be a need. My first infusion could take six to seven hours."

Hawkman raised his brows. "Six to seven hours! Holey, moley, that's a long time to have a needle in your arm."

"They go slow the initial visit. So there's definitely no reason for you to be there and be bored. I'll take plenty to do, along with some flyers to distribute about my books and plenty of reading material. We'll make sure our cell phones are charged and I can call you periodically to let you know what's happening."

He scratched his head. "That's a good plan. I can hang around my office; there's plenty to keep me occupied. Then you notify me a few minutes before you're through and I'll pick you up."

She gave him a hug. "Things are coming together pretty good. So go work today and don't worry."

"If you say so. I still can't get used to the whole damn idea of what's going on."

She patted him on the arm and gave him a kiss on the cheek. "I love you dear, now, get going."

Hawkman left the house and climbed into his 4X4. He hadn't told Jennifer his morbid thoughts about the Carlotta case; they didn't seem appropriate at this time.

Hank Withers lived near the foothills on the outskirts of Medford where a golf course flanked the complex of homes. Hawkman located the address and drove up the curved road to the front of the house. He sat for a moment and studied the structure. Quite a huge place for a man alone. The grounds were neatly sculptured with a low cut hedge along the outer boundary of the property instead of a fence. He liked the effect.

He knew Hank wouldn't be home, but ambled toward the entry in case any neighbors were observing. When he reached the door, he noted the small blinking light near the bell button indicating an alarm system. The double paned glass gave him a view of the hallway leading into what appeared to be a large living room. He walked across the concrete porch skirting the front and gazed around the edge. A dogleg of the driveway extended to the rear, indicating the garage set at the back of the house. He also liked this arrangement. Concrete steps led off toward a narrow sidewalk. Hawkman followed it around the side and ended up at the front of the closed garage.

He stood for a moment with his thumbs hooked in his back jeans pockets and observed the back yard. The shrubbery continued completely around the property. Grass covered the ground, but no flower beds graced the enclosure. Very easy care and neat appearing. Drapes covered the windows, preventing him from peeking inside. He moseyed around to the front where a security vehicle had pulled up beside his 4X4. A uniformed guard climbed out and proceeded to walk around the SUV. He looked up when Hawkman made his appearance.

"You have business here, sir?"

"Hoping to catch Hank, but guess he's already at work. Nice place." Hawkman put his booted foot on the running board. "You guys keep a check on these homes?"

"Yes. Part of their fees when they build up here. We make

notes on strange vehicles seen in the area. I'd never seen yours before, so thought I'd check it out."

"No problem. Got nothin' to hide." He swung into the driver's seat. "Guess I'll go into town and see Hank at the shop."

He turned over the engine and pulled out onto the road. The security truck followed.

Sticking a toothpick into his mouth, Hawkman could see this place didn't have an easy access and he didn't savor the idea of being caught by security patrolling the area. He might have to think about another way of seeing the inside of the house.

He drove to his office and called Delia. "How's Tiffany taking not going to school?"

She laughed. "She thinks it's the greatest thing in the world to play with Princess and watch television until I make her put the cat down and turn off the boob tube to do her homework. Paul made arrangements with the teachers to pick up her assignments everyday."

"Anything unusual to report?"

"No. I've kept my eyes and ears open. Haven't noticed a thing out of the ordinary. How about you? Any more messages?"

"No. We'll keep a vigilance for another week and then if nothing happens, I think we can let Tiffany go back to school. I'll still want you to keep a close eye on her. We can't let down our guard."

"Don't worry. I might even go with her to class."

"Thanks, Delia, I'll keep in touch."

Hawkman hung up and opened the Carlotta file. He'd gone through the sheets a million times, but read through them again, then leaned back, rested his booted feet on top of the desk and thumped the pencil eraser on his chin. After several minutes, a thought formed in his mind. He dropped his feet to the floor and scribbled some notes on the legal pad. Checking the time, he left the office and drove by Tulip's apartment. Her car still sat in front. He parked around the corner.

After several minutes, the waitress dashed out of the house and stopped at the side of the car. While she groped inside her purse, it slipped from her hands and fell to the ground. She yanked it out of the dirt, dusted it off, then rubbed it against her uniform. Hawkman put his binoculars to his eyes, and stiffened at what he observed. Slowly moving the glasses from his face, he watched Tulip jump into the car, back out and speed away. He placed the glasses on the seat and started the 4X4.

He drove out of the complex and headed downtown. He rounded the corner and spotted Tulip parking in a spot a half block from Mom's Cafe. She hurried up the street, her gaze fixed on the sidewalk. Hawkman reached the front door and opened it just as she put her hand out. "Good evening, Tulip."

She glanced up in surprise. "Oh, my, Mr. Casey, I didn't even see you. I'm running so late. Please excuse me, I don't have time to visit. I'll see you inside."

Hawkman took a close look at the purse dangling from her hand and grimaced.

CHAPTER THIRTY-ONE

Hawkman followed Tulip into the restaurant and took a booth. He picked up the menu from the end of the table and watched her scurry toward the back. She immediately returned, tying an apron around her middle. A couple of people were already seated and she waited on them before finally coming to Hawkman's table.

She took a deep breath before speaking. "Please forgive my bad manners. It's not like me to run so late and I feel terrible."

He smiled. "No problem. I couldn't help but notice the Gucci purse you were carrying. How in the world could you afford it?"

"Oh, I didn't buy it. Yesterday was my birthday and I got it as a gift."

Hawkman raised his brows. "Happy belated birthday. My, you must have a suitor who cares a lot about you."

She lowered her head. "My dad gave it to me and I scolded him for spending so much. But he said he got it at a real bargain." Shifting from foot to foot, she poised her pen over the pad. "I better take your order."

He gave her his choice and folded the menu. "I'd be interested to know where he found such a bargain. I'd like to get Jennifer one, but they're too expensive for my pocket."

"If I find out where he bought it, I'll let you know." She then hustled off to turn the order into the kitchen.

Hawkman ate, paid the bill and left. On his way home, he thought about the purse. He couldn't imagine a place in Medford carrying such expensive items. Jennifer might know. He'd even checked the internet for Gucci items after Tiffany had told him about her mother's missing purse. He'd found them at several spots with different price tags. Did Hank know how to order over the net? Would he indulge such extravagance on his daughter, who definitely didn't seem the type? The questions plagued him. He hated to keep reverting back to Tiffany's description of her mother's. But it fit to a tee.

When he reached the house, he went inside to find Jennifer standing at the sliding glass door, staring out across Copco Lake. "Hon, you okay?"

She let out a sigh. "We've got to call Sam and tell him about my situation. I've thought about it all day, and it wouldn't be fair to keep him in the dark. I'd definitely want to know if the situation were reversed."

"I agree. But you had to make the decision."

She stepped away from the slider and Hawkman noticed her eyes were filled with tears. He took her in his arms. "Are you ready to call him tonight?"

"Yes, I think so."

He felt his heart tighten as she pulled away. Before she picked up the phone, she turned to him. "Why don't you get on the extension in the bedroom."

Hurrying, he sat on the edge of the bed and waited until she called out the phone was ringing. He picked up the receiver and placed it to his ear about the time he heard Sam's familiar voice.

"Hi, Sam. This is Jennifer."

"Hey, what's going on at Copco Lake?"

"Not much. Hawkman's working on a case."

"You caught any good trout lately?"

"No, nothing of any size."

Sam's voice softened. "Is everything okay?"

"Not really. I thought I better let you know..." Jennifer's voice cracked. "I've got lymphoma cancer."

Hawkman found himself suddenly standing.

"Good Lord." Then silence on Sam's end. "I better come home."

"No," Jennifer said, her voice quivering. "I'm going to be

all right. I start the chemotherapy Monday. The doctors have assured me they can knock it into remission."

"I want to see you."

"I know. But there's nothing you can do and Hawkman is taking really good care of me. Believe me, I look the same. However, I'll lose my hair, so I'll probably be bald within the month."

"Hawkman, are you on?"

"Yes, son, I'm here."

"How's she doing?"

"Real well, probably better than me."

"Should I come home?"

"Do whatever Jennifer wants. She doesn't need to be upset."

"Will you keep me informed?"

"Yes."

Jennifer regained her composure and proceeded to tell him about the kidney and what the doctors planned on doing. She promised to keep him updated on each event. Satisfied with the decision about Sam not coming home, they finally said their goodbyes.

Hawkman came out of the bedroom as Jennifer reached for a tissue.

"That was the hardest phone call I've ever made. I thought I'd be stronger, but the tears just ran. Do you think he knew I was crying?"

He pulled her close in a hug. "Do you really think it matters?"

She peered up at him. "Probably not. Have you told anyone yet?"

"No, but Williams thinks we're getting a divorce."

Jennifer laughed. "Really?"

"He's asked several times what's my problem. I guess I carry my feelings on my sleeve."

"Now that Sam knows, tell him. It will do you both good."

"When the time is right."

She rolled her eyes. "Men. At least I feel a burden has been lifted off my shoulders with Sam knowing. I don't think it will bother me to inform others now." Reaching across the counter, she changed the subject by picking up a wig catalog. She flipped it open to a turned down page and pointed to a picture. "What do you think of this one?"

Hawkman took the book from her hand and studied the illustration. "It looks like your own hair. Don't you want to get something exotic and different? Maybe be blond for awhile?"

She cocked her head. "I thought about it, but figured if I have six treatments, we're talking close to a year I'll be bald. I'd probably want to look as much like myself as possible. Blond might be fun for a little while, but I'm not sure I'd be satisfied with it after a long period of time."

He handed her the catalog. "Whatever makes you the happiest."

She closed the book and rubbed his arm. "You're very understanding, you know? I've monopolized most of the evening so far and you've been very patient. Tell me what's been going on with the Carlotta case."

"I'll make us a drink and we'll sit in the living room."

"Sounds good."

Once settled, Jennifer leaned forward in her chair. "Shoot."

"I observed something today that bothers me."

Her eyes widened. "Oh, what?"

"Remember when I told you I had Tiffany go through her mother's room and tell me things she thought were missing?"

"Yes."

"She mentioned a black Gucci purse her mother had purchased. She was with her and said it cost a bundle. I researched the Gucci line and they've very expensive. Is there a place here in Medford that sells fancy stuff?"

Jennifer nodded. "Yes, there's a small exclusive store that carries exquisite and costly women's items. I've only been in it once and almost choked at the prices."

"What's it called and where's it located?"

She tapped her chin with her finger. "Oh shoot, let me

think." Then she snapped her fingers. "Elaine's Bouquet, and it's off the beaten track on a side street. It's a quaint looking little cottage that used to be a flower shop. When it closed, Elaine Belmont bought it and turned it into a boutique."

He pointed a finger in the air. "I remember the place. I believe I bought you flowers there once."

"That must have been a long time ago."

He ducked his head. "Yeah, I think while we were courting. So is she making money?"

Jennifer made a face. "Good grief, she only has to sell one item a week to make a killing." She snapped her fingers. "Okay, back to the story about the Gucci purse."

"Today, I saw Tulip Withers carrying a black handbag, identical to the one Tiffany described. She told me her dad got it for her birthday."

Her mouth dropped open. "Elaine never carries two of the same style. Did Tiffany say her mother bought it in town?"

"I didn't ask. At the time I wasn't interested in where she purchased it. But I now have the distinct impression she got it in Medford."

She frowned. "I don't think Hank Withers ever goes out of the area. He never leaves the meat store."

"He might have access to the internet."

"That's possible. I think you need to find out more about the purse."

"I intend to do just that."

CHAPTER THIRTY-TWO

Saturday morning, Hawkman called Delia from the house to find out if she and Tiffany would be home during the afternoon. When she assured him they'd be there, he made an appointment to speak with Tiffany after lunch.

"Is Paul still around?"

"Yes, hold on a minute."

"Hello, Mr. Casey."

"Have you had an opportunity to speak with your daughter about Hank Withers?"

"Let me take this in the other room."

A few moments passed before Paul picked up and Hawkman heard a distinct click of the other phone hanging up."

"Sorry, I didn't get back to you, but didn't have the opportunity. I talked with Tiffany and found out Mr. Withers made three or four unexpected evening visits to the house. He brought special cuts of meat as gifts with the excuse that he figured the ladies needed someone to prepare it for them. Tiffany told me he said things like, 'since your no good daddy up and left you'. And he made other negative remarks about me."

"Did he actually fix the beef or pork?"

"No, Carlotta always had a good excuse for him not to hang around."

"So he never spent an entire evening with them?"

"No. Tiffany said he only stayed a few minutes then left."

"What did she think of those visits?"

"Not much. She laughed about his attempts to be friendly and thought the old man wanted to date her mother, and found this rather comical. However, Tiffany didn't like his snide remarks, but figured he only made them to keep her mom interested."

Hawkman chuckled. "She's definitely intuitive."

"Nothing gets past her."

"Thanks, Paul, this information helps. I'll be talking with Tiffany this afternoon. I won't need to bring up anything about Mr. Withers."

"Okay, see you then."

After hanging up, Hawkman turned toward Jennifer at the computer, and told her about the butcher visiting Carlotta.

Her expression turned to disgust. "Because some old man has a little money, he gets the idea every young and beautiful thing is going to fall at his feet."

"I'm not sure he had courtship in mind."

Jennifer stared at him a few seconds. "You haven't told me everything, have you?"

"No, and not sure I'm quite ready to share my inner thoughts just yet."

She leaned forward and wiggled a finger at him. "You do this to me on every case."

"Yeah, but I usually end up telling you. Anyway, I've got to go into town and talk to Tiffany."

"Tiffany?"

He rose and plopped on his hat. "Yes, I'm going to ask her more questions about the purse. See if by chance there's any identifying mark which might lead me to believe the bag Tulip's carrying belongs to Carlotta."

Jennifer rose from her chair and followed him to the door. "I have a sneaky idea you suspect the Withers of something."

He turned on the step and shrugged. "Just doin' my job."

She folded her arms across her chest. "I see."

Giving her a quick kiss on the cheek, he stepped off the porch and hurriedly headed for the garage. An hour an a half later he parked in front of Delia's house. Tiffany opened the door and her face lit up with a big smile.

"Hi, Mr. Casey. I feel so special. Grandma said you made an appointment to just talk to me."

He smiled. "You are very important, and I wanted to make sure I could see you, so I set up a specific time."

She giggled and curtsied. "Please come in. Have a seat in the living room and I'll get you a tall glass of ice tea."

Hawkman drifted toward the big overstuffed chair. "Sounds great."

Tiffany soon returned with a large plate of cookies and set them on the coffee table in front of Hawkman. Delia trailed behind carrying two large containers of liquid.

"Hello, Mr. Casey." She examined the glasses in her hand. "Let's see, you ordered tea and Tiffany wanted soda."

"Thank you." Hawkman said, taking a big swallow. "Very refreshing."

"If you'll excuse me, I have some things to do in the kitchen."

"Certainly."

Tiffany sat on the couch and pushed the platter of goodies toward him. "Grandma makes the most wonderful chocolate chip cookies." She smacked her lips. "They're so delicious."

Hawkman picked up one and took a bite. "Yes, they're excellent."

She sat back and folded her hands in her lap. "Now what did you want to talk about?"

"Do you recall sometime ago at your house, I asked you to tell me what you noticed missing from your mother's room. Some of the items you mentioned were a couple of dresses, shoes and a black Gucci purse."

She nodded. "Yes, I remember."

Hawkman removed a folded sheet of paper from his pocket and smoothed it out on the table. "Here's a copy of a Gucci purse I printed off the internet. If I'm not mistaken, this is the handbag you described."

Her eyes grew big as she stared at the picture. "Yes, that's it exactly."

"You said you were with your mother when she bought the purse. Where did she buy it?"

"Elaine's Bouquet"

Hawkman leaned forward resting his arms on his thighs. "I want you to think real hard on this question. If we had ten identical purses lined up on a shelf how would you identify your mother's?"

"Can I touch them?"

"Yes, you can handle them and look on every side."

"Oh, then it's easy. On the back of the little gold tab that has 'Gucci' on it, mom took our dremel tool and etched her first and last initials."

"CR?"

"Yep."

"Okay, let's say she hadn't done that yet. If you could only look at the handbags without touching, but you could walk all around them. Is there any way you could tell hers from the rest?"

Tiffany closed her eyes in thought, then broke into a big smile and clapped her hands. "Yes."

"How?"

"One day, not long after Mom bought the purse, she had it on the kitchen table while she painted her nails. They weren't quite dry yet when the paper boy came to the door to be paid. She opened the clasp to get her billfold and smudged one of her nails. After she paid him, she realized there was a spot of red on the handle. It made her so mad. She took a cotton swab with some fingernail polish remover on it and dabbed it off, but it left this tiny white mark. Mom tried to hide the small dot with shoe polish, but it never stayed black." Tiffany made a little circle with her fingers. "It was so tiny, you could hardly see it, and I asked her who would notice it on the inside of the strap. So she finally gave up trying to cover it and decided not to worry about it anymore."

Hawkman grinned. "You are something else, to remember all those little things."

Tiffany's expression turned solemn. "Have you found my mother's purse?"

He gazed at the child for a second. "I'm not sure. But

you're like a little angel sent down to give me the clues I needed. I think you'd make a great detective."

Her eyes lit up. "Really? Why?"

"Because you're so observant. And detectives have to notice everything to be any good."

Tiffany crinkled up her nose. "I think I'd rather be a woman private investigator when I grow up." She picked up Hawkman's half-empty glass and jumped up. "Can I get you some more tea?"

"No, thanks. I think you've told me everything I need to know. So, I'll let you have the rest of your day. By the way, where's Princess?"

"I told her she had to stay in my room while I had this important meeting. I'll go get her really fast. She'd like to see you."

Delia walked in about the time the child dashed toward her bedroom. "Is she okay?"

"Yes, she's getting Princess so I can say goodbye."

Tiffany dashed back into the room with the feline cradled in her arms. "I had to wake her. Guess she decided to nap while I took care of business."

Delia covered her mouth to stifle a laugh. "Smart cat."

Hawkman stayed a few more minutes and played with the kitten. "You've trained her well."

"Grandma showed me some tricks and we've had good luck with getting her to do what we want." Tiffany cocked her head and looked up at Hawkman. "When can I go back to school? I'm getting awfully bored."

Hawkman reached over and patted her on the shoulder. "I'm sure you are. Maybe the middle of next week. I'll let your dad know. Right now I want you safe."

She scuffed a shoe on the carpet. "I know. Be sure and tell my Dad or Grandma as soon as you can. I miss my friends."

"I will. And thanks for the cookies and tea"

Hawkman left the Ryan household and headed for the police station. On the way, he punched in Detective Williams' number on his cell. "Just wanted to check to be sure you're there."

"Hey, this is my first home. Get your butt over here; I need a break."

"I'll be there in less than ten minutes."

Hawkman entered Williams' office to find the detective buried in paperwork. "I thought all this would end when they got you a helper."

"I still have to sign every damn paper that comes through here."

Pulling up a chair, Hawkman sat down in front of the desk. "First of all, I better clear up something. You're thinking Jennifer and I are having marital problems, right?"

"Yeah, what else can I think? You're a grouch to be around lately."

"I know, but we didn't want to tell anyone until we knew a little more and talked to Sam."

"What the hell are you talking about? Surely, Jennifer's not pregnant."

Hawkman couldn't help but grin. "I wish it were that simple. She's been diagnosed with lymphoma cancer."

Williams flopped back in his chair and blew out a breath of air. "My God! What a blow!"

"Yeah, I know. The doctors have assured us they can knock it into remission and she'll be fine. She starts her chemotherapy on Monday."

The detective placed his arms on the desk. "Oh, man, I'm so sorry to hear such news. But thankful they can do something about it."

"They've done a lot with cancer research and treatments. Of course, we don't know what to expect. Jennifer is taking all this news a hell of a lot better than I am. The doctor told her she'll lose her hair and she's already ordered a wig. Her first treatment will be six or seven hours long and she's prepared for it. I'm walking around like a numbskull. She finally pushed me out of the house and told me to go work on the case."

"Man, with such a heavy load on your mind, have you been able to concentrate?"

"Barely. I'm trying. Otherwise I'd lose my mind." Hawkman leaned forward putting his elbow on his thighs. "I think I'm onto something, and I'm going to need your help."

CHAPTER THIRTY-THREE

Williams dragged a paper pad from under a folder and took a pencil from the glass container. "What have you discovered?"

Hawkman explained about Tiffany describing the Gucci purse her mother had purchased. Then about how he'd discovered Tulip carrying an identical handbag. When he inquired where she'd bought it, she informed him her dad gave it to her for a birthday gift. "I'm going to try an examine it more closely, then check with Elaine's Bouquet. From what Jennifer told me, this shop doesn't carry duplicate styles. I could be wrong, but if I can trace this purse back to Carlotta, we've got a hot case brewing."

"Sounds like you have this line of investigation under control. How do you need my help?"

"If suspicions arise concerning this item, we'll need to confiscate it. Then I'm going to need a court order to search Hank Withers' house and store."

"What do you expect to find?"

Hawkman aired his gruesome thoughts to the detective and watched his reaction.

Williams grimaced. "Man, that's pretty gross stuff."

Hawkman nodded. "I hope it doesn't come about, but my gut tells me I'm getting closer all the time."

The detective stood and crossed the room to the coffee maker. Dumping his cup of cold brew into the waste basket, he turned to Hawkman. "Wanta a mug of java?"

"Sure. Thanks."

Once settled back at his desk, Williams placed his elbow on the surface and rested his chin on the pedestal of his hand.

"This case could get sticky. You've got to be certain before we make a move. We're talking about someone who's been in this community for years and has the highest respect from the people who live here."

"I know, but sometimes people crack if they have pressures in their lives."

"Do you think Tulip's involved in this caper?"

Hawkman sighed. "Right off the top of my head, I'm not sure. But it will come out sooner or later whether she is or not."

"What about Carlotta's husband or his mother?"

"I can't see Paul involved in murder." Hawkman waved his hand in a hovering motion. "But Delia's another story. I'm keeping an open book on her."

"You have your work cut out. As I told you, we have the Carlotta case in our open files now, so if you get some good evidence, I can approach a judge and get a court order to search the Withers' properties."

Hawkman stood. "Thanks, Williams. I'll keep you updated."

"Tell Jennifer my thoughts and prayers are with her. I hear chemo is hell. Be sure and support her through this ordeal. It's not going to be pleasant."

"I intend to."

Hawkman left the detective's office and drove to the cottage containing Elaine's Bouquet. He climbed out of his vehicle with a small paper pad and went to the front entry where the business hours were posted. It stated she opened Monday through Saturday from ten until six. After jotting down the information, he returned to the SUV and tossed the pad on the dashboard. Maybe he'd run by tomorrow while waiting for Jennifer. He had a couple of things on his agenda to help keep his mind off his sweet wife undergoing chemotherapy.

He dropped by the office to retrieve the Carlotta file before returning home. When he entered the room, he noted the red message light blinking on the phone. He hit the button, then stopped in his tracks.

"You don't pay attention. I told you to forget about

Carlotta, but you just keep digging. She's gone forever. Let it go. Otherwise, someone's going to get hurt."

Same muffled voice, but the intent came through loud and clear. The caller ID stated it again initiated from a pay phone on Main Street. He burned the information onto a CD and stuck it into the file. Then called Paul.

"I just received another message. Don't let up your guard on Tiffany. I think we better keep her out of school another week. I know she'll be disappointed, but it's better to be safe than sorry. And by all means keep her in your sight; don't let her go out with anyone, even someone you think you can trust."

"I hear you," Paul said in a strained voice. "This is getting mighty scary."

"Yes, it is. I'm working on a lead right now and hope it develops so we can bring this case to a close. I'll keep you informed. Just keep a sharp eye on our little girl."

Picking up the file, he left the office and headed home. When he arrived, it pleased him to see Jennifer behind the computer in the dining room area. He strolled over and gave her a peck on the cheek, then pointed to a piece of tape on her arm. "What's with the Band-Aid?"

She glanced down and laughed. "Oh, I neglected to take it off. I almost forgot I had to have a blood test before the chemo, so had to drive all the way into Medford to the lab. Fortunately, they're open on Sunday. Also picked up my prescription for the oral chemo. You won't believe it, but I have to take fifteen pills a day for five days."

"What!"

"Yes. You heard me right."

"All at once?"

"No, spread out through the day."

"When do you start those?"

"Monday."

"Good Lord, how will your body handle all that potent stuff?"

She held up the prescription bottles. "I've been researching the CVP regimen I'll be on. The infusion consists of Vincristine and Rituxin, just like the doctor explained, plus some other stuff, which I'll find out tomorrow. The orals are these: twelve Cyclophosphamide and three Prednisone tablets a day."

"You'll be gagging by evening."

Jennifer grinned. "I think you're right. And for sure by Friday."

"So what are the side-effects of all this stuff?"

She sighed. "Well, let's not go into those. There's plenty, but I might not suffer them all. Let's keep our fingers crossed. In fact, maybe you should read some of the literature the doctor gave me, so you'll be prepared too."

"I will. Where's the packet?"

"It's on the table by our chairs."

He started toward them.

"Wait, before you get involved with those, are you hungry?"

"No."

"Then let's talk about something different for a little while. Tell me how the case is developing. Anything new today?"

"I'll fix us a drink and tell you what happened."

"Good." She put her computer to sleep and meandered into the living room. Scooting the cancer booklets aside, she flopped down in her chair and waited patiently as Hawkman mixed a gin and tonic.

He handed her the glass and sat down. "Will you be able to have liquor while on chemo?"

"I don't see how a drink in the evening will harm me. Especially after they've pumped me full of battery acid."

Hawkman chuckled. "Me, either."

"Okay, tell me blow by blow what happened when you saw Tiffany."

He related how the child had greeted him, told him about the Gucci, and how he'd pursued the topic. "When she asked me if I'd found her mother's purse, it really threw me. But I decided not to lie and told her I wasn't sure. Then I told her I thought of her as a little angel bringing me clues, also how she'd make a great detective because she observed things and could describe them so accurately."

"You did a great job of distracting her. That was quick thinking."

"Thank you, my love. But how she answered made me suppress a smile. She told me she'd rather be a woman private investigator."

Jennifer laughed. "Good for her."

"Now as far as my examining the handbag, I'm not sure how to proceed."

She gazed at the ceiling tapping her chin with a finger. Then snapped her fingers. "I've got it."

"How?"

"After my chemotherapy tomorrow, it should be close to dinner time. We'll go to Mom's Cafe. Maybe there's some way I can get a glimpse of the purse."

Hawkman raised his brows. "Do you think you'll feel like going out to eat?"

"I understand they give something in the infusion to help cope with the chemo, so I'll probably be fine. Also the doctor gave me a prescription to take today and tomorrow to help my body accept the stuff. So I'll probably do okay the first day or two."

"I just don't want you overtaxed."

Jennifer waved a hand in the air. "I won't be and it will give me something to think about besides cancer." She pulled her feet up into the chair. "Okay, what happened next?"

"I stopped by my office and found another threatening message on my answering machine. Same muffled voice."

Jennifer's mouth turned down in despair. "Oh, no. Did it mention Tiffany again?"

"Not this time, but it didn't have to. The implication was there. So I called Paul and told him to keep her home another week. We have to make sure no one gets to her."

"This must be a horrible, sick person doing this. Can you tell if it's male or female?"

"No, too distorted. I'd just left Detective Williams, so I haven't told him about the call yet."

She raised a brow. "Why'd you go see him?"

"Oh, just to shoot the breeze." He again, decided not to tell her his thoughts on the Carlotta case. "I did tell him we weren't getting a divorce. And told him why I'd been such a grouch. It shook him up and he's concerned about you. Told me to tell you his thoughts and prayers are there."

"That's sweet of him."

"He's really a nice guy."

She grinned. "I know. But I don't think you're leveling with me."

"Why do you say that?"

"Because you two guys don't get together to just blab. You've got something up your sleeve. And you need his help."

"Jennifer, you're uncanny, but I'm not saying any more. I don't have proof of my thoughts and until I do, I'm not talking."

"I'll try to understand. Meanwhile, I'm going to hit the shower, go to bed and read."

She shut down the computer, and headed for the bedroom. Hawkman picked up the literature on the cancer and chemo side-effects. As he read, he felt the hairs prickling on the back of his neck and a tingling sensation radiate down his spine.

CHAPTER THIRTY-FOUR

Jennifer arose early and dressed, then nudged Hawkman. "It'll take us an hour and a half to drive to Medford. I'm supposed to eat breakfast, and pack myself a lunch."

"Can I do anything to help?"

"No, just get ready and join me in the kitchen."

By the time he joined her, she'd piled bacon, toast, and eggs on his plate, and half eaten her own portion.

"Honey, slow down. We have plenty of time."

She rubbed her forehead. "I know. I'm a nervous wreck. I started the first dose of oral chemo an hour ago. I'm taking it with me, but have to wait two hours after I eat before I can take it again. I'm taking the prednisone with my breakfast."

He stared at her. "How do you feel?"

"Okay, so far."

They were soon on their way to the infusion center. Hawkman parked in the lot and carried her bag of items inside. While she registered, his gaze traveled the length of the room and he sucked in a deep breath. He'd never seen anything like it. People were already in the recliner chairs that lined the walls. Bags of liquid hung from the intravenous carts, and tubes were attached to their arms or led from stents in their chest. Many wore hats or turbans, some slept, while others read or visited.

Jennifer took his arm and brought him out of the stupor. "Come on, the nurse is taking me to my chair."

"You have your own?"

"Honey, go with the flow. We're learning," she whispered.

They followed the woman, and once seated, the nurse put

a yellow identification band around Jennifer's wrist, then took her blood pressure and temperature.

"Everything looks good. Your tests are great, so we might as well get started." She handed Jennifer a couple of Tylenol and a Benadryl with a cup of water.

"Can I have a copy of the report?" Jennifer asked, after swallowing the pills.

"Sure. I'll get it for you as soon as I get the drip going."

Hawkman turned away as the woman inserted the needle into Jennifer's left wrist vein. He'd seen much worse, why did this bother him? When he glanced at his wife's face, he immediately knew the reason. He loved her more than words could ever tell and he could hardly stand the idea of her body being invaded. His mouth felt dry and he swallowed hard, then pulled a chair next to her. "You okay?"

"Yes, these gals are good. I hardly felt the needle."

He glanced up at the bag hanging from the pole. "That says 'saline'. Wonder why it goes in first?"

"She said something about flushing my system."

"Interesting."

"Honey, there's no reason for you to stay. Let's find out approximately how long this session will be, then you might as well go do something productive. I asked the gal at the desk if we could use our cell phones in here and she said yes. So, I can call you when I'm about through; then I'll meet you out front."

The nurse returned with Jennifer's copy of the blood test. "Here you go."

"Thank you. Can you tell me how long this session will be?"

She studied the chart. "This is your first time, so we'll take it slow. I'd say six and a half to seven hours. You'll probably be through around four."

Hawkman reached down and scooted Jennifer's bag of goodies closer to the chair. "Can you reach everything?"

"Yes, thank you."

"Okay if I call you in the middle of the day?"

She patted the pocket of her vest. "Yes. I have my cell phone handy."

He leaned over and kissed her lips. "I love you."

"I love you, too, sweetheart."

His heart pounding, he left the room and hurried out of the hospital. He could hardly bear the thought of leaving her with strangers, but he had to trust them. They were like angels in disguise, responsible for making her well. He sure couldn't do it.

He climbed into the 4X4 and left the door open a minute to let out the heat. After checking his watch, he reached for the pad of paper on the dashboard and verified the time Elaine's Bouquet opened. He inserted the key, slammed the door shut and pulled out of the lot. Driving toward downtown, he tried not to think about Jennifer, but couldn't help seeing her brave face flash through his head. He knew she must be scared spit less.

As he pulled in front of the cottage, he didn't spot any other vehicles, then saw the sign being flipped over to read 'open'. Good, he thought. I'll be able to ask questions without a bunch of ladies buzzing around.

He entered the small, but well organized shop. Purses and jewelry were tastefully displayed throughout the one room. He also noticed each item had some sort of mechanism attached so they couldn't be swiped. Good idea, he thought, wandering through the maze of expensive items. Suddenly, a loud boisterous voice greeted him.

"Well, good morning. It's seldom I see a man in the shop this early in the day."

Hawkman turned and faced a short chunky woman, dressed to the hilt in a dark purple pantsuit, white silk blouse and a matching purple tam tilted to the side of her head. Her gray, curly locks twirled around the hat edges, making it appear the hair held it in place. The jewelry around her neck and wrist along with the long dangling earrings all matched her outfit. Her make-up even showed a tinge of purple on her eyelids, cheeks and lips. She had a contagious smile and Hawkman couldn't help but grin.

"You must be Elaine?"

She held out a short stubby hand. "I sure am, honey. And may I ask who you might be?" Stepping back, she gazed into his face. "Oh wait. I know you. You're Tom Casey, the private investigator. Not many men sport an eye-patch and a leather cowboy hat."

He took her hand. "You're right."

"I met your adorable wife, Jennifer, a couple of months ago." Then she covered her mouth with her fingers. "Oh, my, I must quit giving away my secrets. Most men about die when they hear their wives have been in this shop."

He chuckled. "No problem. She can come and look around anytime."

Elaine guffawed. "I love it. Now what can I help you with? Is she having a birthday?"

"I'm really here on business. I'd like to ask about a couple of your customers."

She wiggled a finger in the air. "As long as I don't get anyone into trouble, I'll answer."

"Fair enough. Did you sell a Gucci purse to Carlotta Ryan?"

Her brows furrowed. "I understand the young woman has disappeared."

"Yes. We're trying to locate her and I'm tracking down any lead I can find."

Elaine walked along the counters and rearranged items. "She bought a black leather Gucci about a month and a half ago. I remember it distinctly, because she had her young daughter along. The girl kept telling her mom it's too expensive. Lovely child, but I wanted to wring her neck."

"But she did buy it?"

"Oh, yes, and I gave her a good deal."

Hawkman restrained from asking how much of a bargain. He figured maybe twenty bucks off the going price. "Have you sold an identical purse to anyone else?"

She looked horrified. "Oh, Mr. Casey. I never carry two of the same style in this store. Can you imagine how my customers would feel in this small town if they met each other toting the same handbag." She put her hands on her ample hips. "That would be disgraceful!"

He stepped back in surprise. "Pardon me. Guess men don't think along those lines."

She pointed a long purple fingernail at him, then threw back her head and whooped. "I wish you could have seen your face."

"So you obviously didn't sell another purse that even looked like the one you sold Mrs. Ryan."

"No. I don't even carry a similar style." Then her expression turned solemn. "Has there been any word from Carlotta?"

Hawkman shook his head. "I'm sorry to say, nothing."

"Oh my, it certainly sounds like foul play."

"Hard to say. We'll keep looking."

"I hope she shows up."

"Thank you for your help."

She raised a finely arched eyebrow. "But you only asked me about one customer."

"You answered my other question when you said you never sold but one of each style."

"I see." She narrowed her eyes. "It sounds like you've spotted the purse."

"Possibly, but it could mean someone bought one just like it somewhere else."

"True. But if you get a chance to look inside the handbag, you'll find my little brand burned in one of the corners."

Hawkman gave her a questioning look. "What do you mean?"

"Hold on a minute and I'll show you." Disappearing behind a curtained door, she soon reappeared carrying a long thin metal rod with the circumference of a pencil. Picking up one of the purses on display, she carried it to the counter where Hawkman stood. She pointed at the end of the rod as she held it near his face. "See this?"

He studied the small branding iron. "Yeah. It's got the initials 'EB' on it, but the letters are backwards."

"Right, so that when I put the heated rod down on the leather they brand my store initials into the surface." She pulled the tissue out of the bag she'd carried forward and held it toward the light so Hawkman could see down into the bottom. "Look closely at the right hand corner. See my little identification?"

"Hey, that's really clever. It's so small no one would notice. Do the companies mind you doing that?"

A grin twisted the corners of her mouth. "I never asked. And I doubt my customers even see it."

"Have you done this to all your purses?"

"Sure have."

"Thank you, Elaine. I appreciate your confiding this to me. It will help in my investigation."

"Good luck. I hope you find that girl or whoever did away with her. This world is getting way too evil for my book."

Hawkman left the shop with new energy. He could hardly wait to tell Jennifer about Elaine's brand inside the handbag. Now, finding a way to check Tulip's would be the next challenge.

CHAPTER THIRTY-FIVE

Hawkman drove to his office and called Jennifer from the landline. She answered immediately.

"Hello, Hawkman, this is Chemo Jen, how may I help you?"

He laughed. "How'd you know it was me?"

"Few people have my cell phone number and who else is going to call me while I'm in the infusion center?"

"You're obviously doing okay."

"No problems so far. There's a little discomfort having a needle in your arm, but not bad."

"I'm glad. You still think you're game for dinner at Mom's?"

"Absolutely, I'm looking forward to it."

He proceeded to tell her what he'd discovered at Elaine's. "It gives us several clues to identify the purse."

"Now, let's hope I can get my hands on it without making her suspicious," Jennifer said. "But if she's involved in anyway with Carlotta's disappearance, it won't be easy. I'm real excited about being a part of this case, but I don't want to botch it either."

"You won't. I'll see you in a few hours."

"Okay."

***

Jennifer slipped her cell phone into her vest pocket and pulled the blanket up around her legs. She glanced up at the ceiling and decided the next visit she'd ask them not to put her under the air conditioning vent. Hawkman definitely didn't need to be here; she saw the horror in his face when they poked that needle into her wrist. Her big brave man had a pussy cat heart. She smiled to herself when suddenly, a very strange warm sensation soared through her body. She called for the nurse.

"Yes, Ms. Casey."

"I have this hot feeling in my chest. Is that normal?"

The nurse immediately adjusted the drip, then waited a few moments. "Is it still there?"

"Yes."

"I'm going to cease everything for a while and call your doctor."

Jennifer felt a slight tinge of fear creep down her back.

The nurse returned. "Is the warmth still there?"

"Yes, but it seems to be subsiding. What'd the doctor say?"

"He said to stop the medication until the feeling went away, then to start it again. So let me know as soon as it's gone."

After five more minutes, Jennifer called her back. "It seems to have disappeared."

The nurse smiled. "Good." She flipped the levers on the tubes running to Jennifer's wrist. "Let me know if the sensation recurs."

"Okay," she nodded as she felt the cool fluid enter her veins. Extracting a mystery novel from her bag, she leaned back in her chair and opened the book. Her eyelids felt heavy and she drifted into sleep. Soon, she awakened to the sound of a loud male voice in a chair not far from her. He was telling his neighbor they were giving him a dose of potassium and magnesium. Because his blood test showed their levels had dropped so low, it prevented him from getting his chemo. Jennifer took a mental note of the conversation and decided she'd ask for a copy of her blood test every time, also how she'd prevent such an incident from happening.

She checked her watch and noted lunch time wouldn't be for another hour, so decided to take a dose of the oral chemo. The warmth she'd felt earlier hadn't returned, which eased her mind. She didn't want anything to prevent her from getting the treatment.

Her thoughts went to the Gucci purse. How could she examine it without making Tulip uneasy? Hawkman had questioned her several times about Carlotta and if she had any inkling they suspected the purse belonged to the missing woman, it could make her very edgy.

Jennifer glanced down at the novel and tried to read, but the Benadryl hadn't worn off and drowsiness caused the print to blur. She adjusted the recliner to a more upright position, hoping this would keep her awake.

Observing the rest of the patients in the room, gave her ideas for characters in her upcoming mysteries. She took out her notebook and jotted down the reactions she noticed in different people. Some were comical and others very serious. They came in a variety of shapes and sizes, but had one thing in common; they were all fighting different types of cancer. She took a deep breath and put her notes away. As she leaned back, her stomach growled rather loudly, causing the woman next to her to giggle.

"I think it's time to eat something," Jennifer said, laughing. She removed the lunch she'd brought from the sack and piled the goodies on the shelf attached to the chair arm. She'd decided to treat herself with a soda, chips, steak sandwich and candy bar. Everything tasted wonderful. Then she needed to go to the bathroom. Having watched one of the others roll their portable intravenous gear, she got up, unplugged the unit and guided it toward the small room. When she returned, she settled back in her chair and opened her book again. The drowsiness had left and she could easily read without fear of dozing off.

She chatted with her neighbors, passed out some of her book flyers and asked a few questions. Time passed pretty fast, and before she knew it, the nurse stood in front of her with a small vial in her hands.

"Now it's time for your chemo," she said, checking the wrist band.

Jennifer glanced up at her puzzled. "What's been going into my veins all this time?"

"Everything that gets your body ready for this. Then we

flush you out again. So once the Vincristine is injected, you'll be ready to go home in about fifteen minutes."

"You mean I've been here for over six hours, just getting ready for that?"

The nurse grinned. "Yes. Seems odd doesn't it?"

"Must be pretty potent stuff."

"It is. Be sure and drink plenty of water when you get home."

Jennifer gave Hawkman a call. "Okay, hon, meet me out front in about fifteen or twenty minutes."

"I'll be there."

Jennifer packed up her belongings while the last of the solution dripped into her body. By the time the nurse removed the needle from her wrist, took her blood pressure, and set up the next appointment, time had moved closer to thirty minutes. She hurried out the door toward the elevator, then dashed to the front entry. Hawkman sat in the 4X4, staring at the door and drumming his fingers on the steering wheel. The minute he spotted her, he jumped out, ran around to the other side of the vehicle, and held open the door.

"Hi," she said, climbing into the passenger seat.

When he got into the driver's side, he reached over and planted a kiss on her lips, then sat back and studied her for a moment. "You certainly don't look any worse for wear."

She chuckled. "Did you expect me to turn into some sort of ogre?"

"Who knows, I've never seen someone after they've had chemo."

"Well, I'm not sure what will happen in a few days. I very well might become a monster. Talked to some of the people up there and they say the effects don't hit for a day or two. So, I'm going to take advantage of today and tomorrow." She looped her finger around her pony tail. "And I'll probably lose my hair before the next treatment."

Hawkman looked away. "Do we have to talk about it?"

She lowered her head and looked at him out of the side of her eyes. "Will you still love me if I'm bald?"

He laughed. "No, of course not. I only love women with hair."

She playfully punched him on the shoulder. "You're so mean."

Putting an arm around her, he pulled her close. "Are you still on for dinner at Mom's?"

"I'm famished. However, I don't have a plan on how to examine Tulip's purse without making her suspicious."

"Maybe I should hire a purse snatcher."

"Oh, sure. Williams would just love that."

Hawkman found a parking spot near the front door of the restaurant. "Whoops, they're not open yet. We're a few minutes early."

"That's okay, I'll just relax."

"Are you feeling okay?"

"Yes, just tired. It took a lot out of me up there today."

"I can only imagine, as it drained me, just knowing you were getting that stuff pumped into your veins."

She poked him on the leg and pointed toward his left. "Isn't that Tulip coming up the sidewalk?"

Hawkman rolled down the window. "Hey, Ms. Withers, what's the special tonight?"

She jerked up her head and shaded her eyes with her hand. "Oh, Mr. Casey." Moving closer to the 4X4, she looked past him. "Who's that with you? The sun's right in my eyes."

"It's me, Jennifer."

Tulip's face lit up in a big smile. "When is your next book coming out. I love your stories."

"Soon."

"Good, I can hardly wait."

Jennifer's cheeks flushed. "Thank you. I didn't know you were a fan."

"Oh, yes, ever since the first novel." Then she glanced at Hawkman and back to Jennifer. "Why are you guys sitting out here in the car?"

"Waiting for Mom's to open."

"You better get in there soon. The special on Monday night

is fried chicken and we're always packed. You won't be able to find a booth if you wait too long."

"Oh, Tulip, is that a Gucci?" Jennifer asked, pointing to her handbag.

She blushed. "Yeah, my dad got it for my birthday. I probably shouldn't be carrying it to work. But heck, it's the only place I go so I can show it off."

"Can I see it? I'd really love to have one."

When she held it up, Jennifer reached across Hawkman and took hold of the straps. Hawkman thought he saw a sign of fear in Tulip's eyes when Jennifer lifted the purse from her hand.

"I better get inside before the crowd gets here."

"It's beautiful," Jennifer said, examining it closely before handing it back. "Do you know where your dad got it?"

She shook her head. "No."

"Does he ever shop on the internet?" Jennifer asked.

"Sometimes." She glanced at her watch. "I've got to run. You folks better get inside if you want a seat." Tulip scurried toward the entry, and disappeared behind the door.

Hawkman quickly turned toward his wife. "Were you able to spot anything on the purse in such a short time?"

"I spotted a tiny bleached spot on the handle and the back of the Gucci symbol is scratched up like trying to hide a previous name or initial."

"That's a start. Both of those clues go along with what Tiffany told me." Hawkman eyed the street in front of the cafe. "I think we better go inside or we won't get a seat. Look at the people heading toward this place."

They lucked out and got the last booth. Jennifer checked the menu. "Their chicken must be darn good. Let's try it."

"Sounds okay with me."

Tulip finally reached their table. "Boy, good thing you guys got in here as soon as you did, or you'd be stuck at the counter or standing. Mondays are always this way. You want to order the chicken?"

"Yes," Hawkman said.

"You won't be sorry. It's delicious. Iced tea or coffee?"

"Iced tea," they said in unison.

She wrote it down on her pad, then placed the menus back in the rack at the end of the table. "Be back shortly with your order."

Hawkman glanced toward the door as several people entered the establishment. "Don't look now, but Hank Withers just walked in. Guess he likes chicken every once in awhile."

CHAPTER THIRTY-SIX

Hawkman eyed Hank as he moved up the aisle and headed for the front of the restaurant where a lone seat at the bar remained empty. When he came alongside their booth, he stopped and displayed a big smile.

"Well, hello there, Mr. Casey. See you like Mom's fried chicken too."

Hawkman stood and extended his hand. "Good seeing you again." He gestured toward Jennifer. "Have you met my wife?"

"Yes. She's been in my shop a number of times. How are you, Mrs. Casey?"

She smiled. "Fine, thank you."

"We understand you purchased a Gucci handbag for Tulip's birthday and wondered if you got a good deal. Jennifer wants one, but they're too expensive for my wallet, " Hawkman said.

Hank shook his head. "Women and their fads." Then he glanced toward the door and pointed. "Ah, I better grab that seat up there or I'll be out of luck with this crowd moving in. I do enjoy Mom's chicken dinner. Get tired of beef and pork." He waved and hurried toward the vacant stool.

Tulip appeared carrying two plates heaped with golden brown pieces of poultry, mashed potatoes, green beans and a basket of warm rolls balanced on top. "Here you go. Enjoy."

"Thanks, Tulip"

"Hank sure avoided my question," Hawkman said, as he munched on a chicken leg.

Jennifer dabbed her mouth with a napkin. "I'm being scrutinized."

Hawkman looked over his shoulder just as Hank turned

his attention to the plate of chicken his daughter placed on the counter. "Appears something's bothering him."

"I think you're going to have to corner him to ask pertinent questions. Do you think he's dangerous?"

"Could be."

"Maybe you should get Detective Williams to go with you."

"It's a thought."

After they finished their meal, Hawkman paid the bill and left a hefty tip. He gave Jennifer his arm as she climbed into the 4X4. "I must say they serve a good dinner. I noticed you were able to eat quite a bit. You must be feeling pretty good."

"So far, fine. And you know I love fried chicken."

He walked around the vehicle and slid into the driver's seat. "What's the regimen you have to follow for the rest of the week?"

"When we get home, I've got to take two more doses of the oral chemo, about an hour apart, and then I'll be through with today's batch. I have four more days of these, then I can recoup for three weeks before the next treatment."

"At least you have a break in between."

She told him about the small vial of chemo. "I couldn't believe I'd been prepped to receive one little needle's worth."

"Must be potent stuff."

"That's exactly what I said to the nurse. And she responded with, 'very', and drink lots of water." She dug into her duffel bag and grabbed a bottle of the clear liquid. "In fact, I'll take a few swigs right now."

When they arrived at the house, Hawkman observed Jennifer taking another dose of the cytox, then she arranged the medications on the cabinet. "Good grief, it looks like a pharmacy."

She grimaced. "I know."

"By the way, have you been over to the store and talked to Amelia about what's going on?"

"No."

"I think you should. She's always available and can call on

one of her kids to take over if you need someone while I'm at the office. It would certainly ease my mind. It takes me over an hour to get home and you might need help immediately."

"You're right. I'll talk to her in the morning."

"I'll go with you. In fact, think I'll hang around tomorrow and see how you're doing."

Jennifer pointed at the phone. "Looks like there's a message."

Hawkman punched the button. The voice of the urologist came across explaining he wanted to place a stent into Jennifer's ureter to relieve the pressure from the kidney. And he'd like to make arrangements for the procedure. Could she please call his office as soon as possible. Then he gave a number.

Hawkman noticed Jennifer had her lower lip drawn in between her teeth. A sure sign the call made her nervous. "You know, you don't have to go through with this."

She turned toward him as if she'd just snapped out of a trance. "What?"

"No one says you have to consent to the stent."

"I certainly don't want kidney failure on top of everything else."

"True."

"It just seems everything's happening at once."

He walked around the breakfast bar and put his arms around her. "You're going to do just fine."

At that moment, the phone rang. Hawkman reached over and picked up the receiver. "Hello." He smiled and handed the phone to Jennifer. "This will perk you up."

"Hello." A big grin lit up her face. "Hi, Sam."

***

The next morning, Hawkman slipped out of bed, and noticed Jennifer had the covers tucked around her body as if she were cold. He pulled on his eye-patch, then took his clothes and dressed in the hall bathroom so he wouldn't disturb her rest. Not sure what to expect, he put on a pot of coffee and debated whether to cook breakfast. He'd read people on chemo sometimes lose their appetites and he certainly didn't want to make her feel obligated to eat if she didn't feel like it.

He stared out the kitchen window as he sipped his coffee, and his mind wandered to Hank Withers. It appeared the man had intentionally avoided the question about the purse. The things Hawkman needed to ask the butcher weren't going to be easy, especially if he had anything to do with Carlotta's disappearance.

His thoughts were interrupted when Jennifer entered the kitchen wrapped in her winter robe.

"I'm freezing. I'm putting the electric blanket on the bed. I got so cold during the night, my teeth chattered."

Hawkman looked baffled. "Is this part of the chemo?"

She shuddered. "I don't know, but it must be. I'm cold by nature, but this is different. I feel like it emanates from my bones." She took two tablets from the cytox bottle on the cabinet and gulped them down with a full glass of water. Shivering, she wrote the time down on a pad of paper. "One dose gone and four more to go; next, the prednisone."

"You want me to fix you a bite to eat?"

"Not for an hour. I'm going to stand under a hot shower, then dress in warm clothes." She poured herself a cup of coffee, tightened the terry robe around her body and proceeded to the bedroom.

Hawkman wondered what to expect for the rest of the day. Soon Jennifer returned dressed in a pair of lightweight sweats.

"I feel better and warmer now."

"What would you like to eat?"

"They told me I could consume whatever I wanted and not to worry about diets or anything. The main thing was to eat." She wrinkled her nose. "But nothing sounds good."

Hawkman's eyes twinkled and he rubbed his hands together. "How about a piece of toast lathered in butter, bacon and an egg fried in the grease?"

"That sounds delicious."

He stepped back, startled at her reply. "You never eat an egg fried in bacon grease and you always eat your toast plain."

She threw up both her hands. "I know, but it sounds wonderful. I'll have it."

He hurried to the stove. "I'm going to get things going before you change your mind."

Jennifer looked up at the wall clock. "While you're fixing breakfast, I'll call the urologist and work out a time for the surgery."

Hawkman finished the preparation just as she hung up the phone. "Well?" he asked, placing her plate on the breakfast bar.

"A week from Thursday. So keep that date open." She wrote it on the hanging calendar above the phone. "At least I'll be through with my first session of chemo."

CHAPTER THIRTY-SEVEN

Hawkman found the next few days frustrating. Jennifer's appetite disintegrated and her energy level fell to almost nothing. Even putting one foot in front of the other seemed an effort.

Friday morning, she'd risen early and Hawkman found her sitting on the couch in the living room wrapped in a blanket. "Honey, is there anything I can do to make you more comfortable?" he asked.

She shook her head. "Wish I felt like doing something. I can't even work on my book because I can't focus and I'm so cold."

A sharp knock at the entry caused both of them to turn their heads. He opened the door and Amelia entered, balancing a tray in her hands.

She quickly set it on the counter. "I need to get something with handles on it. That thing is a pain to carry." She headed straight for Jennifer, sat down beside her and took her hand. "Honey, how are you feeling? I researched lymphoma on the computer, plus the CVP treatment you told me about. The side effects don't sound like fun." She patted her arm. "But looks like you still have your beautiful hair."

Jennifer winced. "Give me another couple of weeks and it'll be gone."

Amelia's gaze went toward the kitchen where Hawkman was peeking under the towel she'd draped over the items she'd brought. "Okay, nosey, I'm going to fix your dinner tonight. So if you need to go into town, why don't you go ahead. The kids are watching the store, so I'm free to spend the rest of the day with Jennifer."

He jerked up his head with a sheepish grin. "Are you sure?"

"Yes."

He turned to his wife. "Honey, is it okay with you?"

"Please go. You deserve a break."

"I do need to catch up on the investigation. Do you need anything while I'm in town?"

She pointed toward the counter. "There's a list by the phone."

He found it, stuck it into his pocket, then went back into the living room and kissed her on the cheek. "I'll try and get home before dark."

On his way to Medford, Hawkman chewed on a toothpick and thought about what Jennifer had already been through. Not only did she complain of being cold, but she found it hard to swallow and her jaw ached so badly it almost brought tears. Strange sensations surged throughout her body and she swore she reeked of the horrible medication, even though he couldn't smell a thing. He hoped none of these symptoms were permanent.

Forcing his thoughts away from his wife, he tried to concentrate on the Carlotta case. He'd fallen way behind in his quest and feared new clues might slip through his fingers if he didn't get on the ball.

Paul hadn't contacted him, so he figured nothing threatening had occurred to Tiffany. He wondered if it would be safe to let the child go back to school next week. The girl shouldn't miss any more, as the end of the year was approaching. Maybe he'd take a chance and let her return. Delia would take responsibility for walking her to the classroom, and bringing her home. Plus, she'd more than likely volunteer to help the teacher for several days of the week just to keep an eye on things. He'd give the grandmother a call when he got to the office.

He reached the Medford city limits and decided to drop in on Detective Williams. First, he called to make sure he'd find him there, then proceeded to the police station.

When Hawkman marched into the office, Williams stood and extended his hand. "Good to see you. How's Jennifer?"

"Amelia, the gal who owns the Copco Store, is with her today."

"Oh, yeah. I've met her. Nice woman."

"The chemo is hitting Jennifer pretty hard, but she's a fighter. She has to go into surgery next week to have a stent inserted to protect the kidney."

The detective sat down. "She's getting her share. Hope she gets along okay. I hear chemo is hell."

Hawkman took the chair in front of the desk. "It's not fun watching. I can't imagine what she's going through."

It's been several days since I talked to you. I've left a few messages on your phone at work, mostly about Jennifer. Decided not to call your cell as I didn't have anything pressing to report on the Carlotta case. Anything new on your end?"

"I'm pretty confident the purse Tulip is carrying belonged to Carlotta. Jennifer got a quick look at it the other night and found a couple of telltale signs. Tulip repeated to us Hank had given it to her for her birthday. I hope to talk to him today and find out his story."

"He could swear he purchased it from a flea market or garage sale."

"True," Hawkman nodded. "That's why we need to get into his house and place of business. See if we can find any other clues."

"I can't do much until we know for sure Hank Withers is involved.

Unfortunately, time's against us. He could destroy any evidence before we get there."

Hawkman drummed his fingers on the arm rest. "That's why I feel such an urgency."

"Do you think the man could be violent?"

"I have no idea."

"Why don't I go with you. Sometimes the presence of a police officer gets more information."

Hawkman chuckled. "Or they clam up completely."

"All right, smart ass. Let's go."

"We'll take my vehicle," Hawkman said, as they left the building. When they pulled up in front of the butcher shop, a sign hung on the inside of the windowed door. "Odd, looks like he's closed. I've never known Withers' shop not to be open."

"Me, either," Williams said, climbing out of the SUV.

They both reached the entry and read, "Closed, due to a family emergency. Will return when I can."

"Interesting," Hawkman said. "Wonder what happened and if Tulip went with him?"

"Let's go find out."

"She won't be at work yet," Hawkman said, checking his watch. "We'll have to go to her place."

He rounded the corner and drove into the complex. When he came to Tulip's apartment, his gaze skimmed the lot. "Looks like we might have struck out here, too. I don't see her car." He parked, jumped out of his vehicle and knocked on the door. After several minutes, he returned. "I'll check at her workplace later."

Hawkman dropped the detective off at the police station. "I'll give you a call and let you know if Withers' daughter's still in town."

Williams gave a wave, jogged up the steps, and disappeared inside the building.

Hawkman took a toothpick from the box on the dashboard, and stuck it between his teeth, then drove toward his office. He noticed he'd almost gone through a box of those little wooden sticks; at least it was cheaper than smoking. After parking in the back, he pulled out Carlotta's file from under the passenger seat, left the windows cracked at the top, then climbed out, and locked up the 4X4. Before going up the stairs, he detoured into the bakery.

The baker's eyes opened wide in surprise. "Long time, no see. I thought you'd moved."

After explaining Jennifer's condition to the old man, Hawkman noticed his eyes glistened against the fine white layer of powdered flour covering his cheeks and hair.

"Makes me very sad to hear such news. I do hope she can conquer the 'C' devil. She's a very special person."

"Thank you, Clyde, I'll tell her. The doctors have assured us she can."

"Before you leave tonight, please stop by. I want to send her some of her favorite pastries."

Hawkman touched his hat. "She'll appreciate it."

He trooped up to his office and found the room warm and smelled musty after having been closed for several days. Leaving the door open, he dropped the folder on the desk, and shoved up the windows to air out the small area. He put on the coffee pot and peeled off his jeans jacket, leaving on his shoulder holster and gun. After hanging his hat and jacket on the coat rack, he went to the desk, and noticed the answering machine blinking like crazy. It displayed ten messages.

He poured himself a mug of coffee, sat down, pulled the yellow legal pad to the front of the desk, then punched the play button. The first message came from Detective Williams checking in and wanting to know about Jennifer. The next two were hang-ups, then a tele marketer, Williams again, a couple of messages from former clients, and a person wanting to set up an appointment. The ninth one brought Hawkman to attention. The voice was garbled, and reminded him of the threatening calls he'd received earlier on the Carlotta case; but he couldn't make it out, so decided someone must have had a poor connection. They'd have to try again. The last message came from Paul. "Mr. Casey, could you give me a call?"

Hawkman punched in his number, fearing something had happened. "Casey here. Returning your call."

"Good to hear from you. Mom and I were just wondering if you think it would be safe for Tiffany to start back to school. She's getting awfully restless and the end of the year is almost here. Mom said she'd walk her to the classroom, pick her up at the door and volunteer for recess monitor. This way Tiffany would never be outside without someone watching over her."

"I've been thinking along those lines. Let's give it a go and send her back to school. I'm sure she's bored out of her mind.

But do tell her to be wary. And reassure her, that grandma's only there for her protection, not to spy."

Paul snickered. "Thanks. She'll be thrilled. Any new developments?"

"A couple, but I can't really discuss them yet. As soon as I know something positive, I'll let you know."

He sighed. "It seems things are really dragging."

"True, but without any real evidence, we really have to dig. We'll eventually find out where Carlotta is or what's happened. The police are involved now, and that might speed things up, but I can't guarantee it."

"I'm afraid the longer it goes without any word, the more discouraged I get."

"Unfortunately, you're right, but we won't give up hope."

After ending the conversation, Hawkman leaned back in the chair, rubbed his forehead and wondered when he'd be able to talk to Hank Withers.

CHAPTER THIRTY-EIGHT

Hawkman called the two former clients, then set up an appointment with the probable new prospect in an hour at his office. He felt a little reluctant to take on a new case at the moment, but he'd find out what the person needed before turning it down.

He put in a call to Jennifer, who informed him that she and Amelia were in a hot gin rummy game and didn't want to be disturbed. He smiled to himself when he replaced the receiver. At least, she seemed content and feeling okay, but he knew his wife wouldn't tell him if she was dragging butt.

Putting Carlotta's file aside, he flipped the sheets of the yellow pad over to a clean page, checked the coffee and decided to make a fresh brew. He rummaged in the cabinet for some styrofoam cups and placed them in a stack beside the pot, along with a handful of dry creamers and sugar he kept handy in a small basket. The prospective client gave the impression he might be bringing another person, so Hawkman pushed two chairs close to the desk. He gave everything a final inspection, checked his watch and figured he had a few minutes before they'd arrive.

Wandering over to the window with a mug of java, he stared into the parking lot. His mind drifted to the Withers. He'd drive by Mom's Cafe tonight and see if Tulip showed up. The smell of bakery goods drifted through the open window, which reminded him not to forget to stop by and see Clyde before leaving. A car pulled into a vacant spot near the front of the building. A couple got out and pointed toward the shingle hanging at the front of the stairs. Hawkman figured they were the new customers.

Mr. and Mrs. Jim Thompson needed a private investigator to find a long lost aunt on the wife's side After extensive questioning, Hawkman decided to take the case, as most of the work could be handled on the computer. They happily signed the contract and gave him a deposit. When they left, Hawkman dumped the coffee pot, closed the window, grabbed Carlotta's file, and headed downstairs to the bakery. Clyde held out a large box encircled with a bright blue ribbon, topped with a matching bow, and card.

"You tell Ms. Jennifer I've baked all her favorites today. I hope she enjoys them."

"Anything in there for me?" Hawkman asked, with a faked hurt expression.

The baker laughed. "I'm sure she'll share."

"This is very kind of you, Clyde. She'll be thrilled."

He placed the goodies carefully in the passenger seat, making sure the box sat evenly so the contents wouldn't mash against each other. He stopped at the supermarket and picked up the items on Jennifer's list, then drove to Tulip's apartment complex. Circling the parking lot, he still didn't see her car anywhere, so headed for Mom's. He arrived a few minutes before opening time, so parked and waited. Soon, Tulip drove around the corner and found a vacant slot about half way down the block. Hawkman watched her walk with her head down and shoulders slumped. He got out of his vehicle and met her at the door.

"Hi, Tulip. Went by your dad's shop this morning to buy some steaks. He had a closed sign stating there'd been an emergency in the family. It really surprised me as I've never seen his place not open for business."

She nodded. "Yeah, I know. His brother had a massive heart attack and he wanted to be with him. I'm going to run the store tomorrow. I can be there until almost time for me to come to work here. At least he won't lose too much money."

"That's good of you. But it's going to be a lot of work trying to keep up with both jobs."

"I think I can handle it. I have to get up earlier too, because I'm staying out at his place so I can take care of his pets."

"I had no idea Hank liked animals."

She signed. "Oh,my, he's got a cat, bird and a dog. And they're the biggest babies in the world. They have certain routines you have to follow or they aren't happy."

"How long do you think he'll be gone?"

"Probably two weeks, maybe even longer." Then she took hold of his arm, her eyes wide. "I just heard your wife has cancer. Is she going to die?"

Hawkman stepped back. He'd never let that word enter his thoughts and it shocked him. "Uh, no. She's undergoing chemo treatments and the doctors told her they can knock it into remission."

"That's good news," she said, as she turned toward the entry. "I better get to work."

Hawkman stared at her as she pushed open the door and went inside.

***

The rest of the week Hawkman stayed home with Jennifer as the chemo played its game of hell. She claimed everything tasted like cardboard, so Hawkman ended up eating most of Clyde's delicious baked goods.

But she made him vow never to tell the likable baker. He worked in his home office on the new case and also talked with Paul, telling him the situation. He expressed his sorrow at hearing about Jennifer and assured Hawkman things were going smoothly with Tiffany since she'd started back to school. There'd been no threats nor had they seen anything suspicious around the house. Delia stayed in the classroom and near her granddaughter most of the day.

About the time Jennifer started feeling better, she had to go in for the stent placement. When she came home from the hospital the doctor had given her the pain pill Vicodin, which made her very sick. She vomited and passed out in the bathroom. It scared Hawkman so badly, he wanted to call the medical helicopter to take her to the hospital, but Jennifer insisted she'd be okay.

"Throw those horrible pills away. How anyone could ever get addicted to them is beyond me," she grumbled, holding her stomach as she tumbled into bed.

Hawkman felt beside himself, not knowing what to do as he watched his wife spend three days with horrible pain in her back and right flank.

"Let me call the doctor for a stronger pain killer," he said.

She paced the floor in front of him. "No, I'm going to have him remove this thing. I can't handle this with all the other stuff going on."

"Why don't you lie down and rest?"

"I can't stand to stay in bed. It drives me nuts."

When she called the doctor, he said he couldn't understand the cause of her suffering and ordered an x-ray to make sure the stent hadn't been jarred out of place. The film showed it in perfect position.

Before going to bed, Jennifer decided to ask the surgeon to remove the stent, even though she'd be taking a risk of losing a kidney. But to her surprise, she woke up the next morning with no pain.

"I can't believe it. I think my body has finally decided to accept this thing and quit fighting it. And not only that, I'm hungry."

Hawkman jumped out of bed. "What do you want? I'll go fix it right now."

"Pancakes and bacon sound delicious."

"You got it." He threw on his jeans and a tee shirt, then hurried to the kitchen.

As he stood over the stove frying bacon, Jennifer strolled in slowly, her head bowed.

"What's the matter, honey?"

She held up a handful of hair. "I'm starting to shed. The doctor hit the nail right on the head. It's three weeks since my treatment. Thank goodness I already have my wig and turbans."

He stared at her for a moment. "I can't tell you've lost any."

"This all came out in my comb. It appears it's just going to thin, instead of falling out in clumps."

"Maybe you should just shave your head. Wouldn't that be easier than going through the misery of watching it come out gradually?"

"No, it will be interesting to see how long it takes and if any hangs in there."

"You're a glutton for punishment."

"Think I'll put a scarf on though; I don't want hair falling into my food."

"That's a good idea."

After they ate, Jennifer took a small plastic bag from the pantry. "I think I'll save my hair and see if it comes back the same color and texture. People have told me it could come back different, maybe even curly. At least it'll be an interesting experiment."

Hawkman gazed at her in amazement. "Whatever turns you on."

"You better take advantage of these next few days while I'm feeling okay and do some work on the Carlotta case. Remember, next week is my second chemo treatment."

"It can't be as bad as this one. At least you won't have a stent put in and suffer with a medication that didn't agree with you."

"True, but you can never tell, I've heard each time it acts differently."

"Are you sure you'll be okay here alone?"

"It seems my brain is working this morning and I'm not running into the walls quite as bad. I don't have any energy, but hopefully I can work on my book at the computer. I'm still freezing, but I can always bundle up."

"Okay, if you're sure you'll be okay. Promise to call if you need anything."

"I will."

"I'll stop at the butcher shop and see if Hank's home yet.

If Tulip has the store open, I could pick up a couple of steaks if you think you could eat one."

She tapped a finger on her chin. "Now that sounds mighty good."

"Great. But if you don't feel like eating a big hunk of beef, I'll freeze them for a later time." He buckled on his shoulder holster and turned to give her a kiss. "Wonder how Tulip's managing her father's store and the waitress job?"

"She's probably doing just fine."

Hawkman left the house, and headed for Medford. He didn't want to be gone long, so drove straight to the butcher shop. The bell jingled as he opened the door.

"Be right with you," Tulip called over the buzz of the saw. She had a hair net over her head and hovered over the cutting board, the saw grinding at a bone in the hunk of meat she steadied with her gloved hand.

The saw finally hushed and she turned toward the counter. "Hi, Mr. Casey, what can I get you today?"

Hawkman stood in front of the glass display cabinets and pointed at the filet mignon. "I think I'll take a couple of those."

She pulled two from the tray and held them up. "These okay?"

"They look fine. Have you heard from your dad?"

"Yes, I talked to him last night. His brother's not in good shape. He might be gone longer."

"Sorry to hear it. I notice you're cutting meat here. Doesn't he have a set up at the house where you could do it?"

"No, he doesn't even have a separate freezer, other than the one in his refrigerator. He just uses the big one here to store his own meat."

Hawkman paid his bill. "Makes sense. How are you doing holding down two jobs?"

"It's very tiring. I drop into bed and sleep like a log. But I really haven't minded it too much. I think because I know it won't be forever."

He picked up his bundle and change. "Thanks. I'll be talking to you."

Hawkman drove to his office in deep thought. "Very interesting, Hank doesn't have a freezer at his house."

CHAPTER THIRTY-NINE

Hawkman removed the two steaks he'd bought earlier from the small refrigerator, left the office and headed home. When he opened the front door, he could hear peals of laughter coming from the living room. Then it stopped abruptly as he stepped into the kitchen and put the meat away. Amelia looked his way, wiping tears from her eyes.

"I thought I recognized your laugh," Hawkman said. "What's so funny."

"Come in here and sit down. Jennifer's going to model her new wig."

Puzzled, he meandered over to his chair near the window.

"Okay, you can come out now," Amelia called.

Jennifer waltzed into the room with a red, yellow, green and white clown wig on her head. She had a red round ball stuck on her nose, and bounced around the room like a jester as Amelia snapped pictures. Soon, out of breath, she flopped down on Hawkman's lap. "How do you like it? Thought I'd wear it to the next infusion."

Hawkman guffawed as the red nose fell off and she attempted to catch it. "Where'd you get that crazy thing?"

"It came by United Parcel, and guess who sent it?

"I haven't the vaguest idea."

"Sam, with a note saying, 'You need to be creative'. Can you believe our kid?"

He grinned. "Yep, he has a great sense of humor."

"I called Amelia as soon as it arrived and had her come over to view my new style."

Standing, Amelia placed the camera on the coffee table. "I

needed a good laugh today. Now I better get home and put my supper together."

Jennifer jumped up from Hawkman's lap and gave her a hug. "Thanks for being such a great friend."

She smiled. "Goodnight, you little clown. Glad you're feeling better. Hope the second treatment is easier."

"Me too, I'll talk to you later."

After she left, Jennifer took Sam's letter from the counter and handed it to Hawkman. "I never dreamed he'd remember when I told him I'd lose my hair in about three weeks."

"Kids hear what they want and let the rest slide off their backs."

"He wants to come home, but I'm not sure I'm ready. I feel so lousy during chemo, I don't want him seeing me so sick."

"Tell him to hold off for awhile. You'll let him know when you feel like company. He'll understand."

"I don't want to hurt his feelings."

Hawkman pulled her into his lap again. "Honey, during this time you have to think about yourself. You've spent your whole life thinking about others. But now, it's different. You have to get well, and you can't if you're stressed out. We have to do what's best for you. Your health is the most important thing right now."

She sighed. "You're probably right, but it's hard."

"I know I'm right. If you like, I'll talk to Sam."

"It's okay, I'll tell him." She got up and traipsed toward the bedroom. "Think I'll shed this wig, it's a bit heavy."

"Aw shucks, thought you'd wear it as your everyday attire."

She turned and stuck out her tongue. "I think not."

When she returned, she had on a scarf tied at the nape of her neck.

"How's the hair shedding?"

"It's coming out in gobs. I'd say in a couple of days it will all be gone. It feels so weird. And that isn't the only hair I'm losing."

"Oh?"

"Don't ask." She picked up the camera and headed for

the computer. "I'm dying to see these pictures. If they come out good, I'll send some copies to Sam. He'll get a kick out of them."

She sat for a moment, then giggled. "Come here and look. They turned out great."

Hawkman moved behind her and peered over her shoulder. "Those are a riot," he chortled. "Sam will love them. And you play the role of a clown perfectly."

"I'll print them out later. Right now I want to hear about your day."

"Okay, talk to me while I fix dinner."

"You're really spoiling me, taking over the cooking like you have."

"I figure it's hard enough for you to eat, much less trying to prepare it. It's the least I can do and I enjoy fixing the meals."

She reached up and gave him a kiss. "You're a sweetheart. I thank you for being so thoughtful."

Hawkman unwrapped the filet mignon steaks and held them up. "How do these grab you?"

"Yummy." She settled on one of the kitchen bar stools. "Okay, tell me about your trip to town."

"Had an interesting day. Talked with Paul and all is well with the family. Delia is keeping a close eye on Tiffany and nothing threatening has occurred."

"That's good."

"I dropped by Withers' butcher shop to pick up the steaks, and Tulip is holding down the fort. I asked how the two jobs were going. She told me tiring, but things were under control. I thought it odd her having to cut up the meat during business hours, when her dad always seemed to have it done ahead of time."

"Well, she can't stay at her father's store after hours as she has to go to her restaurant job," Jennifer said. "And she probably doesn't want to get up at four in the morning to do the carving."

"She's staying out at Hank's place taking care of his animals, so I asked if he had a freezer."

"Hank has pets?"

Hawkman nodded. "Yeah, shocked me too. He has a cat, dog and of all things a bird of some sort. Tulip said they were really spoiled and liked a routine."

"Why would you be interested whether he has a freezer or not?"

He scrubbed the potatoes, and placed them in the microwave. "I thought maybe she could prepare the meat at the house, but obviously he doesn't have any equipment there and does all the butchering at the shop. She said he didn't have a freezer at home, only the one in the refrigerator."

Jennifer cocked her head and stared dubiously at Hawkman as he took out the salad makings and cutting board.

"Am I not doing this right?"

"It has nothing to do with your preparations, it's what you just said."

"Oh, and may I ask what I said that sparked your interest?"

"Why are you so concerned about Hank's freezers?"

He avoided looking at her. "Curiosity, I guess."

She narrowed her eyes. "You're not telling me everything."

"You're right. But I'm not sure I'm ready to tell you my theory. Let's wait until after dinner and we'll talk more."

"I'm not going to let you forget."

After dinner, they migrated to the living room, and Hawkman flipped on the television.

"Not yet," Jennifer said, turning it off. "We're going to talk some more."

He gave her a playful shake. "You do have the memory of an elephant."

"But first I want to tell you, I enjoyed that meal tremendously. Thank you."

"You're more than welcome. Glad it agreed with you."

She snuggled down in her chair and covered herself with an afghan. "Okay, tell me why you're so interested in Hank's freezers."

"Look at you, even the word makes you cold."

"Oh, stop it, you know I've been freezing ever since I started this stupid chemo. Come on, quit stalling."

His expression turned solemn. "This is just my thought, in fact, I hope I'm wrong. But I think Carlotta's been butchered and her body stored in a freezer."

Jennifer's mouth dropped open. "Oh my God!"

CHAPTER FORTY

Hawkman settled in his chair and raised both hands, palms out.
"Now, don't get overly excited. This is only a guess."

"But how did you ever come to such a morbid conclusion?"

He counted off on his fingers. "For one thing, we've found no body. Another, there's no record of Carlotta leaving on a plane, bus or taxi. Thirdly, no one outside Medford has seen or heard from her. And fourth, we have a suitcase full of her clothes with fingerprints all over it. Now, all of a sudden a suspected purse shows up in the hands of Tulip. And she tells us her dad gave it to her as a birthday present."

"That handbag could've come from anywhere, but go on, I can tell there's more."

"No police record of Carlotta Ryan involved in any accidents, and she's not been admitted into any local hospital with amnesia. It also seems odd to me, she hasn't tried to make contact with her daughter, regardless of what type of mother people may consider her. In my opinion, the woman's dead."

Jennifer sighed. "It makes sense. But tell me what gives you the idea Hank Withers might be involved? Other than Tulip's statement he gave her the Gucci. Did he have a motive to kill Carlotta?"

"Yes, he'd like to see his daughter married to Paul."

Jennifer's gazed at the ceiling and exhaled loudly. "You've got to be kidding! I doubt a good-looking man like Paul would give Tulip a second look."

"Hard to say. He might want a normal mother for his

daughter instead of a high-fashion model, someone who would treat her like a growing child instead of an adult."

"Did Paul tell you this?"

Hawkman shook his head. "No. Those are my own ideas coming from what I've observed."

Jennifer pulled the afghan up around her neck. "Tell me how Paul has reacted to Carlotta's disappearance."

He pursed his lips. "I guess like any man. Disappointed and scared. But remember, he's been separated from her for some time and living in his own apartment. Not like they were living together as man and wife under the same roof."

"Did you ever inform him Carlotta had been to see a lawyer about a divorce?"

"No, because Ms. Phillips hadn't even started the paperwork. She spent a lot of time trying to persuade the woman to see a marriage counselor before making a decision. The papers hadn't been drawn up, so I figured Paul didn't need such news right after his wife's disappearance."

"What if he did find out beforehand and knew Carlotta would wipe him out financially if she followed through?" She raised her brows. "Maybe he got rid of her." She leaned forward. "And then there's Delia. A strange grandmother with a weird reading taste for her age. Didn't you tell me she could hardly stand her daughter-in-law? Maybe Carlotta's buried under one of those strange statues around the pool you described." Jennifer shivered. "Makes me even colder when I think of all the people with motives."

About that time Hawkman's cell phone rang. He glanced at the clock. Who'd be calling at ten thirty at night? Snatching it from his belt, he put it to his ear.

"Hello."

A woman's sobbing voice came over the line.

"Slow down, I can't understand you. Who is this?"

"It's Delia. Tiffany's gone."

Hawkman jumped out of his chair. "What do you mean, she's gone?"

"Princess dashed out the front door when a neighbor came

by to return some books. And...and Tiffany flew out the door after the cat before I could stop her."

"How long ago did this happen?"

"About an hour ago. We've called the police."

"Are they there?"

"Yes, and they've searched the entire area and found no sign of her or the cat. We've checked with all the neighbors and no one has seen anything. What are we going to do?" Delia cried.

"I'll be there as soon as I can. Get a hold of yourself. We'll find her."

Hawkman hung up and headed for the front door.

"Wait," Jennifer threw off the afghan and hurried to his side. "What's happened?"

He quickly gave her a run down of Delia's story. "I don't know when I'll be back. Will you be okay?"

Jennifer gave him a slight push. "Of course, just go. Oh, my. I hope you find her."

"The child could be up in a tree after her precious Princess or crawling through a storm drain after her. Let's pray she'll have returned home by the time I get there."

On the freeway to Medford, Hawkman pushed the accelerator as fast as he dared. He didn't need to be pulled over, but he sure didn't want to waste any time either. When he reached Delia's house, black and whites were parked on both sides of the street. The front yard, bathed in light, stood out from the neighboring homes. Just as he stepped out of his vehicle, an ambulance swerved around the corner and came to a screeching halt in front. His heart skipped a beat as he hurried to the entry ahead of the paramedics. When Paul opened the door, his face had the eerie look of a ghost as he directed the emergency crew into the living room. Delia lay on the couch, her skin ashen as the men and women surrounded her with their load of equipment.

"What going on?" Hawkman asked.

Paul pulled him aside and whispered. "She passed out on me. Scared me half to death. I don't know if she's having a heart attack or the stress has gotten to her."

"Where are the police?"

They're combing the area, but so far have found nothing.

"Is Detective Williams with them?"

"Yes. He's helping with the search." He glanced toward Delia. "I think Mother feels guilty for letting Tiffany out of her sight for those few minutes."

One of the paramedics moved toward Paul. "Are you the one who called?"

"Yes, I'm her son."

"Has she been under some stress?"

"Yes. My ten year old daughter has disappeared."

The man put a fist on his hip. "I see. That pretty much explains it. According to the EKG, we don't suspect a heart attack at this time, but she seems very distraught. Does she have any tranquilizers in the house?"

Paul peered over at his mother and threw up his hands. "I haven't any idea."

"I don't see any need to take her into the hospital, but I do suggest you reach her doctor right away and get something to relax her."

"Thanks, I'll do that."

The young man moved back to Delia's side, and Hawkman turned to Paul.

"I'm going out to do a little combing of the area myself. It doesn't appear like you're going to get much rest tonight. I'll return and let you know if I find anything."

Paul rubbed the back of his neck. "I'd appreciate it. I wanted to go out with Detective Williams, but he thought it best I stay here at the house in case Tiffany tried to call." He gestured toward Delia. "And also to be with Mom. I'm going to try and get her to bed, but I doubt I'll have much luck."

Hawkman patted him on the shoulder. "I'll get back to you soon, either in person or by phone." He hurried to his vehicle. Driving around the block, Hawkman spotted several uniformed men going from house to house, but didn't see Williams. Searching each side as he drove down the street, he came to a sudden stop when he noticed a small carcass on the edge of the pavement. He grabbed the flashlight from the glove compartment and jumped out of the truck. To his relief, he discovered a squirrel had met its fate, and not Princess. He widened the area to several blocks surrounding Delia's residence, but found no clues to what had happened to Tiffany or her cat.

He drove back to the house and spotted Williams getting out of his car. Hawkman quickly parked, and hurried toward the entry to catch up with the detective. "Williams, hold up," he called, trying not to be too loud and wake the neighbors.

The detective swiveled on his heel. "Hawkman, when did you get here?"

"An hour or so ago. I've been driving around to see if you guys missed anything. I hope you have good news."

Williams face showed nothing but gloom. "You know how hard it is to tell a father and grandmother that we have no idea what's happened to their child. There's not a person in this neighborhood who saw Tiffany."

Hawkman looked back toward the street. "Boy, that's hard to believe. Usually a lot of people walk in the evening or take out their dogs."

"Unfortunately, this all happened between nine-thirty and ten o'clock. People usually walk before dark, and are inside watching the news by then. Mrs. Ryan said she'd just stopped by Tiffany's room and scolded her for not being ready for bed when her friend stopped by to return some books. The cat followed her down the hall and when she opened the door the feline hightailed it outside. I guess Tiffany went screaming after the animal. Mrs. Ryan, being preoccupied, couldn't chase her down. A bad set of events taking place all at once."

"Did Delia go out after the person left?"

"Yes, but she couldn't find any sign of the child or the cat."

"How much time had elapsed?"

"Not more than fifteen minutes, she says."

"And she didn't see any cars or anything suspicious?" Hawkman asked.

"She was focused on the child and not much else. That's why the woman is in such a state of panic right now. She feels it's all her fault."

"You know Paul had to call the paramedics?"

"Yes, I checked in with him shortly after they came." Williams scratched the back of his head. "You got any ideas?"

Hawkman grumbled. "My main suspect is back east for a couple of weeks or longer visiting a sick relative. You think we've got some outsider who happened to see a little girl out in the night?"

Williams scowled and hit his fist into the other hand. "I hate to think it, but that's how it appears."

"How was Tiffany dressed?"

"In a nightgown."

Hawkman kicked a pebble and sent it skittering across the sidewalk. "Dear God, that makes things even worse."

CHAPTER FORTY-ONE

Detective Williams moved toward the door. "I want to get a picture and description of Tiffany so I can send it out over the Amber Alert system as soon as possible. Its proved to be a good system for locating missing children. The faster we can get it displayed, the better."

"Excellent idea. I'm going to do some more scouting. Not sure what I'm looking for, but I can't hang around doing nothing."

Hawkman scurried back to his vehicle and drove aimlessly for an hour before he found himself at Tulip's apartment complex. He had no idea what drew him here, since he knew she was house-sitting at her father's place. Circling the area, he didn't spot her car and her flat was pitch black.

Resigned to the fact he couldn't do much at three in the morning, he decided to go home and snatch a couple hours of sleep. Depending on Jennifer's condition, he'd continue the search in the daylight hours.

Hawkman arose the next morning to find his wife in the kitchen drinking coffee, her bald head hidden by a pretty mauve colored turban. "That's a good color on you?"

"Thanks, but don't get used to it." She refilled her cup. "Did you find Tiffany?"

He snatched his mug off the top of the refrigerator. "No. It's like she disappeared into thin air. Williams is afraid some maniac spotted the nightgown clad little girl. It makes me sick to my stomach. I'm going back out today, if you're feeling okay. The police are out in full force. They've probably already got her abduction up on the Amber Alert."

Jennifer sat down on one of the kitchen stools and ran her finger around the coffee cup rim. "It gives me the shivers to think of what could be happening to that precious little girl right now."

Hawkman rubbed her shoulder. "Let's pray nothing. Maybe she wandered too far and things look different at night, so she might have just lost her bearing. She's been preached to for a couple of weeks about being wary of strangers. Her fears could have caused her to hide from the very ones searching for her."

She reached up and patted his hand. "I hope you're right."

"So how are you feeling?"

"Fine and my next treatment isn't until Monday, so I'll probably be okay for several days. Hopefully that will give you time to find Tiffany. The only thing I ask is if you'd pick up the thing I need in town. With my immune system taking such a beating, I don't want to be around the public."

"No problem. Where's your list?"

She picked up a small paper pad off the counter, ripped off the top sheet and handed it to him. "You can get everything at the market, so you won't have to run from store to store. I really appreciate it. And there's no hurry for any of those items."

"I'll pick up anything you want."

"The main thing right now is find that little girl." She stood. "Shouldn't you eat?"

"No appetite. I'll grab a bite in town if I get hungry."

She gave him a hug. "Good luck on your search."

Hawkman left the house and headed for Medford. He called Paul only to hear a very tired voice come over the line. "This is Casey. Any news?"

"Nothing. We're worried sick."

"How's Delia?"

"She happened to have some Valium and took one last night after the police left, but only if I promised on my life to wake her if I heard anything."

"I discovered over my police scanner, they have Tiffany's description on the Amber Alert. You never know who might call in with a good lead. The police will check out all of them."

"The waiting is the drain. It's really getting to me."

Hawkman could hear the catch in Paul's voice. "I'm going to talk to Detective Williams, then I'll search on my own again. I'll give you a call later today."

"Thanks, Mr. Casey."

When Hawkman reached the city, he headed straight for the police station. He'd already contacted the detective and knew he'd be there for a short period of time. Parking in the lot, he hurried up the steps only to find Williams surrounded by local reporters in front of the building. Hawkman could hear the news people asking about Tiffany Ryan and watched the detective as he cleverly answered some of their repetitive questions.

Williams finally raised a hand. "I've told you all I can without jeopardizing this case. Interview over." He turned and walked into the station. The gang with their microphones hooked to recorders and notepads in hand were stopped at the door by several uniformed officers.

Hawkman made his way around the group and followed Williams to his office. After they were both inside, the detective slammed the door.

"Damn reporters. They ask some of the dumbest questions I've ever heard. What's happened to journalism? Don't they teach them how to report anymore?" Grumbling he sat down at his desk.

"You did a good job of turning them off."

The detective leaned back and sighed loudly. "Well, I've barred the whole bunch from coming into the police station or we'd have them swarming in here like a bunch of bees. My men know to stop them the minute I step inside."

"Yeah, I noticed. Good idea." Hawkman stood observing Williams. "Did you get any rest last night?"

"No. And we haven't found the little girl either. We've had a few calls from people thinking they'd seen her, but nothing panned out. You have any suggestions?"

"I don't even know which way to turn. Yet, I feel she's close." Hawkman adjusted his hat. "I'm not going to waste any more time. Just wanted to check and see if you've come up with anything before I proceeded. Why don't you try to get a few hours sleep. You look beat. Keep your cell phone nearby and I'll contact you if I come across any leads."

Williams raked his fingers across the bristles on his chin. "Yeah, I must look like death warmed over. Think I'll do what you suggest and go home for awhile. I could use a good shower and a few winks."

The two men left the office.

In the hallway, the detective poked Hawkman's arm. "Let's go out the back way. I'm in no mood to face those unanswerable questions again."

They parted ways at the corner, and Hawkman headed for his SUV. He glanced back and grinned. Williams said the reporters would be waiting and sure enough they were crowded around the front door of the station.

He drove toward town and stopped at the butcher shop. The bell on the door jingled as he stepped inside. It surprised him to see a young Asian man behind the counter. "Hello, who are you?"

"My name John," he said with a big grin, showing a row of nice straight teeth. "I help Mr. Withers with shop."

"Is he back from his trip?"

"No, but soon. Ms. Withers needed me this morning. She'll be here at noon. Can I help you, please."

"I'm curious. How often do you help at the shop?"

He gave Hawkman a big toothy smile. "Oh, maybe twice a week."

"You cut the meat, too?"

"Oh, no. I only help sell. I know nothing about butchering. That's Mr. Withers' specialty." He laughed nervously. "And Ms. Tulip Withers."

"I need to talk to Ms. Withers about business. You say she'll be in at noon. How come she's not here this morning? I understood she'd take care of the shop for her dad while he's gone."

"She called early and asked me to open the store. Said she

had things to do before coming in." He threw back his small shoulders. "I very trustworthy, have key."

"I'm confident you are. I'll come back after lunch."

"You have name? I can tell Ms. Withers to expect you."

"Yes. Tom Casey."

John pointed a finger in the air. "I know you. You private investigator. I hear about you. You once a spy."

"That was a long time ago."

Hawkman turned to leave, but stopped when John spoke again.

"You no buy any meat?"

"Not this morning."

"Is there trouble?"

"Why would you ask?"

John's shoulders sagged. "You serious man. Came in here all business, but no buy anything."

"Tell Ms. Withers I'll be back."

Hawkman left the butcher shop wondering if Tulip had word of her father's return. When he arrived at his office, he sat down at his desk and booted up the computer. He'd run a search on Mrs. Thompson's aunt before leaving the office yesterday and sent a query to several assisted living homes. Three answers awaited him. The last one hit the jackpot and stated the woman now resided at a place in her hometown called The Homecare Facility for Alzheimer's Patients.

He picked up the phone and called the Thompson's. They appeared very relieved the aunt was still alive and thanked Hawkman profusely for locating her. Now they could handle things from here on out.

Hawkman had no more replaced the receiver than it rang. When he answered, the muffled voice hit him like a shot between the eyes. 'I told you something would happen if you didn't drop the case.' He stiffened and punched the record button, but the line went dead. He glanced at the caller ID and noted it came from the pay phone. This time the voice sounded familiar.

CHAPTER FORTY-TWO

Hawkman stared at the instrument for a few seconds, then punched the play back button. Unfortunately, he'd only caught the last two words on the recorder. Hardly enough to make any sort of identification. But this time he thought there was something about the tone of the voice he'd heard before, or was it just because he'd already received several of these calls? This person obviously had Tiffany. He prayed the kidnapper hadn't harmed her. He swiveled the chair around with his back to the door and contemplated calling Detective Williams. He felt in his gut Tiffany was being held somewhere in the area. The call had come from the same pay phone on Main Street as the others. Maybe he should ask the store owners closest to the phone if they'd noticed a person making a call. He slapped his hand on the desk. No busy clerk would pay that much attention.

He picked up the handset and punched in the detective's number. At that moment, a change in the light of the room made him twist in his chair.

***

Detective Williams never reached home before he received an urgent call to come back to the station for some unfinished police business. Things eventually calmed down and he finally caught a moment to stretch out on the small day bed in his office. He'd no more dozed off when his cell rang. He fumbled in his pocket for the phone, and put it to his ear. "Hello," he grumbled. But all he heard was a groan and a loud thump, like someone had fallen. He sat up and glanced at the caller ID.

Slapping it back on his ear he held it tightly. "Hawkman, are you all right?" A gasping voice came over the line.

"Call an ambulance, someone just tried to kill me."

Williams immediately dialed the emergency number, and called for a back-up as he dashed through the lobby. Two officers trailed him, jumped into their black and white, then followed the detective's unmarked vehicle with sirens blaring.

When they reached Hawkman's office, the ambulance had already arrived and were rushing up the steps. Clyde, in his white apron and floured hair, stood outside his bakery with wide eyes.

The detective took the steps two at a time and gulped when he spotted the red smeared carpet. Hawkman lay on the floor where the paramedic had cut off his shirt and jacket, revealing slashes in his upper and lower arm. After the young man called for the stretcher, he glanced up at Williams.

"He's lost a lot of blood."

"Has he been shot?"

"No. The wounds appear like deep cuts."

Williams leaned close to Hawkman's face. "Who did this?"

"Don't know, everything blurred," he whispered. "I had my back to the door when he came in. On me before I could make a move. Barely missed getting it in the back."

The second paramedic gave the detective a little nudge with the stretcher. "We need to get him to the hospital."

Williams jumped back out of the way. "Sorry."

After the ambulance left, the detective turned to his officers. "Tape off the area and get the lab boys over here. Maybe they'll find some fingerprints. Have to wait until I talk to the doctor or Hawkman to find out exactly what made the injury. But I suspect a knife, so search the alley and in the trash bins for any suspicious looking weapon."

He jogged down the stairs where Clyde still stood spellbound by all the activity. "Did you see anyone come into Hawkman's office?"

Blinking, he stared into space, then slowly twisted his head back and forth. "No." He gestured toward the bakery, "My store sets back a few feet and I can't see who goes up those stairs. I'm usually at the back with my ovens and only come out front when I hear the bell ring above my door. I hurried outside when I heard the sirens." Clyde grimaced. "Is Hawkman going to be okay?"

Williams patted him on the shoulder and a cloud of flour dust lifted into the air. "I'm sure he'll be fine. It doesn't appear his injuries are life-threatening. I'm going to the hospital to check, but I'll be back shortly and let you know how he's doing. My officers will remain here to secure the upstairs."

"Thank you." Clyde turned with his head bowed, and strolled back into the bakery.

When Williams climbed into his vehicle, he didn't want to waste any time, so left the red light on top and punched the siren. As he squealed around the corners, his thoughts went to Jennifer. Would Hawkman want him to contact her? He'd wait until a physician had examined the private investigator, then he'd have something to report. When he reached the hospital, he quickly found a parking place, and rushed into emergency. At the desk, he showed his badge. "Did you just admit Hawk...uh, Tom Casey?"

She glanced at the clipboard on the counter. "Yes, Detective Williams, the doctors are getting him ready for surgery."

Williams snapped up his head in surprise. "Surgery? How serious is he hurt?"

"All I can tell you is his condition needs special attention."

"Whew, didn't expect anything but stitches," he said, and turned away. The detective slowly walked outside and decided to call Jennifer. This is just the news she needs to hear while going through the effects of chemotherapy. He pulled his cell phone from his pocket and punched in Hawkman's home number.

"Hello, Jennifer, Williams here." He heard her suck in a deep breath.

"You wouldn't call here in the middle of the day if something wasn't wrong."

Now he knew why Hawkman always said his wife had great

intuition and could practically read his mind. "Hawkman's in the hospital, but he's going to be all right."

"What happened?"

The detective told her what he could. "I didn't know whether to call or not, but when I got here and they said he was going into surgery, figured I'd better."

"I appreciate it. Will you be there for a while?"

"Yes."

"I'll get to the hospital as soon as I can."

"Should you come here and be exposed to all these sick people?"

"That's not an option at the moment. See you in about an hour."

He opened his mouth to object, but she'd already hung up. Exhaling loudly, he called the officers he had on duty at Hawkman's office. "Did you find any clues? Not a fingerprint anywhere? How about a sharp edged weapon?"

Williams paced the sidewalk as the officer talked. "This has got to be the damnedest thing I've ever come across. A child has disappeared without a clue, then an attempt on Hawkman's life and no inkling of who did it. This is a frustrating situation." He stopped, and listened. "I know, you're doing the best you can. I'm just thinking out loud. Make sure Hawkman's place is locked up, then tell the baker man downstairs Hawkman's going to be okay. Then you two go ask some questions door to door. See if anyone spotted a vehicle driving up the alley or noticed a person going up to his office around noon. I'll check in with you later." He slapped shut his cell phone and stalked back into the waiting room. When he caught the eye of the clerk, she shook her head, so he flopped down in a chair and snatched a magazine from the end table.

Unable to sit still, Williams crossed and uncrossed his legs while watching the door for Jennifer's arrival. Finally, he got up and confronted the woman at the counter. "Come on, surely Tom Casey's out of surgery by now. He couldn't have been bunged up that bad."

"Hold on a minute and I'll go check."

He shifted from one foot to the other while thumbing his fingers on the counter top. Suddenly, someone tapped him gently on the shoulder. He whirled around and faced Jennifer. "Hello, sweetheart." And put an arm around her shoulders.

She wore a solemn expression and her eyes were shadowed with worry. "Is he all right?"

"I've just asked the gal to go find out what's going on. He's been in surgery for over an hour. I didn't think he'd been cut up that bad."

She took a deep breath and bit her lower lip. "Who did this?"

"Don't know. He says it happened fast, had his back to the door and didn't see anything."

Jennifer closed her eyes for a moment. "I wanted to put a bell on that door a long time ago, but he wouldn't hear of it. Bet he won't argue anymore."

"Stay close to me, I don't have any contagious disease. And you don't need to be around any people who are coughing and sneezing. We can't afford to have you sick." He held her away from him and looked into her eyes. "How are you doing? Looks like you've still got your hair."

She forced a faint smile. "It's a wig. I'm as bald as a cue ball."

"Man, you bought a great match." He grinned. "You're still beautiful."

"Thanks."

About that time, the attendant returned. "Mr. Williams."

He whirled around. "Yes."

"They've just rolled Mr. Casey into recovery. He's doing fine. They had to repair muscle and tendons. I told the surgeon you wanted to speak with him."

"Good."

Jennifer stepped up to the counter. "I'm Tom Casey's wife. How long will it be before I can see him?"

"Probably an hour, then they'll move him to a private room. Check back with me and I'll be able to tell you the number."

"Thank you."

They stepped toward a row of chairs just as the surgeon, still in his scrubs, hustled around the corner. "Detective Williams?"

Williams raised a hand. "Over here."

The doctor hurried toward him. "You wanted to see me?"

"Yes. What kind of weapon made Casey's wounds?"

"I'd say a long knife. Not the normal switchblade type, more like a sharp carving one. The cuts were very deep."

Jennifer reached over and touched the doctor's arm. "I'm his wife and got here as soon as I heard the news. Where are the wounds?"

He pointed to the upper part of his left arm and forearm. "There were two swipes, one here on the upper area, which was the worst, and one on the lower part. But both required extensive repair."

Jennifer grimaced. "Will that arm be disabled?"

"It'll take awhile to heal, and he'll definitely need therapy. But I believe it will be fully functional in time."

"When can I take him home?"

"Tomorrow around noon, if there are no complications."

CHAPTER FORTY-THREE

After the doctor disappeared down the corridor, Jennifer and the detective meandered toward the far corner of the waiting room and sat down. She stared at Williams as he stifled a yawn and noticed his eyes were bloodshot.

"How long has it been since you've had any sleep?"

He shrugged. "I don't remember."

"You look beat. Why don't you go home and get some rest. There's nothing you can do here."

He rubbed his eyes. "Are you going to stay all night?"

"Probably. But I can curl up in a chair in Hawkman's room and catch a few winks."

"How are you feeling?"

"I'm doing just fine and my next chemo isn't until Monday. I'll have my patient home by then and in case I need other help, Amelia's just down the block."

"You realize you're not going to be able to keep him down."

She nodded and let out a soft sigh. "I know."

Williams stood and straightened his rumpled jacket. "If you're sure you don't need me, I think I'll take off. I'm pretty wiped out." He surveyed the area. "Stay as far away as you can from any coughers. We don't need you down too."

She patted him on the back. "Don't worry, I'll be careful. It looks like the place is thinning out, and they'll have Hawkman in a room before long. You go home and get to bed."

Once the detective left, Jennifer settled back in the chair and opened the mystery book she'd thought to grab as she dashed out the door. Soon, the clerk at the admitting desk called her forward.

"Mrs. Casey, they have your husband in room four twenty-five." She pointed down the hallway. "Take the elevator on the left."

"Thank you."

When she got to the room, she hesitated a moment outside the door and caught her breath. It seemed only walking a few steps left her winded. She straightened her shoulders, and stepped over the threshold. Hawkman lay with his arm bandaged from his shoulder down to his fingers. He turned his head and looked at her with groggy eyes. "Honey, you shouldn't be here."

She placed her purse and jacket on the chair, then crossed over to the bedside. Taking his uninjured hand, she brought it to her lips. "Wild horses couldn't have kept me away."

His left eyelid fluttered. "Where's my eye-patch?"

Jennifer fished through the plastic bag containing his personal items and finally found it in his jeans' pocket. She slipped it over his head.

"Thanks," he said, adjusting it over his eye. "Is Williams around?"

"No, I sent him home. The man appeared utterly exhausted. He couldn't even remember when he'd last slept."

"When can I get out of here?" He tried to sit up, but groaned. "Damn, that smarts."

She pointed a finger at him. "Just lay still. You're not going anywhere. If you behave yourself, they might let me take you home tomorrow." She eased down on the bed. "Do you feel like telling me what happened?"

His eye closed. "How about after I take a nap."

***

Saturday morning, Jennifer took Hawkman home and tucked him into bed. "Now you have to stay here for at least two hours or I won't fix you anything to eat."

"Boy, you really know how to hurt a guy. By the way, where's my 4X4?"

"It's still at the office. I gave Detective Williams the keys this morning when he dropped by the hospital. He said he'd bring it home sometime today when he could grab a free officer to follow him. Also, he said he wanted to talk to you about what happened."

Hawkman flinched and glanced down at his bandaged arm. "I'd like to get my hands on who did this." Then he gazed at Jennifer. "I think I'll be able to take you to your chemo treatment on Monday."

She shook her head. "Not this time. Amelia's going to drive me. She has to do some shopping in Medford for the store, so it's perfect timing."

He slammed his right fist against the mattress. "Why in the hell did this have to happen now?"

"Don't get yourself all upset over the situation. It occurred, and we'll take it from there. Main thing is to let the arm heal, then get you into therapy. You heard the doctor. It's going to take awhile to get it back to normal."

He stared into her face. "You know I can't stay down, Jennifer. I've got to find Tiffany before it's too late."

She sat on the foot of the bed and gnawed her lower lip. "Can't Detective Williams take over? This person tried to kill you. Next time he might succeed."

"He won't get a second chance." Hawkman tossed back the cover and threw his legs over the edge of the bed. When he tried to stand, his body dropped back to the mattress, and he clutched his head.

She jumped up and came to his side. "What are you trying to do?"

"I can't wear my shoulder holster with all this crappie bandage wrapped around me. I've got to get my .22 mag Black Widow out of the gun case and check it out so I can carry it in my boot."

"I'll get it for you. Stay in bed. You can't do anything today, you're too weak."

He grit his teeth as he slumped back onto the pillow. "I hate this helpless feeling. And my arm hurts like hell."

"The doctor prescribed some pain pills, so I picked them up at the pharmacy. Do you want one?"

"No."

Jennifer went into Hawkman's office and worked the combination on the gun vault. She retrieved the small box containing the Black Widow pistol, closed the door and twirled the knob. "He always keeps his weapons in immaculate shape, I don't see why he's worried about it," she grumbled, marching back into the bedroom.

She found him standing again and struggling into a pair of Levi's. Dropping the gun onto the bed, she helped him tug up the pants and buckle the belt. He pointed out the sliding glass door of their bedroom.

"I just spotted my 4X4 coming around the bend. Detective Williams should be knocking on the door any minute. Can you grab me a shirt out of the closet? One with snaps or buttons down the front, yet big enough to fit over all this tape and gauze."

She quickly flipped a shirt off the hanger and tugged it over his large shoulders as he slipped his right arm through the hole and fastened it.

"Thanks. I'll take care of the gun later. Right now I better talk to Williams."

Jennifer helped him get situated in his chair overlooking the lake just as the doorbell rang. She welcomed the detective and his side kick, then ushered them into the living room. "Can I get you a cup of coffee or a glass of iced tea?" she asked.

"Coffee sounds great," Williams said.

"Excuse me if I don't stand, but I find myself a little lightheaded," Hawkman said, extending his right hand. "Thanks for bringing my vehicle home. I really appreciate it."

"No problem. I also need to ask you some questions about the attack. You feel like talking?"

"Yeah, but I don't know how much help I'm going to be. I had my back to the entry and just punched in your cell phone number when the light suddenly changed in the room. I looked around to see who'd entered the office. I immediately spotted this long blade poised above my head and heard a swishing sound as it moved downward. I dropped the phone and lashed out with my left hand to stop it. I felt a searing pain surge through me and blood poured from my arm. I guess if I hadn't twisted around, I'd probably be dead. Thank goodness you answered the phone."

The detective furrowed his brows. "What do you mean by a swishing noise?"

"I'm not sure, but it resembled a sheet hanging on the clothes line being whipped by the wind."

"And you never actually saw the person?"

"No, it happened so fast. All I recall is a blurred silhouette, like a fast moving figure in an old time movie."

"You think this person could have been wearing a long coat?"

Hawkman scratched his head. "Very possible. The movement of the arm going up and down could have caused the illusion."

"It's odd you never saw a face."

"Wish I had, but it seemed obscured by a hood or something. I'm not sure. The door blocked my view as the attacker ran out, then I went down."

The detective rose from the couch. "We've got to get back to the station. Take it easy and I'll let you know if we come up with anything."

"Williams, you know whoever did this has Tiffany. Time is moving fast and we've got to find the child."

CHAPTER FORTY-FOUR

Jennifer followed Hawkman into the bedroom and watched him lift his cowboy boots out of the closet. Then he moved over to the dresser and fumbled in one drawer after another.

She placed her hands on her hips. "What are you looking for now?"

"My ankle holster."

"It's in the gun cabinet. Want me to get it?"

"Please."

She went into his office again, realizing there would be no way to stop him, so she might as well be on his side. Maybe she could talk him into waiting to go into town until tomorrow. Another good night's sleep would give him more strength and he'd be less vulnerable. Her husband had been through much worse and she knew he'd get through this, but worry still raced through her heart. Whoever attacked him was very evil. When she thought about how the knife could have gone through his back, shivers raced down her spine. She needed him now more than ever.

Retrieving the small holster, she went back into the room, handed it to him, then sat down on the edge of the bed and watched as he attempted to strap it around his right ankle with one hand. She struggled within herself not to reach over and help, so she sat on her hands. "Honey, I hope you're not planning on going out tonight. You're still awfully weak."

"Don't worry, I need more rest. But I plan on going in early tomorrow morning. There's a few things I've got to do."

"How bad does your office look. Are we going to have to replace the carpet?"

"Yeah, it soaked up a lot of blood. It's probably stained beyond repair."

"Why don't I go in with you and take care of whatever needs to be done."

He jerked his head around and glared into her eyes. "No way. You're not about to get involved in such a strenuous project. You need all your strength to handle the chemotherapy. I'll hire it done"

She folded her arms across her chest. "I feel so helpless."

He reached over and grabbed her wrist. "Honey, the most important thing in the world right now is for you to get well. The chemo is knocking down all the good stuff as well as the bad and we don't want you sicker. So the best thing is to keep you as healthy as possible through this ordeal and I'm going to help you accomplish this goal. This wound I've acquired will heal in no time, but you've got months to go."

She sighed. "You're right, but it sure gets to me when my activities are so limited."

"Time will pass quickly, and you'll be back to your normal self before you know it." He directed his attention back to tugging on the cowboy boots with one hand, then placed the gun in the holster on his right ankle. "I need to get used to this rig again. Been a long time since I've used it."

The rest of the evening, Jennifer found herself chuckling as she watched Hawkman practice pulling the small Black Widow pistol from his boot. "You remind me of the hero in a cowboy movie."

He laughed. "Let's hope I can perfect a fast draw before I have to use it."

***

Early Sunday morning, Hawkman arose and left the house quietly. His arm ached like hell, but he wouldn't let it interfere. He'd learned many years ago how to deflect pain with his mind. Now it was time to bring the talent back into use.

When he arrived at his office, he called Howard's Carpets and set up an appointment for late Monday morning. They'd installed the current rug, so they were familiar with his location.

He then headed down the stairs to his vehicle. The bakery stood dark and quiet as they were closed on Sundays. When he stepped into the alley, he spotted a young boy about ten years old tossing a hard ball into the air and catching it in his gloved hand.

"Nice catch," Hawkman said, smiling as he reached for the door handle.

The boy strolled over. "Thanks. Hey, I know you. My Dad told me your name's Hawkman and you used to be a spy." Then he pointed to the bandaged shoulder. Wow, did that person hurt you bad?"

Hawkman gave the boy his full attention. "What person?"

"The one in the witch's cape."

He dropped his hand and stared at the boy. "Tell me about it."

"You know on Friday. I saw the ambulance come after the person left, so figured you got into a fight or something."

"Why weren't you in school?"

The boy frowned and ducked his head. "I had a stomachache and didn't feel good. So my Dad picked me up at lunchtime and brought me back to his workplace." He dropped the mitt and ball to the ground, then pointed down the way. "He's a welder and works in the shop down there. I was sitting in his truck out back, cause I didn't feel like smelling all that burning stuff and it's hot in there too."

"So what'd you see?"

"At first, I didn't pay too much attention." He pointed toward the opposite area off to Hawkman's right. "Because lots of people park their pickups behind the stores to load up heavy stuff."

"What kind of truck?"

The boy shrugged. "I don't know the make, but it looked old."

"Do you remember the color?"

"Dirty dark green"

"So what made you notice this particular vehicle?"

"When the person climbed out of the cab in a funny cloak, and the sun's rays bounced off something shiny in his fist, I just watched to see what he was going to do."

"What'd he have in his hand?"

"It looked like a long knife."

"So you're saying this was a man?"

He clenched his hands behind his back and screwed up his mouth. "Gee, not sure, I never saw the person's head, because with the hood up, it made a shadow."

"Could you see any clothing underneath the cloak?"

"No, because the cape, came clear down to here." He bent over and touched his ankles. 'But the person did have on some sort of boots. I could see those."

About that time, a loud whistle echoed through the air.

"Oh, that's my Dad. I gotta go."

"Jason, where the hell are you?"

Hawkman glanced down the alley to see a big, potbellied man, hands on hips, standing outside the back door of the welder's shop.

The lad snatched up his mitt and ball, then hightailed it down the asphalt.

Hawkman moved to the rear of the 4X4 and watched the boy run down to his father. He waved, and the man returned the gesture. Climbing into his SUV, Hawkman grimaced as he settled into the seat. Even though the doctors had bandaged and taped his arm to his body, any movement made it hurt like hell.

Backing out of his parking spot, he studied the area where the boy indicated the pickup had parked. He searched his mind for anyone with such a vehicle, but no one came to mind. At least now, he felt assured he'd actually heard the swishing sound of fabric.

He drove downtown and parked in a slot near the butcher shop. Taking his time, he exited the vehicle. It seemed if he moved too fast, it made him lightheaded. He strolled into the store and it surprised him to see Hank cutting meat behind the counter.

"Be right with you," he called over his shoulder.

When Hank turned around, Hawkman thought he detected a trace of fear flash through the man's eyes.

"Uh, what can I sell you today?"

Hawkman leaned his right side against the cooler. "When did you return? Didn't expect to see you for another week or so."

Hank kept wiping his hands on the towel. "My brother took a turn for the better, so I flew back last Thursday night. I really hate to be away from the shop too long. But Tulip took good care of things."

"She seemed to manage both jobs fairly well."

The butcher gestured toward Hawkman's left side. "What happened?"

"Got into a little accident."

"Bad?"

"Yeah."

"Sorry to hear it."

Hawkman's gaze fanned the wall behind Hank. "Where are your freezers?"

The butcher pointed to a door leading into what looked like an office. "Back there. I have two: one big walk in where I keep sides of beef and pork, then a chest type where I keep small wild game, like birds and such. Sometimes, people want those types of meats for special guests."

"I've never seen a butcher's work place."

Hank motioned for him to come around the end of the counter. "Since there are no customers right now, I'll show you about."

He led Hawkman through the building, and pointed out the big cooler, then opened the freezer with the wild game, indicating the wrapped packages of quail, grouse, squirrel and rabbit.

The bell rang at the entry and they hurried to the front.

"Thanks for the tour. Enjoyed it." Hawkman said, as he stepped out the door.

Hank gave a wave and proceeded to wait on the shopper.

Climbing into his vehicle, Hawkman leaned his head back on the rest and closed his eyes for a moment. The tour around the shop had worn him out. His shoulder ached from the the weight of his arm and bandages, he slid his right hand underneath the wounded limb and pushed up. It seemed to relieve the pressure. After he remained still for about ten minutes, and concentrated on ridding himself of the pain, he felt it ease and his energy return.

He drove by Tulip's complex and spotted her car at the apartment. But before confronting her, he wanted to drive out to her father's place. If the security guard caught him again, he'd have to think of some excuse.

Driving into Hank's exclusive neighborhood, Hawkman decided instead of parking in front of the house, he'd pull into the driveway and follow it around to the back. He stopped alongside the rear of the building, climbed out, and hurried to the small window in the garage. Using his right hand to shade the glass from the sun's glare, he found himself staring at a pickup which fitted the young boy's description.

CHAPTER FORTY-FIVE

Hawkman stepped away from the garage and glared at the house. His heart leaped when he spotted a white cat staring at him from the inside ledge of a curtained window. He hurried forward and placed his hand on the glass. The feline rubbed her head against the surface and Hawkman spotted the small gray circle of hair between her ears, glistening like a crown. "Princess", he said aloud. He snatched the cell phone from his belt and punched in Williams' number.

"I think you better get a search warrant for Hank Withers' house." While Hawkman paced the back yard talking to the detective, the Security guard drove up, exited his vehicle and strolled toward him.

"You again?" he said, fist planted defiantly on his hips. "Mr. Withers is working."

Clipping his cell back into place, Hawkman faced the man. "Yes, I know, but you probably should contact him. His place is about to be searched by the police. He might want to come home, so they don't have to break down any doors."

"Who are you anyway?"

"I'm a private investigator looking into a murder. I've just called the authorities and they're on their way."

The man's face turned pale and he hastened back to his vehicle. Hawkman could see his gaze darting nervously toward the house as he talked on his car phone.

For the next thirty minutes, Hawkman conferred back and forth with Detective Williams.

"The cat will be our ace in the hole," Williams said. "Are you sure it isn't Hank's."

"Hell, no, I'm not sure. I don't know what his animal looks like, but there aren't many cats with the markings like Princess. If Tiffany's in this house, she's probably drugged, and we need to find her fast. It's been over three days and you know how crucial time is. The pickup in the garage fits the description the kid gave me. I'd bet my bottom dollar it's the one driven to my place and Hank may have well been my attacker. There's definitely something fishy going on here."

"But I thought you said Withers was out of town for two or three weeks."

"I found out today, he got back Thursday night."

"He couldn't have kidnapped Tiffany."

"Have you ever thought he might have hired someone to snatch her to throw the blame off himself. This way he's got an airtight alibi."

"You've got a point. I'm going to the judge right now."

"Hurry up, or I'm going to knock down a door."

"Don't do it. You could ruin the whole case."

"Well, hang up the damn phone and get your butt in gear."

Hawkman hurried over to the window again, then circled the house trying to find an uncurtained window, but all were covered. He even called out Tiffany's name several times to no avail. When he heard tires squealing on concrete, he lurched around. Hank Withers screeched to a stop, jumped out of the car and barreled toward the private investigator.

"What the hell's going on?" he bellowed.

Hawkman had transferred his Black Widow from his boot into his right pocket, and his hand clutched the handle. "You've got some questions to answer, Hank."

"What about? The Security man acted scared to death. Said you were investigating a murder."

"That's right. Carlotta Ryan's. I understand you visited her on several occasions, bearing gifts of prime cuts of meat. But she turned your advances down, so you decided to get rid of her."

Hank glared at him. "You're crazy."

"Am I? Wouldn't you like to see Tulip married to Paul?"

"Not bad enough to kill his wife."

Hawkman pointed toward the garage. "When did you last use that pickup?"

"About two months ago."

"That's odd. Someone saw it in the alley behind my office two days ago."

"Whoever told you that is mistaken. It's got a flat tire."

"Show me."

Withers went to the front of the big garage, twisted a key into the padlock and swung open the doors. He caught his breath and stared in rigid silence at the truck.

Hawkman moved behind him. "Which tire's flat, Hank? The spare?"

The butcher turned slowly, his face drained of color. "I don't know what to say. The left rear was flat when I left."

About that time, Williams' unmarked car followed by a black and white bounced into the driveway. Several other patrol cars surrounded the house. The officers jumped from their vehicles with brandished weapons pointed toward Hank Withers.

When the detective approached, Hawkman motioned for him to follow as he walked into the open garage. He moved toward the front of the truck and peered into the window of the passenger side, then pointed at a garment which lay crumpled on the floorboard along with a pair of brown leather work type boots. "I hope your lab guys are coming?"

"They're on the way."

"Have them hit this truck and garage." Hawkman left the building and strode toward the back entry of the house. "Let's get inside."

Williams held out his hand in front of Withers. "You can make this easy or we'll break the door down. Head lowered, Hank rummaged in his pocket, then handed over the keys. Hawkman and the detective hurried through the door and into the kitchen. A large parrot in a cage squawked loudly, a small dog barked furiously until his master walked in, then two cats scurried toward other parts of the house.

Hawkman followed the white kitten to a closed room.

The animal meowed and glanced up at him with a pleading look. He shoved open the door, and the feline bounced upon the bed, tread in a circle around the neatly spread comforter, then purred loudly while rubbing its head against the pillow. Hawkman dashed out of the bedroom and searched every room in the house. When he found nothing, he stormed back into the kitchen and grabbed Hank Withers by the collar of his jacket. "Where's Tiffany?" he spat, yanking the man toward him.

"I don't know what you're talking about."

"Like hell you don't!" He felt the man wilt under his grip and shoved him into a chair. Princess crept into the room and rubbed against Hawkman's leg. He pointed to her. "Where'd you get this cat?"

"Some stray my daughter brought in while I was back east."

"Okay, tell me about Tulip's purse. Where'd you get it?"

Hank's gaze sank to the floor. "I never gave Tulip that handbag. In fact, her birthday isn't for six months. I don't know why she concocted such a story."

Hawkman spun on his heel, and dashed out the door.

"Where you going?" Williams yelled.

"Grab that white cat when you leave."

CHAPTER FORTY-SIX

When Hawkman climbed into his 4X4, he glanced at the area where the technicians were hovering over the pickup, dusting for fingerprints and gathering evidence. His gaze narrowed on one of the men with rubber gloves lifting out a long cloak from the passenger side of the vehicle. He gently folded it and placed the garment into a large plastic bag. Then he picked up the boots, tagged them and put them into a container.

Hawkman stuck the key into the ignition and the engine roared to life. One good thing about an automatic, you could shift into reverse with one hand. He slowly maneuvered around the lab's van, then followed the driveway around the house. Williams' car blocked the exit, so he had to bump across the drainage ditch in front of the house. It jarred his arm so badly, he let out a yelp and swore under his breath, but he couldn't let the pain get the best of him right now. Once on the asphalt, he shoved his boot down on the accelerator and sped toward town.

He swerved into the complex of Tulip's apartment. Instead of stopping in front of her unit where her car sat, he went around the corner and parked. He checked his gun and shoved it back into his pocket instead of dropping it into the ankle holster. Taking a deep breath, he sat a moment and tried to relax his throbbing arm. After several minutes, he climbed out of the vehicle and strolled toward Tulip's flat. When he reached the door, he wanted to bash it in, but decided he'd better ring the bell. Tulip opened it immediately instead of peeking out the window. Her face paled when she looked up at him.

"What do you want?"

"We need to talk."

"I have nothing to say to you."

She tried to slam the door, but Hawkman braced his foot against the bottom, then shoved it open with his good hand. He stepped inside, and pushed it closed with the heel of his boot.

Tulip backed away, her gaze darted from him to the closed extra bedroom. "Why are you here?"

"Just came from your dad's place. He said he never gave you that Gucci purse. Where'd you get that handbag, Tulip? Did that belong to Carlotta? Princess was roaming around your dad's house and he said you told him it was a stray you took in. Want to tell me about where you found her."

Her gaze rotated from side to side as she backed toward the small kitchen. "I don't know what you're talking about."

Just as he moved closer, a moan came from the other part of the house. A faint voice called out. "Tulip, help me."

Hawkman turned his head for a split second. But out of the corner of his eye he spotted the light reflect off of something shiny. He whirled around in time to see Tulip's arm swing the long blade above her head. Grabbing a small kitchen chair, he shoved it between them. She let out an animal cry, then kept advancing, and waving the butcher knife.

Hawkman pulled his gun and pointed it at her heart. "Stay back, Tulip, I don't want to shoot."

She suddenly lurched around him and ran into the extra bedroom. Hawkman dashed in behind her as she approached the bed. A small body lay curled in the middle of a bright red spread, her hands and feet bound to the post. Small glassy eyes squinted as Tulip lifted the knife above her head, clenching it with both hands. Tiffany screamed as Hawkman's weapon fired.

Tulip crumbled to the floor. He slowly made his way around her fallen form, his gun aimed at the woman's head. Her arm jerked and Hawkman quickly stepped on the blade. He didn't dare take his eye off the woman as she wasn't dead and he only had the one hand. Hawkman yearned to get the ropes off Tiffany and call the police, but his only option was to stay put with his gun aimed at Tulip. He hoped Williams had figured it out and would be here shortly.

Tiffany stared at him. "Aren't you Mr. Casey?" she asked in a soft voice.

"Yes, sweetheart. And as soon as the police get here, we'll get you untied."

She blinked her eyes several times as the tears spilled down her cheeks. "I'm so glad you're here. And why do you just have one hand?"

He smiled. "It's only for a little while."

"What happened to your other one?"

"Someday I'll tell you all about it. Right now you just save your strength. Help is on the way."

Tiffany closed her lids. "Okay."

Hawkman glanced at the large chest freezer sitting on the opposite side of the room and a chill ran down his spine. He felt the knife under his boot move and bared down harder. "Stay still, Tulip. You're bleeding and the more you move, the more blood you lose. We don't want you to die before the police and ambulance arrive."

He heard the front door bang open and someone shout, "Police."

"In here," Hawkman called.

Williams ran in with his gun drawn. "What the hell!" He reached down, grabbed the sharp tip of the butcher blade and removed it from under Hawkman's boot, then handed it to one of the officers to bag. Tulip moaned as the detective tried to help her up. "Looks like she's been shot."

"I had no other alternative; she attempted to stab Tiffany. Make sure you call for two ambulances. I don't want the child riding in the same vehicle with this murdering bitch. Just let her lay there. Then as soon as we get Tiffany on her way to the hospital, I'll call Paul and Delia."

"Is the child okay?"

"I think so. It appears she's been drugged and needs attention. Get her untied from the damn bed," Hawkman said. Then he glanced at the detective. "Did you bring the cat?"

"Yes," the detective said, motioning for the officer holding Princess to come forward. Williams quickly untied Tiffany's restraints and helped her into a sitting position.

"My arms and legs hurt," she groaned as she tried moving.

"They'll feel better in a little while," Williams said, handing her the feline.

Tiffany's face broke into a big grin as she cuddled the animal. "I didn't think I'd ever see my little Princess again."

"You probably can't take her into the hospital," Hawkman said, "but I'll bring her home."

After the ambulances arrived, the first one loaded Tiffany onto a gurney and took off. The second one had to tether Tulip to the stretcher, and two officers were assigned to her vehicle.

Once the ambulance carrying Tulip disappeared down the street, Hawkman pocketed his gun, then immediately called Delia and Paul telling them the good news. Both were in tears, and said they were headed for the hospital. He reached down and ran his hand along Princess' soft fur as she curled up on the bed cuddling against the pillow. He turned toward Williams and pointed at the freezer. "See if you can open that thing."

The detective tried to budge the lid. "It's locked."

"Get a locksmith."

The detective pulled out his cell phone and then looked at Hawkman with an incredulous expression. "You really think..."

Hawkman nodded.

It took close to an hour for Williams to locate one of the certified locksmiths. When the man arrived, he worked on the chest type freezer for only a few minutes before he popped the lid, then slammed it shut and stepped back in horror, falling backwards into a nearby chair. "Oh my God!"

"What's wrong?" Williams asked as he stared at the ashen faced man.

He pointed a shaking finger at the big white box. "There's a body in there," he gasped.

The detective quickly opened the lid, then moved his head slowly toward Hawkman. "You were right. We've found Carlotta Ryan."

Hawkman peered into the cavern of the freezer. "At least she isn't butchered like a piece of beef."

"How the hell did Tulip cram her into this thing without a fight?"

"Probably drugs."

He dropped the lid and told the locksmith he could go. After the man hurried out the door, Williams ran a hand through his hair. "Wonder why Tulip didn't kill the little girl?"

Hawkman sat on the chair and elevated his hurt arm with the other hand. "I don't think she planned on killing Tiffany until I showed up. She knew the child was the key to any relationship with Paul. If anything happened to his daughter, she could kiss it all goodbye. She probably had some weird plan on how she'd return Tiffany to the family. When I showed up tonight, she figured every thing had gone awry."

The detective called the coroner and the lab technicians. When he hung up, he sighed. "This has been one hell of a case. It's going to be interesting to hear more answers during Tulip's trial."

Hawkman stood, scooped up Princess and the two men walked out into the front yard.

"Do you think Hank had anything to do with this scheme?" the detective asked.

"I did up until earlier today when I saw him check the pickup for the flat. His face literally dropped when he glanced down and saw the inflated tire. He never questioned his daughter about anything, and believed everything she said. But when Tulip said he'd gotten her the Gucci purse for her birthday, he began to doubt her. He's going to be shocked about Tiffany and Carlotta. I don't think he had any idea what she'd really been up to."

When the coroner's wagon arrived, the two men watched them load Carlotta's frozen body into the van.

Hawkman carried Princess to the 4X4 and told her to 'stay' on the passenger seat. She obeyed and curled into a ball as he drove away. Stopping at the pet shop, he bought a thin white rhinestone studded collar. At a nearby jeweler, he purchased a small silver bell, engraved with the name 'Princess', and had it attached to the glittering piece of leather. Then he headed for Delia's place.

THE END

EPILOGUE

After six months, Jennifer's cancer went into remission and she didn't have to take any more chemotherapy. Her kidney suffered no damage and worked perfectly after the stent removal. Now she's waiting patiently for her hair to grow back, her energy to be restored, and prays the lymphoma cancer never returns.

Tulip Withers was convicted of first degree murder in the case of Carlotta Ryan and was sentenced to spend the rest of her life under maximum security in the Oregon State Penitentiary. Three months into her incarceration she was killed by a prison inmate.

Hank Withers closed the butcher shop, sold all his property and went back east to settle near his ill brother.

Paul Ryan sold the dwelling where Carlotta had resided, then bought another home near his mother, where he, Tiffany, and Princess now live. Tiffany still spends most of her time with Grandma Delia.

Author, Betty Sullivan La Pierre